WOLF OF ASHES

DARK MAGIC SHIFTERS 1

EVERLY FROST

Frost, Everly
Wolf of Ashes

Cover design by Claire Holt with Luminescence Covers
www.luminescencecovers.com

For information on reproducing sections of this book or sales of this book,
go to
www.EverlyFrost.com
everlyfrost@gmail.com

DISCOVER THE EVER REALMS

Seven series. One world.

Suggested Reading Order:

Bright Wicked
Storm Princess
Assassin's Magic
Soul Bitten Shifter
Supernatural Legacy
Dark Magic Shifters
Kingdom of Betrayal

Well, hello there, Darkness,
come on in.

CHAPTER ONE

"*You were loved.*"

That's what my mother whispered to me when I was a little girl shivering in her lap because I was afraid of the scraping sounds that would echo through the damp stone wall beside our cell.

"*You were loved.*"

She'd remind me over and over like a ward against the perpetual night that surrounded us. While she shared her food with me, stretching out the scraps our jailer fed us. While she wrapped her arms around me to keep me warm from the freezing cold in winter.

Even when she struggled to breathe at the end.

"*You were loved.*"

I soon came to understand that she chose her message carefully.

What mattered was not that there was love in my life before I'd been born, but that it was in the past.

I was loved.

She was loved.

Until we weren't.

Now I crouch in the center of my cell, my threadbare, black dress barely covering my backside, listening to the unusual sounds through the solid, stone walls.

I'm accustomed to hearing soft snarls from animals I can't identify, along with the occasional low moan—of pain, not pleasure.

But these are two voices I've never heard before.

Neither of them belongs to my jailer. He calls himself Zadkiel. He's an angel with the blackest hair, the whitest wings, and a smile that makes my stomach turn.

The higher pitch of one voice tells me it's female. The other is male. Both are muffled through the thick, stone walls that make up my cage.

Four stone walls. Impenetrable ones.

I was born in this dark room, and I've never stepped beyond it.

There are small air vents in the ceiling, each located near a corner. Very dim light also filters through those vents but my eyes have adapted to the dark.

I have an old mattress on a wooden frame for a bed, a wooden bucket in the corner for a toilet, and a single, wooden chair, which I rarely sit on. Because, well, that would be civilized. Or so my mother told me every time she rested on it, her head held higher, as if it made her feel like her old self.

I am not civilized.

The cage is magically sealed so that the walls defy any sort of deep scraping or attempted burrowing.

Not that I haven't tried.

Like the animal that I am, I have raked my claws across those stones over and over, looking for any weak patch. After my mother died, I turned my quest into a game, managing to scratch out tiny squares as I tested every inch of stone for a weakness.

The scratches remained on the surface, but my claws sunk no deeper.

Zadkiel found it humorous. So humorous that he would slap me once for each square I made since his last visit. The slap itself didn't hurt so much as the light that filled his palm.

Light magic.

A contradiction to his rancid soul.

Painful to my dark heart.

He taught me that if I try to escape, he will flood the air with light. Once, I made it three steps past him toward the door he'd left inches open to taunt me. His light burned my back so badly that I couldn't sleep for days.

Screaming never did any good, either. As Zadkiel likes to remind me, sound only passes one way through the wall—inward—and he's the only one who knows I'm here.

But now...

Something's happening beyond my cage.

Something new.

I close my eyes and focus on the sounds, trying to hear what the woman is saying. Hers is the first female voice I've heard since my mother died. The man's voice is raised and threatening.

But still, their speech is inaudible. Rising to my feet and hurrying to the wall, I press my ear against the cold surface, desperate to make out what they're saying through the magic coating the stone.

Searing heat suddenly burns across the side of my face.

I jump away from the wall with a cry, staring in shock at the way the rock has turned crimson red, as if it's being heated from the other side.

My eyes widen at the power it would take to burn through stone this thick.

The blaze stops then starts again, much lower to the floor. I jump farther back as it bursts across the stone in a wavy line for several feet, leaving the smooth rocks glowing.

My ears suddenly *pop*.

It's painful and sharp, as if the pressure within my cage changed. My mother once described being carried into the air and the way the weight changed within her ears. I wonder if this is the same kind of thing.

The sensation settles quickly and I crouch low, daring to hold my hand, palm up, toward the glowing stones. I'm wise enough not to make contact. Not yet, anyway.

Searing heat radiates out from the stone, scorching my palm even at a distance, but it's not so much the temperature that intrigues me now.

It's the way the air around my hand shimmers with energy.

Slowly extending the claw on my right forefinger, I press it against the rock.

To my shock, my claw sinks into the stone.

All the way through until my finger is burning from the contact.

The magical seal is gone!

I wrench myself backward so fast that I land on my backside. I don't know exactly how the seal has broken. Possibly because of the heat source on the other side. Or maybe some other magic is at play.

Either way, the seal is gone.

My heart is in my throat, my thoughts churning at the possibility that escape is finally within my reach.

But how to make it happen?

The stone is hot and soft, like heated metal that will soon form a hard surface once more. I know this because my mother taught me all about the properties of metal. All about a lot of things.

She taught me everything she knew. Every minuscule piece

of information, no matter how trivial it seemed, in case it would one day help me.

She taught me basic physics, chemistry, and biology. She taught me math and how to read. She convinced Zadkiel to bring us books, although he seemed only to agree because he could subvert her intentions, never bringing what she asked for: like a children's picture book when she asked for a book on natural sciences.

Sometimes he would bring books in other languages that she couldn't read. But she was never deterred. She would use whatever he brought her, even if only for the illustrations, and would simply change my lesson. Sometimes we got lucky and he brought an encyclopedia, probably because he thought it would bore us to tears. Those tomes were like gold to us.

Mom educated me about humans, supernaturals, the old gods, and all the different kinds of magic.

I learned about lust, greed, sex, envy, politics, basic medicine, technology, and food—and *damn*, I want to try cupcakes one day. The pink, frosted ones with sugar decorations on top.

I learned that the sky is blue, not gray like my cage's ceiling, and that there's such a thing as 'fresh' air.

It was also clear that, for my mother, who had lived under a blue sky and breathed fresh air, being kept in this cage was a misery her body couldn't sustain.

For her final lesson, she taught me about death.

But I found out all by myself the meaning of loneliness.

Now, I carefully consider the glowing stone along with the intense growls on the other side of the wall. I make out the sharp clanging of metal—possibly chains, judging by the way the sounds seem to slither and rattle. Then voices again—both the man's and the woman's—followed finally by retreating footfalls, heavy ones.

Then silence.

I'm not sure if they've both gone, but if I don't try to escape now, I may never get another chance.

Racing to the lone chair, I pick it up, throw my arm across my eyes to protect them from flying debris, and I bash the chair against the wall where it's still cold and hard.

The chair's legs snap off. One of them shatters. And now they're perfect for digging through hot stone without burning my fingers. Assuming the wood doesn't catch fire, but I'll deal with that if it happens.

Crouching low to the heated portion of the wall, I begin gouging the surface as fast as I can, dragging the jagged wood through it. Splinters immediately catch in my palms and I pause to retrieve my mother's old shirt, wrapping the tattered material around my hands and using my teeth to tie it before I resume my task.

The wood isn't as sharp as my claws and it's slower to cut through, snapping off at intervals and frustrating my progress, but I persist until the moment a chunk on the other side falls away.

The opening is only as big as my hand, not nearly large enough for me to slide through, but certainly big enough to allow sounds and smells to rush in.

Oh, the smells. A whole, glorious onslaught of them.

My moment of elation is destroyed by the savage growls and strong scents of dark beasts that make the hairs on the back of my neck stand on end.

Cautiously, I lean toward the hole and then—

A mouth full of teeth gnashes at the opening on the other side.

Fuck!

I catch sight of silvery eyes before I scuttle back from the wall.

The overlapping snarling sounds coming from the other side tell me there's more than one of those beasts, whatever the fuck they are. But the scents are all theirs. Whoever the woman and man were, they're gone now.

I sift through my mother's descriptions of dark creatures and land on a few options for what the snarling creatures could be, but I would need to see more of their bodies to be sure.

Like that's going to happen in any safe fashion.

My hopes are now in turmoil.

If I make the opening big enough that I can escape through it, the creatures will be able to get through to my side.

If I somehow manage to keep the opening small enough only for my body—which is not guaranteed if the beasts are slimmer than me—I'd have to shimmy through headfirst or feetfirst and either way, they'd rip me apart before I made it more than a few inches.

I switch my focus to the door, tentatively pressing on it. It's also made of stone and sits seamlessly in the wall, but it has remained locked. Even if it weren't, I can't be sure I won't step right into the path of the beasts outside.

For all I know, Zadkiel placed those creatures there as a second line of defense if I were ever to get out.

What's worse, now that I've made a hole in the wall, he will see it. He'll know the magical seal was broken and he'll punish me for it *and* I'm sure he'll find a way to fix it.

He could come along at any moment.

Fuck, fuck, fuck!

My heart is in my throat as I face the choice between a fight with dark beasts or a battle with my jailer.

CHAPTER TWO

I crouch low to the ground, taking deep breaths as a sense of finality settles over me.

I'm certain I'll die in a fight with Zadkiel. Of all the things my mother taught me, it's that Zadkiel isn't an ordinary angel. Unlike many other supernaturals, he has the strength to kill me.

But a chance like this hasn't presented itself for twenty-three years. It may not happen again.

If I don't try now…

With a cold determination, I retrieve my mother's old skirt. I was saving it for when my black dress got too ragged, but it's time to take chances. Ripping the skirt into smaller pieces, I wrap one of them around my other palm to protect my skin.

I choose the two sharpest planks of wood from the remains of the broken chair.

Now that I'm armed with more than my claws, I wait, preparing myself for when I hear Zadkiel's approaching footfalls.

Long moments pass.

The snarls on the other side of the wall die down a little.

Then start up again. The beasts seem to be prowling back and forth. Waiting, like I am.

Time stretches. The long minutes become long hours.

At one point, I nod off, only to wake with a start, fear striking my heart, but nothing has changed.

The hours become a day and by then, my hands are going numb. I'm forced to put down my weapons, but I'm prepared to pick them up at a moment's notice.

One day becomes two, and now I'm hungry.

I have one chunk of bread left and half a flagon of water.

The beasts continue to move back and forth in front of the opening I made, but the pitch of their snarls has changed. Every now and then, they make a plaintive moaning sound.

Are they hungry too?

I can only stare at the wall with confusion. *Where is he?*

Zadkiel has never been absent for longer than two days. When the second day stretches into a third, I consider that he might never return. He hasn't brought me food or fresh water, and I haven't heard him come to feed the beasts, either.

My stomach gnaws at me, my mouth is dry, and my head swims.

Is this some kind of new punishment? Does he somehow know that the magical seal is broken and he's waiting for me to become too weak to fight him?

The questions crowd my mind through the increasing hours.

Finally, the snarls outside my cage stop and, when I dare to peer through the little opening, I make out the faint silhouette of a paw and a leg resting on the ground. One of the creatures must be lying close by.

It gives a soft whine, but that's all.

By the fourth day, I have no water left and my choices have run out.

If I'm going to die anyway, better to do it while I have enough strength to fight the creatures outside my cell.

Assuming I can break the wall open now.

Cautiously, I use the blunt end of one of my makeshift weapons to tap the wall. The stone is so brittle that it cracks off at the lightest touch.

I test it on a higher spot and with slightly more force, expecting the wall to remain solid.

Crack!

The sharp sound is followed by a cascade of cracks and then, to my shock, the fissures extend in all directions, a vibration ripples through the wall, and the surface fractures across several feet.

Chunks fall in both directions—toward me and outward.

I leap back just in time to avoid being hit in the head as a portion of the wall above me also collapses.

I'm now completely exposed to attack.

I left one of my makeshift weapons on the bed, but I don't dare take my eyes off the beasts in front of me while I grip my remaining plank of wood in my left hand.

As the dust clears, I find myself facing another cage, but this one has bars and a fully visible door with a latch that looks like it could be broken but has remained in place.

Four shapes move in the darkness. I make out sleek, black bodies, silver eyes that disappear when they blink, and silver claws that extend and retract as the beasts prowl toward me.

They look like panthers and my memory stirs.

But no... They can't be...

Not the shadow panthers my mother told me about. One female and three male. She was convinced these beasts had hidden themselves from the world in a mountain somewhere.

Yet here they are. All four of them. Each with unnaturally silver claws and eyes that betray their species.

Three of them hold back, making it clear that the one in front is their leader. Her slightly smaller bone structure tells me she's the female of the pack.

She's the one whose instincts I have to trigger.

These creatures are the stuff of nightmares.

Just like I am.

Calling on my wolfish nature, I allow my claws to descend and draw my lips back from my sharpening teeth. If I have to shift fully, then I will, but I'd rather conserve my energy.

I was born to tame beasts like this, gather them to my side, and give them a purpose.

The female will obey me if she recognizes the nature of my power.

Lowering my head without taking my eyes off her, I utter a fierce growl, pulling the sound from deep in my chest. It's the snarl my mother taught me that signals to another dark creature that they should leave me the fuck alone or face the consequences.

"Back off," I say as my growl fades. "That's all I ask of you."

The female panther's head snaps up, her ears pricked and alert. She gives a soft grunt, blinking at me in the dark, her silvery eyes appearing and disappearing as her eyelids open and close.

I growl again, more softly this time. "I want my freedom and I'd rather not kill you."

She sniffs the air, her nostrils flaring, and now a curious light enters her eyes. She takes a small step in my direction, her paw landing on a piece of rocky debris that lies between us, but she doesn't come any closer and her claws retract.

I'm sure it's the only sign of subservience I'll receive from this proud creature.

I risk glancing at the cage door. It's so close to my current position and the latch looks broken. It will take multiple twists, but I hope I'll be able to lift the latch—unlike these beasts, whose claws could never achieve the fiddly task.

Carefully, I step up onto the debris, choosing my footing so I don't slip or get stuck. The rocks shift beneath my feet and the panthers twitch, but they don't come after me.

Faster now, I sidestep to the door, keeping the beasts within my sights.

My hand lands on the latch and, after twisting it back and forth and then over its damaged catch, I'm slipping outside the cage and into the corridor beyond it.

With a firm push, I close the door behind me.

Just like that, there are no longer any bars or walls around me.

I'm struck with a sense of space and it's fucking terrifying.

Rows of cages stretch out into the distance, maybe as many as fifteen on each side of the wide corridor. The absence of sound tells me that, other than the panthers and me, there's no other living creature here.

Directly to the left is the solid, stone wall that formed one of the sides of my cell, but facing it from this direction, I would never be able to tell that there's a space behind it. The door's outline isn't visible and all that sits on the wall is a misshapen lever that has the appearance of melted iron.

I turn back to the far end of the corridor. I've never had the chance to look so far into the distance and my vision blurs as I try to scan along the cages to the door that must be located at the end.

I tell myself the impediment to my vision will pass.

I was born an apex predator with the sharpest senses. My ability to see long distances may have been stunted by my surroundings, but I promise myself I'll overcome it.

Stepping away from the cage, I'm preparing to race down the corridor and claim my freedom when I pause.

Inside the cage, the panthers have prowled forward, their bright eyes trained on me.

The female makes a soft, mewling sound, her head held low, but not in an aggressive way.

"You want your freedom, too." I exhale a slow breath, hoping I'm not taking a terrible chance when I open the cage door and back away quickly, increasing my speed when the panthers don't immediately leap out after me.

My matted hair slaps my back in heavy thumps as I run.

Behind me, the panthers move quietly, but they pull to a quick stop each time I turn to glare at them.

Finally, I reach the door to my freedom. It doesn't have a handle. It looks like I might only need to push on it. I'm still gripping one of my wooden stakes and both of my palms are wrapped in the scraps of my mother's clothing.

If only she were with me right now.

My eyes burn with tears I won't shed. Grief is not for me, but rage *is* and I plan on using its heat to avenge her.

Quietly, I place the wooden stake on the floor beside the door, freeing up both of my hands.

I don't know what lies beyond this door. Death could be waiting for me, but I'll face it head on.

"This is for you, Mom," I whisper, planting my palms on the door and pushing it open.

CHAPTER THREE

I expected to step into the same gloomy darkness that fills the prison.

Instead, the brightest light streams across me, drawing a scream of pain to my lips. For a moment, I think it's Zadkiel's power; that he waited for me to taste freedom before burning me with his light.

Dropping to my knees, I fling my arm over my eyes, slowly coming to realize that this light...

It's simply light. Not burning power. Just an extreme brightness like the rays of the sun Mom once described.

Desperately, I try to see my surroundings, needing to know what threats lie around me.

All I can make out is an expanse of wood beneath my knees.

On the surprising side, now that my initial shock has abated, I can't sense any other angelic beings nearby.

As quickly as I can, I untie my mother's skirt material from around my palm and wrap it around my eyes, trying to dull the light.

It helps, but it's not a complete fix.

The brush of fur against my lower back and thighs makes me freeze, but then one of the panthers gives a soft grunt. I recognize the female's growls. The side of her face bumps my knee—at least, I think it's the side of her face. Then her head presses up beneath my right palm—the hand from which I took Mom's skirt.

The other three panthers move around me and I'm completely at their mercy as one of them presses against my back, an insistent movement.

I rise up a little and the female rises with me, her head remaining under my hand.

She gives another soft grunt and then moves forward.

I stay where I am, but she comes back to my hand.

"Do you want me to follow you?" I ask, even though I know she can't answer in my language.

She gives another soft grunt.

I have no other choice.

Around me, the air is so bright that even with the blindfold on, I have to keep my eyes closed. But my ears can hear just fine, and my sense of smell is also helpful to me.

We may be alone in our immediate surroundings, but as we progress forward, I sense the presence of other beings somewhere beyond us.

The faster I can get out of here, the better.

The panther leads me to the right and then her head pushes upward. I don't know what she's trying to tell me until my foot hits a surface directly in front of me and I find myself sliding my foot upward to figure out what it is.

It takes me a beat to realize… it must be stairs. I saw pictures of them in illustrations.

Stepping upward, I shuffle forward, keeping my hand on the panther's head while the other panthers mill around me, their bodies brushing my legs, urging me onward.

I lose count of the steps as we proceed higher and higher,

but along the way, I also realize that the air I'm breathing is pure.

Fresh.

It's filling my lungs for the first time and I fight the dizziness that comes with it, as if this good thing could be bad for me, even though I want more of it.

Finally, I shuffle forward and there is no ledge. I stop abruptly because my toe dips and it feels like I'm standing at the edge of something. I try to open my eyes to see what it could be, but just at that moment, there's a sound behind me.

An opening door.

A voice. The same female voice I heard through the walls of my cage.

The panthers give urgent snarls.

All of them ram into my back and then—

Fuck!

I'm falling through air that feels icy and weirdly welcoming at the same time and then darkness engulfs me once again.

Fucking beautiful darkness.

As I continue to fall through it, I rip off the covering over my eyes but keep hold of it because there's no way I'm letting go of a piece of my mother.

My fall slows and I land gently on a gleaming, marble floor.

The inky-black surface extends far into the distance in every direction—left, right, and up, into a nothingness that is so vast, I can't quantify it.

I'm not sure where the staircase disappeared to because it didn't feel like I traveled that far, but here I am, surrounded by night.

Is this the world?

I quickly dismiss that possibility. There is no blue sky, no grass, no buildings.

Oh, and there are also no walls.

In the next moment, the panthers land behind me, but all I care about right now is the endless space in front of me.

"This is freedom," I whisper, stepping across the marble floor, which cools the bare soles of my feet, a soothing sensation.

My walk becomes a run and then I'm racing as fast as I can through the darkness, taking deep breaths, inhaling the glimmering energy in the air.

An energy that reeks of dark magic.

My magic.

The essence of my heart.

The rapid beat of paws tells me the panthers are close behind, but it's when their footfalls are joined by another sound that I slow and stop, crouching to the floor and listening intently.

In the distance is a swishing noise and it's coming closer.

Rising to my feet, I peer into the darkness, finally making out the shape of a tall figure moving toward me. The newcomer appears to be male, judging by the width of his shoulders and the narrowness of his hips and waist, although his entire frame is thin. A long, black robe rests around his body and it must be the source of the swishing sound because it's dragging across the marble floor.

He seems to bring the darkness with him and a thrill passes down my spine.

Then I make out the shape of the black crown resting around his eyes, obscuring the upper half of his face, its spokes rising up over his forehead and past the top of his head.

My heart leaps at the sight of it.

The immense power in the crown calls to me like food to my starving stomach.

The angry press of the man's lips does nothing to dissuade me from my need to connect with that crown.

Without thinking, I lift my hand, the one gripping the loose material of my mom's skirt, and I reach toward him.

He draws to a rapid stop at my gesture.

If only I could see his eyes; I'm sure he'd be eyeing me cautiously now.

"Keeper of dark magic," I say, greeting him. "I never dreamed I'd meet you."

His lips part, as if I've surprised him. His voice is like a wraith's, a shocked whisper. "You know what I am?"

"Of course," I say. "My mother told me all about you. Everything that *her* mother told her. All the knowledge passed down through the generations from mother to child. All the way from the time of the Vandawolf."

The keeper takes a step back from me, but his shoulders are suddenly hunched. "*Vandawolf.* That's a name I haven't heard for thousands of years." He seems to rally quickly. "If you know what I am, then you know you shouldn't be here."

"Shouldn't I?" I ask, finding my lips curving upward. "Isn't this exactly where I should be? In a place of dark magic?"

He glides forward until we're only a few paces apart and now it feels as if he can see me through the metal covering his eyes. "Not until you die."

"Yes, that's right," I murmur. "It's your burden to collect the magic from dark creatures when they perish. So that their untethered magic doesn't roam free and cause chaos. Technically, I shouldn't be able to step foot here until I die, at which time you will strip the magic from my bones."

He gives me a nod, his lips drawing back from his teeth. "Technically."

"Well, then, I must be here for a reason." I lift my hand toward his face again, my tone becoming a challenge. "Perhaps I'm here to claim your crown."

Now, he jolts backward.

I take a step forward, not letting him widen the gap between us.

That crown.

My mother told me all about it. It contains all of the dark magic the keeper has collected over thousands of years, a power like nothing else. Of course, he can't use it himself. His only purpose is to collect the magic. The rules of his creation stop him from wielding the magic he tethers.

But if I had that crown, I could destroy my enemies. I could cut out their hearts and make them bleed. Death would be a mercy for them.

Growls are leaving my lips and behind me, the panthers are fanning out, as if they're also preparing to attack.

"I forgive you for assuming I would fear you," I say to the keeper. "But I'm not leaving without that crown."

His answer is a snarl, but his voice sounds different now. Deeper, more guttural. "Why do you wish to take it?"

"I would use it to destroy my enemies and claim what's mine." My voice is vehement. "I will do anything to make them feel the pain they've caused me."

He stops moving, his robe wafting around his black-clad legs. "Anything?"

"I will cut to the bone if I have to." My lips draw back as I allow my claws to descend. "To get what is *owed* to me."

My threatening stance seems to please him.

The corners of his lips rise. "Would you cut as deep as your own bones?"

I don't hesitate. "If it means I would see my enemies suffer before I die—*yes.*"

"Oh, I'm not talking about death," he says. "I'm talking about the power in your heart."

Now I'm wary. "My heart?"

He suddenly closes the gap between us. I brace for attack

and the panthers snarl a warning at him, and he stops inches away from me.

The power radiating from him is intoxicating and my head spins to be this close to him.

His voice lowers, a soft suggestion. "I propose we make a deal, you and I."

"What deal?" I ask, my gaze rising from his lips to the crown. I want to see his eyes.

His response is a whisper that sends a shiver through me.

"Give me the power within your heart," he says. "By so doing, you will give me life. With life, I will be able to claim the power in my crown. In return for this, I will give you the vengeance you seek. Whatever you need me to do so you can achieve your revenge, I will do it."

My eyes widen at his proposal.

If I give him the ability to use his power, he's offering to use it for *me*. I was determined to seek vengeance on my own, but it was going to be an uphill battle. Particularly because I don't have any means to make it happen. I don't even have a shred of untorn material to my name.

Now, all the power I could possibly want is within my grasp.

I reach up, suddenly needing to make contact with his body. My fingertips hover the barest distance from his jaw before I dare to breach the gap.

His skin is cool to touch. Ethereal. Otherworldly. And not quite here. As if his form is paper thin.

I know what he is. I know about the power in his crown. But I don't know who he was all those thousands of years ago before he became the keeper of dark magic. I don't know if his heart was always dark or even what kind of supernatural he was.

Would I give away my heart in exchange for his power?

"You're asking for the power in my heart," I say, my eyes narrowed, since I need the organ beating in my chest to stay alive. "What exactly do you mean?"

"I'm talking about the greatest power of a heart," he says, as if I should already know. "The power to love."

Of course.

The decision is easy. All it takes is for my mother's long-ago words to echo back to me.

You were loved.

Quietly, I say, "What use is my heart if there's nobody left to love me?"

His lips soften. I feel his focus like a burn as his hand rises to my chest, his palm pressing over the location of my heart, his fingertips brushing against the bare skin that's reachable through the rips in my dress. A trickle of pleasure travels through my breast and down to my stomach. It's so unexpected that I fight not to gasp.

"If you want my heart…" I whisper, my voice turning into a snarl as I fight the unusual sensation across my skin, "*Take it.*"

CHAPTER FOUR

*T*he keeper's other arm scoops around me, pulling me close.

I sense the thinness of his form and I marvel at the way his wraith-like body can carry the weight of so much power. "I cannot take most dark magic from the living," he says, "but I *can* take the power of a heart since it only exists during life."

I find myself standing eye level with his chin, my gaze lifting to the crown and, up this close, to the shadows behind the metal.

My lips part with surprise when I catch a glimpse of the empty expanse behind his crown, a cavern of pain and despair.

Agony strikes through my chest so suddenly and sharply that I jolt, but his other arm tightens across my back, forcing me to stay where I am. My focus flies down to my chest, where his fingers are clawed and blood is soaking my dress.

A second later, the pain ends as quickly as it began, and his palm flattens against my skin, the final droplets of blood trickling across the back of his hand.

Black blood. The evidence of my heritage.

He lowers his head to mine and whispers against my lips. "I'm sorry if that hurt, but I promise it will be worth it."

That's it?

My forehead creases. "It's done?"

His lips are so close to mine that when I sway forward as I speak, my mouth brushes his. Tingling sensations flow all the way from my lips to my core, making me blink with surprise.

"It's done," he says, the movement of his lips against mine sending another stream of pleasant sensations through my body.

He breaks the contact, leaving me perplexed as he steps back and reaches up to his crown, his hands closing around it as if he's going to take it off.

I lean forward in anticipation, but a second later, he crouches to the floor and bows his head.

I can no longer see his face.

He slips the crown upward. The moment it leaves his head, black hair appears, falling across his face.

Remaining crouched, he rolls his shoulders, shrugging off his cloak, which floats to the floor and settles on the smooth surface with a soft hiss.

His frame is thin and transparent.

But then he rises slowly back to his feet.

My breath catches when his body transforms rapidly as he moves.

His chest fills out, gaining breadth, and his shoulders broaden. His neck thickens, his biceps grow, and his thighs and calves fill out with muscles.

My eyes widen even further when his transformation doesn't stop there.

Flames suddenly flicker around his chin and chest, fire streaming from his mouth as he exhales.

In the next moment, the fire stops and his fingers extend

into black claws that appear deadly sharp and then just as quickly retract.

Next, scales shimmer across his skin, first black in color, then ivory white, then just as quickly, they morph into a dusting of fur that covers his arms and legs before it, too, disappears.

Deep-amethyst wings burst across his back, feathers so long, they drape to the ground before they fully retract. The wings haven't even fully disappeared before electricity crackles between his fingers on both hands, charging the air around us so that it feels like a lightning strike is seconds away.

I can only stare as his form shifts through the characteristics of countless supernaturals from dragons to wolves, bears, harpies, warlocks, and finally...

His skin smooths out to take on a human appearance, settling into a pale-brown color. His tall, muscular form remains sculpted, every perfect muscle gleaming in the dark.

He's completely naked and it's impossible to miss the size of the length between his legs. That is, before energy crackles around his fingertips and clothing appears. Black pants and a gray T-shirt cover his nakedness and cling to his muscles.

He holds his crown in his left hand, but with another crackle of energy, its shape changes, shrinking until it's the size of a ring, which he slips onto the forefinger of his left hand.

Then his head rises, revealing a sharp jaw, high cheekbones, and lips shaped like a god's. He considers me with eyes that flicker through forest green, fierce amber, and finally settle on the darkest brown.

My heart is pounding in my chest, confirming that the organ is healthy and functioning as it should be, but *damn*, it was disconcerting watching this man shift his form through so many different shapes.

"Our deal is done," he says, his voice a deep rumble, the wraith-like hiss completely gone. "Tell me what vengeance you seek and I will make it so."

My lips part. I'm ready to speak, but I pause.

Deals are tricky. The keeper of dark magic has taken the power in my heart and now I need to assert my claim in return.

Despite all the lessons my mother taught me, the only information she refused to give me was the identity of the man responsible for her imprisonment when she was six months pregnant. All I know is that he is male.

Oh, she talked about the supernaturals in her life, but she never told me which man betrayed her. Which man so coveted the chance to rule the most powerful empire of dark creatures that they would condemn her to die in a cage.

I think she must have known that, if I ever escaped, I would seek revenge against that man.

But her final words will never leave me.

"We may be creatures of dark magic, but we were loved."

Now, I allow my hatred to rise as I voice my answer carefully. "You will help me kill the man who murdered my father, imprisoned my mother, and stole the empire that should have been mine."

The dark magic keeper smiles. "Then let the age of dark magic begin."

CHAPTER FIVE

a shiver of anticipation passes through me, overshadowed only by my hunger and thirst.

Unwilling to admit any weakness in front of the keeper, I say nothing about the gnawing ache in my stomach and instead prepare to ask him how the fuck we'll get out of this endlessly dark place.

The keeper surprises me when he taps his chest, his gaze becomes distant, and he says, "You're hungry, but there's no food or sustenance here. Neither can I conjure any. We need to leave this realm as fast as we can."

He sweeps his arm around me and hustles me to the right. "This way. Quickly."

I'm not sorry if he's taking me somewhere to get food, but the level of tension in his body indicates his sudden urgency isn't because of my empty stomach. "Why the hurry?"

"Now that I've shrugged off my cloak, this realm will become a vacuum, clinging to whatever dark magic it can. We don't want to become trapped here."

The panthers stay close to my heels, their black bodies blending into our surroundings so completely that it's only when they glance up at me with their silver eyes that I can place them in the dark.

"What will happen to the dark magic that's left untethered from creatures who die?" I ask, feeling a twinge of responsibility that doesn't sit well with my dark nature.

"That's no longer my problem," he replies.

My guilt only increases. *Fuck and damn.* "But—"

The keeper stops me, his arm remaining around my waist, his gaze devouring my face as he turns me toward him. "The balance between light and dark will reset itself. Such is nature. It's a problem that the creatures of the light will face. *We* do not have to concern ourselves with it."

I narrow my eyes at him. "Are you saying that the balance may tip and reset in favor of darkness?"

His eyes brighten. "I'm counting on it."

He gives me a wolfish grin, revealing momentarily sharp teeth that quickly transform back into their more human-looking shape. That is, the shape of humans I've seen in faded illustrations in dusty books.

He ushers me through the dark, moving confidently as he follows a path that's certainly not clear to me.

As far as I can discern, the only change in our surroundings is the temperature. The farther we venture away from the place where I first fell into this 'realm'—as he called it—the colder the air around us becomes.

Unbearably cold. Even for me.

It's as if our surroundings are pushing back against us.

My footfalls begin to slow and so do the keeper's.

The impact of the frosty air on the panthers is visible. Their outlines become clear as ice forms on their pelts, and shivers ripple across their backs.

I wrap my arms around myself, my teeth beginning to chatter. "Maybe we sh-sh-should have b-b-brought your c-c-cloak with us."

"Are you cold?"

I glance at the keeper, only to find that, in the seconds between me looking at him before and now, he's somehow acquired a puffy-looking jacket, long pants that appear to be made from a thick material, and calf-high boots with fur turned over at the top.

I catch the fading electricity around his fingers, which would indicate he conjured the clothing for himself.

He gives me a grin, as if he's very pleased with himself.

"What the f-f-fuck?" I practically spit at him, but I'm sure my saliva is freezing on my tongue. "S-S-So you can't make f-food, but you c-can make clothes? Will you m-make clothes for m-m-me?"

"Of course." His hands are now covered in mittens, but energy crackles around them once again. "All you have to do is ask."

I snark at him. "Oh, is that all?"

He takes a longer look at me, his forehead slightly pinched as if he's perturbed. His gaze has the effect of making me a little more pleasantly warm when it follows the flow of my black hair, lingering on the blonde tips before passing down my curves to my toes.

I can only guess he's scrutinizing my shape for the purpose of conjuring clothing that will fit, but as far as my appearance goes, I don't know what I look like.

Our jailer never gave us a mirror. My mother once described my features to me: golden eyes, black hair with gray streaks that turn to blonde at the end, and high cheekbones.

I was able to feel the shape of my face to verify her description and I could see the strands of my long, matted hair by pulling it forward, but the only way I've seen my eyes is in the blurry reflection off metal surfaces.

The keeper ceases scrutinizing me and returns his attention to the way forward, urging me onward once again.

He moves so quickly that for a second, I think he's going to leave me in my cold clothing after all, but he waves his left hand in my direction as he moves.

A bright-yellow jacket takes shape and wraps around my chest and arms. It's puffy enough to make my arms stick out a little at my sides and long enough to cover my butt. A moment after that, warm pants appear around my legs, wrapping from my waist to my ankles. And finally, a snuggly pair of boots covers my feet.

All while I continue to hurry along beside him.

Suddenly, I'm warm all the way to my bones and it feels like I'm walking on clouds.

It's an uncanny feeling. I'm weirdly pampered.

I wonder if this is why people wear shoes.

I have hard calluses on the soles of my feet that protected them from the stone floor of my cage, but *damn*, I could get used to this sort of comfort.

My teeth stop chattering now that my body is protected against the freezing air. "What about the panthers?"

The keeper's focus continues to remain directly ahead as he pushes onward, his footsteps slowing even further when the air becomes colder.

At my question, he waves his left hand in the air again. Energy crackles around his fingertips and lights up the space around us.

Doggy jackets appear on the panthers, the kind I've seen in children's book illustrations of cute puppies belonging to even cuter kids. The jackets are made of pink-and-white checkered material that's fluorescent and glows brightly in the dark.

"Delightful," I mutter.

One of the male panthers yelps and tears at the material with his teeth, quickly ripping it sufficiently to shimmy out of it. He gives me a self-satisfied grin as he resumes shivering in the cold.

I supposed he'd rather freeze than wear such a brightly-colored jacket.

The female panther doesn't attack her new coat, but she turns her eyes up at me and gives me a hard stare.

"Not impressed, huh?" I ask.

She bares her teeth at me before she slinks along beside me.

A step ahead, the keeper draws to a stop.

"Here," he says. "There's a weakness in the boundary. Something on the other side must have been eating away at it." His brow quickly creases. "I'm not sure what could be waiting for us if we go through this way. I sense it isn't the natural world..."

"What do you mean 'not the natural world'?"

Even as I ask my question, he peers back the way we came and the tension in his shoulders grows. I, too, sense the increasing pull in our environment, which tugs at my back even as the cold pushes at my front.

"It's this or nothing," the keeper says. "We'll have to chance it."

Black claws grow quickly from his fingertips and he pushes them through the air in front of him, pulling the darkness apart with the same action he'd use to open curtains.

"Quickly," he says. "I can't hold it open for long."

I squint at the much brighter light spilling through the gap he's created. It's impossible to see what lies beyond the narrow opening, and I hope the keeper isn't sending me to my death.

I'm reassured when the female panther darts through without hesitation, followed quickly by the three males, all four of them disappearing within seconds.

I step in behind them, crouching so I can slip through the parted darkness beneath the keeper's arms. The freezing-cold edges of his realm brush my shoulders as I pass by, and I feel the sting all the way through the puffer jacket like icicles ramming into me.

Fuck, that hurts!

It's as if the realm itself is trying to grip and tear at me to stop me from leaving.

I grit my teeth against the pain, push forward with all my might, and in the next moment, I've left the keeper's realm behind.

In the second before the brightness of my new surroundings overcomes me, I glimpse a landscape that's charred and burned. Two lines of trees stretch out in arcs on either side of me. Their trunks are burned out, their branches either shattered and lying in pieces on the ground or dangling from their scorched bodies. Only a few brown leaves remain on them.

A stone wall sits immediately behind my current position. It rises as high as my shoulders, but it's crumbling so badly that I suspect I could knock it over with a gentle push of my fingertips.

Where I'm standing, there's a gap in the stone wall, the jagged edges appearing dangerously sharp, and it feels somewhat like I stepped, not from the keeper's realm, but through the opening in the wall into this place.

Ahead of me, the shadow panthers have padded onto a flat, square courtyard that extends about thirty paces into the distance. It's paved in marble that might once have been white but is now burned black. It isn't a gleaming black like the floor of the keeper's realm. This marble is striated with inch-wide fissures that appear to be filled with lava.

Lava that's still cooling down.

Heat waves fill the air around me and swirl through the center of the courtyard, where an empty pedestal sits.

On the opposite side of the courtyard is an impenetrable brick wall, this one rising all the way up into the hazy air, its top hidden in clouds of black smoke.

That's all I see before the brightness of the heat waves makes my eyes sting and the burning heat hits me like a punch to the face.

CHAPTER SIX

H̸ot! So fucking hot!

I'm instantly bathed in sweat. A flood of it slides down my face and between my breasts.

"Clothes," I gasp. "Too hot!"

Squeezing my eyes shut against the light, I rip at the jacket, boots, and the pants, flinging them off as quickly as I can. As soon as they hit the ground, they vanish into nothing. Ahead of me, the female panther and the two males still wearing jackets are also tearing theirs off, helping each other to remove them.

Now that I've got the warm clothing off, the hot air rushes in and it's only marginally better now that I'm only wearing a threadbare bra and underpants.

As quickly as I can, I wrap the strip of material from my mother's skirt around my eyes again. The other material from her shirt remains around my left hand and, although it makes my palm sweaty, I'm not letting it go.

I'm aware of the keeper stepping up behind me and a soft, swishing sound that is presumably the sides of his realm sealing together.

His voice sounds at my ear. "I can make you a new blindfold if you wish."

"No," I say, more sharply than I intended, but the hunger pains in my stomach are making me angry. "This belonged to my mother. I will never part from it."

Besides, the material is so perfectly threadbare that I can see my surroundings through the weave without experiencing the acute glare. Although 'glare' is probably not quite accurate. I have a feeling this place could be dimly lit compared to the outside world, given that the only lighting is the glow from the cooling threads of lava.

"As you like," the keeper says.

I catch a flicker of electricity before the clothing around his own body changes. This time, he becomes bare-chested. A pair of jeans covers his legs and sturdy-looking boots appear on his feet. I'm gratified that his skin glistens with sweat, which tells me he's feeling the heat too.

He offered to make me a new blindfold, which I don't want, but even the callouses on my feet won't protect me from the temperature in the courtyard ahead of us.

"Boots," I say, staring at him expectantly, even though I know he can't see my eyes.

He looks back at me, his head tilted slightly, as if he's waiting for more.

His inaction, the increasing heat, the gnawing emptiness in my stomach, and my dry mouth make me even more irritated. "You told me all I have to do is ask. I need boots."

"Please," he says, pointedly. "Boots, *please*."

I glower at him. "Asking isn't begging."

"Saying 'please' doesn't amount to begging."

I swipe at the sweat dripping down my brow, sighing into the heat. "I need boots… *please*."

"As you like," he says.

Knee-high leather boots appear on my feet. They're so soft

and fit me so perfectly that it feels like… Well, Mom once described silk sheets to me and I imagine these boots feel a lot like that.

Other than the boots, I'm still only wearing my underwear, but I don't give a shit about my near-nakedness. I'm accustomed to the cold and this heat… *Phew…* It's nearly too much.

I saunter toward the courtyard, pretending I'm not so thirsty that I want to crawl out of my own skin. The panthers gather around me, deftly avoiding stepping on any lava fissures.

"Not the natural world?" I arch an eyebrow at the keeper. "What you should have said is that we were about to step into literal hell."

He gives me a grin that I find more than a little wicked, as if he'd be delighted to escort me on a vacation to the underworld.

"This isn't hell," he says, studying our surroundings. "I sense the light magic that was used to create this place, and it has the same stench as the magic that was used to create the place you came from." He gestures in the air. "This is a pocket of the veil."

"The veil." I flinch at his mention of it. "Then this place was created by angels."

According to what Mom told me, the veil is the space between the natural world and the heavenly realm. Within the veil, pockets have been created and doorways into those pockets are hidden throughout the United States. Our cage was located within such a pocket.

"Indeed," the keeper is saying. "Only angels with the strongest light magic can create pockets in the veil like this one. Are you familiar with Sentinels?"

I'm too fucking familiar with Sentinels. They're supposed to live in groups of three within the veil, guarding precious objects. If any other supernatural were to manage the nearly impossible task of finding and infiltrating a pocket of the veil, the Sentinels would fight to the death to keep that object safe and stop that supernatural from leaving.

"My jailer was a Sentinel," I say, my response clipped. "Ordinary angels can't hurt me, but Sentinels can."

"With their soul light." The keeper's lips press into a thin line. "There are not many Sentinels, but the few who exist are extremely powerful and can inflict severe damage on creatures of dark magic."

My shoulders have become hunched, the memories of burning pain returning to me.

The keeper's right hand lightly brushes my cheek, drawing my gaze upward. His other hand taps his chest. "Your anger is warranted."

For a moment, his face fills with pain, and I wonder if it's his pain or mine. He tapped his chest like that before when he sensed my hunger.

The tension around his eyes eases and his voice becomes even softer. "In this case, it's lucky for us that this pocket of the veil was created, because it has provided us with a conduit from my realm to the outside world."

As he speaks, he inclines his head back toward the crumbling gap in the stone wall before turning toward the solid brick wall ahead of us. "This way. Step carefully."

The panthers stay close to me, but they don't seem so concerned anymore about the cooling lava on the ground, happily padding toward the center of the courtyard as if they belong in this hellish landscape.

Well, I suppose it suits them.

"You're not fucking hellhounds," I chastise them as I plot a careful path between sizzling fissures.

Not like my mother. She was a hellhound. A magnificent one. Strong against every other supernatural, except a fucking Sentinel.

Sometimes I wonder if she would have survived our cage if she'd chosen to remain in her fully-shifted form. After all, dark spaces didn't frighten or diminish her. By choosing to spend so much time in her humanoid form—a form that needed fresh air and a blue sky and nutritious food—her body had weakened irreversibly.

She once told me she tried to stay in her shifted form as much as she could when I was a baby, snatching an hour here and there while I was sleeping. But she couldn't care for me in that form. Couldn't feed me, change me, or rock me to sleep. By the time I could look after myself, the damage to her body was done.

I press my hand to my heart, where it still hurts, and cast a glare at the keeper's back.

Surely, by taking the power in my heart, he could have taken all of the pain too?

I glance down at the nearest male panthers, only to find them grinning up at me, their lips drawing back from their silver teeth. I don't imagine for one second that they're smiling at my pain. I called them hellhounds and it seems they don't mind that title one fucking bit.

I'm not sure how the female feels about it because she's prowled ahead of me and now travels at the keeper's side.

He surges ahead, nearly at the pedestal that sits in the center of the courtyard, and I make myself keep up, even though my thirst is unbearable.

"How did I even get into your realm?" I ask, uncertain if he'll give me an answer.

"For some time, the walls between my realm, the veil, and the natural world have been thinning. You fell through an opening that the Sentinels haven't been able to close." He gives a soft sigh. "Until I had a heart's power, I wasn't able to escape through any of those openings."

He slows his pace and pauses at the pedestal. "Ah," he says, as if he has just realized something. "A powerful object rested here. Something that didn't belong in this pocket of the veil."

He narrows his eyes at our surroundings. "Whatever the

object was, it was powerful enough to have burned through the walls of my realm. It must have created the openings like the one you fell through."

He crouches briefly to the floor and lays his right palm flat against it. His head tilts a little to the side as if he's trying to sense something.

When I draw level with him, he says, "Death also happened here. But not the death of dark magic creatures. Light magic is heavier around this location."

He gestures at the wall we're headed toward, and his brows draw down as if he's warier now. "A battle raged all the way to that wall, beyond which I suspect it probably continued." His eyes narrow and he appears deep in thought. "Or perhaps it started from that direction and moved over here. Then back again."

I follow his line of sight. Maybe if I weren't so hungry, I would be able to discern the danger he senses. "How can you tell?"

"I can follow the streams of magic like footprints. They cross the courtyard multiple times and sometimes leave the ground."

As he finishes rising to his feet, the dark light in his eyes becomes intense and a sheen of golden scales forms across his skin. Dragon scales or serpent scales; I'm not sure which.

"Winged creatures fought here," he says, sounding very certain and more than a little unhappy. "Powerful ones."

I speak aloud the conclusions I'm drawing from his body language. "You're concerned."

He nods. "This battle was recent. It could still be raging out there or it could be over. It's unclear what we might be stepping into when we pass through to the natural world."

He chews his bottom lip and turns back toward the way we came. "The level of power I'm sensing is worrying. We should avoid these beings at all costs."

I'm surprised that any creature would give the keeper of

dark magic a reason for pause. The fact that he seems to be contemplating heading back the way we came tells me he's serious about the threat level we could face.

But his words also trigger my anger.

I may be tired, thirsty, and starving, but I step up to the keeper as he considers me quietly. I'm so close to him now that I have to tip my head back to see his face. "I'm not afraid to fuck with powerful creatures. I lived my life imprisoned by one. If I meet that Sentinel again, I will kill him. No matter the cost to me. Even if he burns me to the bone. I'm done with fear."

The keeper's nearness is intoxicating and the crown-shaped ring he's wearing radiates power that only serves to feed my anger.

"*I will fear no more,*" I say.

He stares down at me, his eyes grazing my face, a disconcertingly intense study. Then his tension fades and his lips rise. "No more."

Without taking his eyes off me, the keeper inclines his head at the far wall—the one that extends all the way up into the haze and will provide our exit. "Let's go. Be prepared."

CHAPTER SEVEN

*T*he keeper walks straight toward the stone wall, and the panthers follow him.

When he reaches it, he stops. "I'll walk through first," he says. "Count to ten and then come after me. I will have either subdued any threat by then or drawn them away from you."

Without waiting for my agreement, he steps into the wall as if it's made of nothing but air and disappears through it. The female panther darts after him.

"But—" I'm left with the three male panthers, who gather close around me like guards. Their heads are held low and they growl at the wall.

I wish I had names for them, but names carry power and must be chosen carefully. I promise myself that once I've reached a safe place where I can breathe easily, I'll figure out what the panthers should be called.

In the meantime, I force myself to count backward from ten, murmuring each number beneath my breath.

Finally, I reach one and I hurry forward, not wanting to admit to myself how much it has unsettled me to lose sight of the keeper. I've been alone for so long that having this man and all of these panthers near me feels as necessary as breathing.

I extend my arms and squeeze my eyes shut as I approach the wall, half-expecting to find it solid, but the air tingles around me and that's the only feedback I get before I realize that I've stepped all the way through.

I'm prepared to find myself among enemies—attackers on the other side of this stone—and my claws are extended in readiness.

There's nobody else here but the keeper and the panthers. The female pads up to me, nudging my hand with her head, as if to reassure me.

"We're alone," the keeper says. His visible skin is covered in black scales that extend from his cheeks down his neck and bare chest and arms like armor. "For now."

I exhale and retract my claws, allowing myself to study the space around me.

I'm startled by the fact that it appears to be some sort of cell.

It's so similar to my cage that I can't stop my shudder.

Actually... it's *smaller* than my cage.

All of us together are filling the space and it feels cramped.

I cast a disapproving glance at the barest of necessities within the cage. A mattress on a wooden frame. A single chair. Although this cell also has things I didn't have: a lidless toilet, instead of a bucket; a single blanket; and a small desk.

The bars across the front of the cage are warped and appear to have been torn open.

On the other side is a small, open area that ends with a set of stairs leading upward.

The whole place appears to be hewn out of rock.

"I think we're underground," I say, drawing conclusions from the appearance of the walls, ceiling, and floor.

"I agree," the keeper says, his eyes narrowed at our surroundings. "But I've never seen this place before."

I find his comment curious and my forehead creases. "How would you have seen it before?"

He gravitates toward the side of the cell as he replies. "Every time a creature of dark magic died, I had the chance to see the world around them and to experience their memories. Only briefly, mind you. Their memories would slip away quickly. But over time, I accumulated knowledge about the world. Buildings, places, technology. I watched the world change." He taps his temple. "And I built a map in my mind. But this place is not on it."

"Which means... what, exactly?"

"Dark creatures have never died here. We should assume, therefore, that this could be a stronghold for creatures of another kind of magic. They could be light magic, elemental magic, possibly even old magic. Regardless, this place could have been fortified enough that dark creatures might never have set foot here."

"Great," I say dryly. "Even more perfect than the possibility of running into powerful creatures of light magic is the chance we've found ourselves inside one of their strongholds."

The keeper has paused at the side of the cell, and now he stares at a strip of material hanging on a nail there. He makes a humming sound in the back of his throat and his eyes are narrowed as he peers at it.

"What is it?" I ask.

"A sash, perhaps. Or a blindfold." He scoops the material up in his big hand and inhales deeply. The shape of his eyes changes as he takes in the scent of the material, his pupils becoming distinctly reptilian. Combined with the black scales covering his skin, it has the effect of making him appear serpentine.

He drops the material quickly. "This isn't good," he murmurs to himself.

I may be desperate for food and water, but I don't like the

way he suddenly reconsiders our environment as if it might be even more dangerous to us than he first suspected.

"What's wrong?" I ask, a sharp demand for answers, and then I attempt to soften it with: "Tell me. *Please.*"

"I'm familiar with the supernatural who owns this sash," the keeper says, pointing at the strip of black material that has settled back against the wall. "I recognize her scent. She's an angel of great strength, but she isn't pure like most angels."

I'm surprised by his description of the angel. "'Not pure'?" I ask. "What do you mean by that?"

He gives me a suddenly gleaming smile. "She won't hesitate to judge and kill what she hates." His smile drops from his face. "Which will include us."

Huh. I'm not sure I'm so scared of an angel who doesn't conceal her true intentions behind a countenance of supposed purity. It's the fakers who make me want to tear apart the world.

"It sounds to me like she's more darkness than light," I say, wondering if this angel really would kill me. After all, I've never hurt a soul. Not yet, anyway.

The keeper acknowledges my statement with a grunt. "We must proceed carefully."

He prowls across the cell, steps over the remains of the mangled bars, and moves toward the staircase.

"We already were," I grumble, surprised by the sudden feeling of defeat that rises within me.

I knew escaping my cage wouldn't be easy, but the path to freedom has brought me into new dangers I wasn't anticipating. I swore I was done with fear and that I would fight every enemy who steps into my path, but...

My body's growing weaker by the minute. I'm not at my full strength, although the reality is that I've never been at my full strength. With minimal nutrition, my jailer ensured I was never as strong as my full potential.

My legs wobble as I take a step and I mask it by pausing near the strip of material hanging on the wall.

I could fear this material as a symbol of the being who wears it.

Or… I could face that fear. Literally.

With a snarl, I pull the black sash from the nail and wrap it around my own head. Its opacity is complete; it blocks everything from view, which means it could be useful if the light in the outside world proves too much for me.

Of course, I will need to ignore its scent. A powerful mix of justice and rage.

Not pure, huh?

I can feed on the rage the owner of this material left within its folds, but this justice… It carries the sense of punishment being meted out quickly, efficiently. Ruthless but clean.

My definition of justice is blood and pain. Delivered with extreme prejudice.

Removing the sash from my face, I tie it around my waist like a belt. I am no longer concerned about the woman who wears this sash.

No, make that *used to* wear it.

It's mine now.

Even though the temperature in this cell is comfortable to me, I recognize that I'll need to ask the keeper for new clothes soon, if only because walking around in my underwear will attract attention. In the meantime, I remain decked out in my bra, my underpants, my mother's old shirt tied around my left hand, a strip of her skirt around my eyes, and now this sash around my waist.

It takes me a few seconds to plod across the cage to meet the keeper at the base of the stairs at the far end of the room. Again, I mask my weakness by acting as if I'm studying my surroundings as I move.

I try to keep the desperation from my voice as I ask, "What's the difference between food and clothes? Why can you make one, but not the other?"

"Clothing is an illusion," he says. "Food must be real."

My brow creases. "But the warm clothing didn't feel fake."

He lifts his chin. "That's because it was a *good* illusion. It tricked your brain into believing you were warm. It would even trick someone who touched your clothing into believing the clothing was really there. If I conjured food for you in the same way, you would believe your belly was full."

His smile fades. "And yet you would waste away. Better to feel your hunger and thirst than to die because of deceit."

"Oh." *Well, that makes sense.* "So if you want to get rid of me, you could simply feed me fake food."

He reacts to my claim quickly and with surprising force, pulling me toward him. One of his arms sweeps across my back, while his other palm rests against my jaw, his fingers splayed over my cheekbone, his position ensuring that I don't look away from his eyes.

"I made a vow." He growls, baring his teeth at me. While his teeth resemble a wolf's, black scales ripple across his naked chest and up the sides of his neck that look distinctly *dragon*. "You will live to have your revenge."

I try to take a breath, fighting the effect of his bare skin against mine, the press of my breasts against his chest and the contact of my body with all the other hard parts of him. "Do you really think I'll believe deceit isn't in your repertoire?" I whisper.

"It isn't when it comes to you."

I don't believe him. Not completely. He's a dark creature like me. We live on lies and subterfuge.

My hands splay across his chest, testing for a moment his reaction to my touch.

His pupils darken, but his hold on me softens. "I sense your fatigue even if you won't speak of it. Do you need me to assist you to climb these stairs?"

"Don't you fucking dare," I snarl, pushing away from him.

His distance makes my skin cool in the dank air.

"As you like." Without further hesitation, he ascends the stairs, and once again, I follow.

If I had more strength, I would take the lead and assert dominance.

I tell myself I'm simply allowing him to act as my shield.

I'm being wise, not weak.

The stairs advance to a corridor with ivory walls. There's no natural light, only lamps set at intervals along the wall. The brightness isn't too unpleasant, which I hope means my eyesight is beginning to adjust.

An opaque door sits at the far end of the corridor obscuring whatever lies beyond it.

Despite the barrier, my sense of smell is detecting...

What is that?

Something utterly revolting to my senses. It's like flowers... but not flowers.

It sets the hairs at the back of my neck on end.

"Angels," I whisper. "It's fucking angels."

CHAPTER EIGHT

The keeper presses his palm to the door, the same way he pressed his hand to the ground in the burned courtyard.

"I believe you're correct," he says.

"Can you tell if there are any Sentinels among them?"

He shakes his head, humming in the back of his throat, but some of his tension finally eases. "I can't be certain, but I don't sense any strong light magic. Whatever battle was being fought in this place, I no longer sense the presence of those powerful creatures."

I breathe out my relief. Not that I wasn't ready to take them on, but I'm happy I won't have to do it right now. "That's good. Regular angels don't bother me."

The keeper's hand lands on my shoulder. "A trail of blood is not in our best interests. You need a clean path behind you or you'll forever be looking over your shoulder."

I'm already looking over my shoulder. Even now, my jailer could be tracking me. At some point, I'm going to have to tell the keeper where I've come from and what's coming after me.

But right now, standing in a hallway on the other side of what could possibly be a legion of angels, doesn't seem like the time.

I narrow my eyes at him. "I didn't say I was going to kill them."

"Then you'll trust me to deal with any angels we encounter?"

"It depends on how you plan to 'deal with' them."

Presumably, it doesn't involve any blood since he seems against that.

He gives me a smug smile. "You'll see."

I'm ready to protest, but he's already pushing the door open.

The panthers hold back, their growls coming low and soft, as if they're as disconcerted by the smells in our new surroundings as I am. They'll be wary of angels, given what they must surely have experienced at Zadkiel's hands.

The door opens into a large room.

Despite the keeper's belief that there are no *powerful* creatures present, I was bracing for a room full of angels, but there are none in sight.

The walls are cracked, fissures extending across their surface, and chips of paint and plaster are strewn across the floor. It looks as if the entire structure was shaken. I sift through my memory of environmental factors, wondering about the tremors that my mother called 'earthquakes,' but I quickly dismiss that possibility. These cracks are combined with burn marks that indicate targeted fire, the scorch lines streaking across the walls as if from some sort of flamethrower.

I'm glad we haven't been confronted with angry angels, but their absence is becoming more disconcerting.

"Where are they?" I ask, and quickly add, "Maybe those powerful creatures killed them?"

The keeper proceeds at a slow pace ahead of me along the corridor. He shakes his head. "The angels are here. Somewhere..."

His ears take on the shape of a wolf's while his nose

elongates and thickens like a bear's. "I can hear and smell them." He growls before his features return to their humanoid shape. "There's a legion outside this building. I hear the clanking of metal and scraping of soil."

I shudder. At the peak of my abilities, I should be able to sense what he can sense. The fact that I can't tells me I'm in bad shape.

He proceeds cautiously through the room, checking our surroundings as he moves.

My only concern is for us to find the way out.

Well, that is, until another scent fills my chest.

Food.

Mindless with the need for sustenance, I veer in the direction of the mouthwatering smells. I don't know what kind of food it might be—it doesn't smell so bland as anything I've eaten. It must be something with layers of flavor, given the variety of combined scents wafting my way.

The keeper's hand snakes around my forearm before I can move away from him. "How badly do you want to eat?" he asks, indicating that he too, can smell the food. But of course he can.

"Badly." Although in many respects, it's my thirst that matters more. My stomach tightens painfully at the promise of food. "Enough to say *please* a hundred times."

"Very well," he replies. "I think it's safe enough for us to take a detour through this broken place and deal with its inhabitants when we need to."

I'm practically running when he leads me to the left, a final burst of energy pushing me onward on the trail of the delicious scents.

We enter another room, this one with a glass ceiling that's shattered. Sharp pieces litter the floor all around the room. Again, the far walls are charred as if a fire burned across them.

But what stops me in my tracks is the darkness above us.

A twinkling darkness.

One of the few things that could take priority over food.

I want to see it better, and my hands rise to my face to remove my makeshift blindfold, but I remind myself that even the soft lighting could cause me pain, so I stop myself.

"The sky," I whisper, trying to see it through the weave, all the way up there. "Is that the night sky?"

The keeper pauses ahead of me, tipping his head back briefly, before he surprises me by reaching for my face and urging me to look at him instead of up through the broken ceiling.

"The light in this room obscures the night sky's beauty," he says. "Do not look upon it here. I will show you the beautiful darkness when the time is right."

Beautiful darkness.

My focus is now on the keeper's features, the streaming shifts of color through his eyes, one moment luminescent, the next so black that I feel like I'm falling into an abyss.

I struggle to tear my eyes away.

Then the scent of food breaks through again, and my hunger prevails.

I tug in that direction, but the keeper's hold on me tightens.

"What is it?" I ask.

He inclines his head at the patterned glass that litters the floor. "I know that glass. I've seen it in the memories of dark creatures who tried to invade this place and never got closer than the outside walls. I know where we are now."

The pain in my stomach makes me reckless. "Okay, well, unlike them, we're already inside, and there's food—"

"No," he says. "This is a place called 'the Cathedral.' We can't stay here."

"Cathedral?"

"The stronghold of the Philadelphia Order of Angels. These angels are known for their ferocity. Whatever battle was fought here appears to confirm it. We need to leave."

"Philadelphia," I whisper. "*Fuck.*"

More worrying to me than the identification of our location is the fact that we're still in Philadelphia. My cage is here. Zadkiel lured Mom to this city under the guise of helping her. I was hoping that, by traveling through the dark keeper's realm and then through a pocket of the veil, I'd moved far away from my cage.

As for the Order of Angels, every major city has one. Each is led by a Serene Commander—a warrior angel stronger than the others.

The fact that we're now standing within the stronghold of the Philadelphia Order means that my jailer could also be here. Even though he's a Sentinel, and they usually keep to their pockets of the veil, he's also an angel, which means he would have a right to come here.

In fact, if there was some battle he was called to help fight, it could explain why he disappeared for a few days. Even now, he could have discovered that I've escaped and might be on my trail.

"No." I groan against these possibilities, fighting my need to escape, which is now at war with my desperate need for sustenance. "But there's *food.*"

The scents wafting through the archway on our left are driving me to madness. If there's a fight ahead of me, I need to be stronger for it.

I jab my finger in the direction from which the smells are coming. "*Food.*"

"We don't belong here," the keeper says, more gently than I was expecting.

My response is harsh in the face of his calmness. "We don't belong *anywhere*. Everywhere we go will be dangerous for us. I'm not afraid, remember?"

Just telling myself that doesn't banish the fact that I should be afraid, but it does allow me to put my anxiety in its place and replace it with another emotion.

"I'm hungry. I'm dehydrated." My voice becomes a low, dangerous growl. "And now I'm *angry*."

"You're hungry-angry," the keeper says, nodding as if this is a thing.

"Angry-hungry." I growl, but I end on a whimper when he continues to hold my arm. "And thirsty. I'm really thirsty. Please?"

The panthers, too, whine up at me and then turn to the keeper, their eyes big and pleading as they look to him.

He makes an unhappy sound in the back of his throat. "There are safer places to eat and drink, but the fact that you've admitted this weakness tells me you're not going to manage the journey."

"Weakness!" I spit. "Don't insult me right now. Did you not hear the part where I'm *angry*-hungry?"

He appears completely unmoved by my fury, but he releases my arm. "As you like."

Immediately, I launch myself in the direction of the arched passageway to the left of the damaged room.

The keeper stays close behind me, and the four panthers spread out around me in the corridor. I follow what feels like a short maze of hallways, the cooking smells growing stronger until I finally reach a partially open door.

From within the room beyond it, there also wafts the floral scent I detected before, and once again, my instincts are at war.

There's danger in that room. Just as the keeper warned.

The female panther's soft growls reach my ears as the keeper looms in behind me. I proclaimed to him that I wouldn't hesitate to fuck with powerful creatures, but the floral scent is giving me pause.

His shoulder brushes mine. I expect him to tell me he told me so and tug me in the other direction.

Instead, the sudden blackness of his eyes takes my breath away.

He reaches past me and pushes open the door.

With the movement of his hand, dark light resembling thin threads of mist appears around his fingertips and travels across the space in front of us. Tendrils whoosh around the door's edge and reach across the air.

As the light streaks into the room, I take in the layout in a heartbeat.

It's a place for cooking. My mother would have called it a 'kitchen.' I recognize the shapes of electrical appliances that could be ovens and stoves, although they're more streamlined than the ones my mother described. She did warn me that technology was rapidly changing and that it would likely continue to change over the years.

A very large table is located in the center of the room, and on the other side of it stand two women.

One of them is holding a knife and chopping what I think are potatoes.

The other is mixing something I can't yet see in a large metal bowl.

As soon as the door opens, their heads snap up and their white wings extend, gorgeous wings that beat suddenly and sharply, carrying the women up into the air even as the keeper's dark light drifts toward them.

Whatever magic he's conjured, it's going to reach them too slowly for my liking.

I'm not about to wait for his dark light to do its work.

Even in my weakened state, I prepare myself to fight.

CHAPTER NINE

 y black claws extend with a *snap*, their muted color making them harder for any opponent to see.

I know the basics of cutting throats and disemboweling bodies and how to avoid both happening to myself. Mom taught me how to fight dirty. If only I could have used those techniques on our jailer.

The younger of the two angels, despite lifting off the ground, is still holding on to her mixing bowl. It sits snugly against her left side while she grips the wooden spoon in her right hand as if it were a blade.

Some sort of milky-looking sauce splashes from the spoon as she points it from me to the keeper. "Stay back, dark beasts."

Her voice is sickeningly ethereal. I can't help but wrinkle my nose even as I stride toward her.

The older woman is far less outspoken, her hand shaking where she brandishes her knife in our direction. Maybe, despite the keeper's assertion that these angels are fierce, she doesn't know how to use the blade.

"Bright saints, have mercy on us," she whispers, her wide eyes seeming glued to the keeper, her trembles extending all the way out to the tips of her wings.

A glance at him tells me why.

His features have morphed in the space of seconds.

Two blood-red horns project from the top of his head; his eyes have become glowing, crimson orbs; black clothing covers him from his neck to his ankles; and a scaled tail with a sharp tip at the end rises up behind him and flicks in the air.

Pure devil.

I can't help my crooked smile as I draw to a halt only a few paces from the table. I was planning to leap up onto it and launch myself through the air at the angels, but my weak body defies me.

I brace for them to come at me, but it seems the keeper's appearance has frozen them in their tracks.

As the younger angel coasts the air, edging backward, her gaze flies wildly from the keeper to the panthers. Then to the blade shaking in the other angel's hand. Then to her wooden spoon—which she seems to finally realize is less-than-adequate for this task—before her darting gaze lands on me.

Her eyes widen even further when she seems to recognize the sash I'm wearing around my waist, her jaw dropping a little. "That doesn't belong to you!"

Hmm. Interesting that she's more outraged about the sash than she is worried about her life.

She brandishes the wooden spoon at me and I raise my eyebrows at it. "Really?"

Her cheeks flush bright red and her lips part as if she's about to issue a retort.

Well, she has pluck, I'll give her that.

Before she can make another sound, the keeper's dark light reaches both angels.

The tips of the tendrils brush their chins and curl around their necks.

As soon as the magic touches them, their eyes become blank and they drop softly to the floor, although they're still gripping their would-be weapons.

"You don't need to be concerned about us." The keeper's voice is soft and his eyes are entirely black now as he focuses on the two women.

The moment he speaks, they relax, as if they believe him.

He continues in a mesmerizing croon. "We're not your enemies. *No.* We've simply come here for food and water and nothing more. You will fill three jugs of water and leave them on the table. You will serve us two of the meals you're preparing. Finally, for our beasts, you will prepare bowls of water and bring fresh meat. We will eat, drink, and then we will go."

His voice remains quiet, but there's a harder edge to it as he continues. "While we're here, you will not look at us. When we're gone, you will forget we were here. If you do this, you will not be harmed."

"Speak for yourself," I mutter. My hatred of angels extends beyond my captor to their entire race. Even if the keeper has forbidden me from spilling their blood.

The keeper side-eyes me while the women retract their wings and place their cooking implements back on the table. They immediately set about retrieving jugs, plates, and food, ignoring us the whole time.

I watch them warily, waiting to see if they wake up from the trance the keeper placed them in.

When they don't, I take a moment to study them more closely.

The younger angel has bright, blue eyes and auburn-blonde hair, and by the unholy saints, she smells like fucking spring. Her scent is so bright and cheerful that it turns my stomach.

The older angel has dark-brown hair streaked with gray and delicate wrinkles around her eyes and mouth.

I have no way of knowing if either of them is affiliated with my captor. My only certainty is that they are not the same kind of angel as he is. The energy around them is far weaker.

Beside me, the keeper's ears briefly take on the shape of a wolf's before he resumes his former countenance: light-brown skin, deep-brown eyes, and no tail or horns in sight. "The other angels are still outside," he says. "But we should stay alert."

My stomach pinches, a nasty, empty feeling that reminds me just how much I need water and food. "I'll be prepared to run."

But only if I manage to scoop up a jug of water first.

As soon as the younger angel places a flagon of water on the table, I grab it and drink the whole thing as fast as I can.

Thank the dark saints.

I groan with relief, licking the final droplets off my lips as I pull out a chair and sit at the table.

The angels don't bat an eyelid, proceeding to place bowls of water and pieces of raw meat on the floor for the panthers. Then they serve out plates of food for me and the keeper and push them across the table toward us. All without looking at us.

Each plate is laden with food they took from the hot oven.

I sink back against the chair, not yet reaching for the food. I've never been drunk, but I imagine it feels a lot like this. My mouth is no longer dry, my body feels stronger, and my thoughts are sharper.

I grin at the keeper as I slouch happily in my chair.

He takes small sips of water, and it makes me wonder how long it's been since he's drunk anything—or even needed to.

I'm more cautious with the food since I'm not certain how my body will tolerate it. I recognize most of its components as vegetables.

The keeper also eats slowly, pushing the pieces around his

plate. He stabs them with his fork and examines them, sniffing them carefully before he puts them into his mouth and chews.

Every now and then, he pronounces the name of the food. To the small pebbles of yellow vegetables, he says, "Corn."

To a chunk of orange that is straight on one edge and curved on the other, he says, "Carrot."

"Yes." I've never eaten either before now. Even if Mom hadn't told me about corn and carrot, I'd recognize them from children's books. "Did you see them in the memories of dark creatures who died?"

He gives me a nod. "Centuries ago, it was common for dark creatures to die in taverns. Even now, many deaths happen in places where food and beverages are served." He shrugs. "Alcohol seems to bring out the worst in us."

He arches his eyebrows at me as if he's baffled before he returns his focus to the piece of carrot, which has remained impaled on his fork. "Also, I think I must have eaten carrots in my life before I became the keeper."

I'm not surprised by this. According to my mother, each of the four keepers of magic was a supernatural with a life and even families before they became a keeper.

He peers at me before I can ask him more. "What about you?"

He knows nothing about me. Not where I came from before I met him in his realm, or what my life was like, or what food I may or may not have eaten. He seems to be able to discern some aspects of my feelings and needs, which he indicates by tapping his chest. I'm not sure of the extent to which that also gives him the power to see my memories.

"How much does my heart tell you?" I ask.

"It tells me what you're feeling in the present moment," he replies. "Your physical and emotional state."

"Does it allow you to see my memories?"

His eyes twinkle. "If it did, do you think I would have asked if you'd ever eaten corn?"

I snort. "You might've. Just to throw me off."

He arches his eyebrows at me. "Remember, I have no deceit when it comes to you."

"So you say."

He sighs, as if my disbelief pains him. "Then let me answer your question more clearly: I can't see your memories."

I study him for a moment. If he's lying, I can't tell. "I've never eaten corn."

"Do you like it?"

I tip my head, an ambiguous response. "It's mushy."

He grunts. "It's better on the cob."

"On the cob?"

"I believe it grows on a thing called a 'cob.' Apparently, it tastes great with butter."

On the other side of the table, the women continue to ignore us, and the longer they do, the more curious I am about the power the keeper used on them.

When he channels the essence of a wolf or a dragon, or even the electrical currents of a warlock's power, he takes on the physical attributes of that same power. I'm curious now about whether or not the power he used to make the angels obey him was connected to his devilish appearance.

"What magic did you use on these women?"

"Demon power," he says, confirming my theory. "Demons have the strongest powers of persuasion, although it usually requires physical contact with the target to make it work. Over time, I've accumulated the dark magic of many demons, so it seems the combination of my voice and dark light is power enough."

I narrow my eyes at him, contemplating his choice of words. "It *seems*? You mean you didn't know for sure if it would work?"

"I don't know for certain how any of this magic will work,"

the keeper replies, studying his hands. "Not until I try it. Next time, I'll make the dark light move more quickly toward its target. I'm grateful you hesitated before spilling their blood."

I grimace since it wasn't hesitation but exhaustion that stopped me from leaping across the table at them.

Aside from that, I'm a little alarmed by his admission that he doesn't know how his magic will work until he tries it.

So many things could go wrong...

I shake off my misgivings since the dark light seems to have turned out okay.

Or... maybe not.

My attention is suddenly drawn to the younger of the angels.

She twitches and her blue eyes focus on me.

I stare back at her in alarm as she stiffens.

"Uh, keeper...?" I reach for him without taking my eyes off the angel. "I think she's waking up."

He's immediately on alert, glaring at the woman. "That's inconvenient. The compulsion must be wearing off."

I'm already sliding off my chair and preparing to either fight or get the hell out of here. Both will be easier now that I feel strong again. "Well, do something about it, yes? Unless spilling angelic blood is suddenly appealing to you."

The keeper extends his hand and dark light flicks from his fingers, speeding across the air and hitting the angel in the face like a splat of food.

"There's no need to be afraid." He speaks quickly. "We aren't even here."

The dark light sits on the surface of her skin and, for a second, I don't think it's going to work a second time, but in the next moment, the woman's eyes go blank and she resumes her task.

The keeper makes an unhappy sound in the back of his throat. "It seems my power of compulsion has a time limit."

I reach forward and shove the bowl of stew away across the table. "That's okay. Vegetables weren't doing it for me, anyway."

I grab the second jug of water and gulp it all down, checking the panthers' progress eating their food. I'm happy to see that they've gnawed the raw meat all the way down to the bones.

They lick their lips and grin up at me.

"Burgers," the keeper suddenly says. "We need burgers."

"Huh?" My forehead creases until I remember that a burger is a combination of meat and bread. "Oh, yes, I know burgers."

The keeper mimics the shadow panthers when he licks his lips as he backs away from the table. "Apparently, they're delicious."

The angels continue to go about their chores and I give them a quick backward glance before I follow the keeper from the kitchen into the corridor beyond it.

The maze of hallways leads us back to the atrium with the broken glass ceiling. From here, I can sense the way the air moves through the hallways beyond this room.

Now that I'm not starving, my senses are back to full speed and so are my thought processes.

I can discern multiple possible exits, but before I can point out the nearest one, the keeper surges ahead of me in that same direction.

His ears have shifted again into the shape of a wolf's, so I assume he's channeling his strongest aural abilities to determine the quickest way out.

Before we can take more than a few steps in that direction, the air fills with a dangerous scent.

It's like inhaling cold, winter air, but not the icy air in the keeper's realm. This scent is crisp and pure.

An angel appears in the doorway ahead of us, blocking the way.

She's quite possibly the most beautiful creature I've ever seen, but then, as of now, I can count the number of females I've laid eyes on at exactly four. That's if I don't count the female panther.

The only imperfection on her perfectly smooth, porcelain skin is a faint smudge on her left cheek. It could be from soot or dirt. I have no way of knowing which.

Her gaze rakes over my underwear-clad form and across the keeper. She draws a sharp breath and her hand flies to her hair, withdrawing a golden pin in the blink of an eye.

I'm not sure what she thinks she's going to do with a hairpin. Poke me in the eye, maybe?

In the next moment, it transforms into a golden sword with a gleaming, sharp blade.

Okay, well, she could definitely poke me in the eye with that.

"Who are you?" she demands to know, her voice strong with not even a hint of fear in it as she holds the sword in front of herself.

I'm immediately on the back foot, but the keeper is relaxed.

He throws me a reassuring smile before he extends his hand and dark light streams from his fingertips. At the same time, he says to the newcomer, "You will allow us to pass."

I hold my breath as the light shoots across the ten paces between us and to the angel, hits her squarely at the base of her throat, and sinks into her skin.

"I will not," she replies, remaining clear-eyed.

Wait... what?

The keeper falters a little and his brows draw down, but he tries again, sending a darker stream of magic toward the angel. This torrent wraps around her throat like a noose and tightens beneath her chin, throwing dark shadows up across her beautiful features.

"You will—"

"Don't waste your breath," she snaps.

She wriggles her shoulders and stretches her neck from side

to side, and the dark light shatters, the pieces vanishing into nothing as they fly away from her body.

"Compulsion power doesn't work on me." She strides toward us, her boots crunching on the fallen pieces of glass and grinding them into the floor, leaving a trail of sparkling dust in her wake.

"I am the Serene Commander of the Philadelphia Order," she says. "You are dark creatures trespassing on hallowed ground, and that gives me the right to end you."

CHAPTER TEN

*T*he angel storms toward us, her sword held ready. "Prepare yourselves to meet your keeper."

If only she knew...

I glance at the keeper standing right beside me, but there's no time for smirking. Unlike the angels back in the kitchen, power billows around this woman. If she's the Serene Commander, then she's the strongest warrior angel in this Order, and my instincts are telling me I'm in trouble.

My black claws extend as far as possible—a full two inches—and my breathing becomes harsh as I brace for her attack.

Beside me, the keeper launches into action.

His hand wraps around my arm. "I have another way out! Come with me. Now!"

I spin to follow him, but it's too late.

The angel has released her wings, which carry her across the distance far faster than I would have ever anticipated, and now her golden blade slices down through the air between us.

The keeper is partly turned away, his hand still wrapped around my wrist, and I don't have time to shout a warning. I shove at his back, knocking him out of the sword's path before it can cleave off his arm where it's extended toward me.

In the next moment, I leap backward, narrowly avoiding the arc of the angel's blade as she adjusts the trajectory toward me instead of him.

She lands and retracts her wings but doesn't stop coming after me, her sword slicing across the air toward the side of my throat.

In the background, I'm aware of the panthers hurling themselves toward her back, and of the keeper bursting with crackling energy that twines around his entire body. But I'm also aware that he may not be able to release his power unless he gets a clear shot at her.

Just as her sword would reach my throat, I throw myself forward but down, sliding through the broken glass on the floor. I cut up my bare knees and shins, but I grit my teeth through the pain.

The Serene Commander clearly wasn't expecting me to so willingly injure myself, and she doesn't follow my movement fast enough. I slide beneath the blade toward her legs.

I'm already twisting mid-slide, my left hand pushing upward, my claws closing over her hands where she holds the sword. If I weren't pushing upward for the purpose of deflecting her weapon, I could ram my claws through her wrists and tear her hands right off.

But my target is also her stomach and lungs, a much deadlier blow.

As my left hand pushes up, my right hand swipes across her torso. My claws are strong enough to disembowel her and cut open her ribs, rending her lungs apart.

Unluckily for me, her reflexes are as sharp as mine.

Her wings sweep outward, the force of their sudden extension so great that she not only knocks the leaping panthers out of the air but sends shards of glass scattering across the floor on either side of me.

A single beat takes her up and beyond my reach, but not so fast that she avoids the very tips of my claws.

They nick her stomach before she's airborne above me.

At the same time, I narrowly miss the swipe of her sword as it wrenches back through the air with her, an inch from the right side of my face.

I snarl up at her from where I'm now kneeling on the floor, the panthers gathering around me. I'm acutely aware of the smears of black blood coating the floor behind me and the drip of blood across my calves where I kneel.

Up in the air, the Serene Commander snatches at the torn material of her white dress, her eyes wide in apparent disbelief at the short lines of red blood blooming across her stomach. Mere scratches. Surely, too shallow to be of concern to her.

Her glare rakes across my face, then fixates on my blindfold and her fingers twitch. Perhaps she's imagining ripping it from me. As her wings beat the air, they send wind swishing around me, ruffling the panthers' fur and billowing my knotted hair.

The energy crackling around the keeper intensifies, and I'm surprised he hasn't released it now that the Serene Commander is located away from me in the air. An easy target.

I risk a glance at him, only to find him focused on the Commander's face and not on her sword. His forehead is puckered and his head is tilted, as if he's thinking hard about something.

Whatever it is, I hope he makes up his mind soon.

The Serene Commander allows the torn material across her stomach to settle back into place.

"You will pay for that," she says, her lips twisting before she swoops down again.

The air rushes around me at her approach.

I jump into a crouch, balanced and ready to leap upward before she can pounce on me.

"Panthers! With me!" I cry as I harness the strength in my legs and leap upward.

The female panther jumps in time with me, close to my side, while two of the males are a beat behind us. Their jumps are perfectly timed to reach the angel's wings as she extends them slightly to control her descent.

I sense the fourth panther crouched on the floor to my left, watching and ready, and it occurs to me that these beasts have been together for a long time. Their hunting skills may well be rusty, but *damn*, they can move.

Despite leaping later than I did, the two males reach the Serene Commander first, their powerful bodies a mass of pure muscle driving them upward. Their jaws close around her wings, ripping feathers.

At the same moment, the female panther and I connect with the angel's torso, the female panther's jaws narrowly missing tearing off the woman's ear, but her claws rip at the angel's left shoulder.

My claws impale her right side.

There's a flash of fear in the Commander's eyes, but she still has her sword and it cuts far too close to the female panther's body. My muscles tense at the last moment and I use my leverage to shove the Commander to the side, knocking her toward the ground.

Her sword sails over the female panther's head. Feathers fly through the air around us as they're torn from her wings with the force of her fall.

I land on the floor at a crouch and the panthers land smoothly around me.

One of the males spits a white feather from his mouth, pushing out his tongue, as if he's never tasted anything so revolting.

The Commander isn't idle, but she's clearly realized that her wings are a liability. Hell, I could have told her that. Wings are a fucking nuisance unless you really know how to use them.

She retracts them as she hits the floor in a clumsy roll. Her sword also disappears into her fist—no doubt so she doesn't chop her own limbs off by accident—but I'm sure the weapon will reappear at her command.

She regains control over her body as fast as I expected she would and her tumble becomes smooth. Within seconds, she's back on her feet and charging toward me again.

Blood drips from both of her shoulders, but she seems intent on ignoring the wounds. They're only flesh wounds, so I'm sure she'll heal fast.

My eyes widen when her weapon takes on the form of a club a moment before one of the male panthers jumps at her. She throws herself to the floor just like I did and slides beneath his trajectory. The club connects with his left shoulder with a *smack* that sends him sprawling across the floor. Twisting and launching herself upward as she slides, she thumps the other two males, one rapid swing after the next as they attempt to attack her. Both of them yelp and slide across the floor and I snarl with anger that she could have broken their bones.

Well, I suppose she isn't the Serene Commander of this Order for no reason.

My hand shoots out, halting the female panther even as her legs bunch beneath her. She looks ready to tear out the angel's throat, but I don't want her injured. "No. Stay clear."

I'm gratified when she obeys me, retreating a few paces across the floor and out of the angel's path. The female panther stops close to the keeper, who has continued to stay out of the fight. The light has died down around his body and he's watching me intently with very human-looking brown eyes.

The tension around his mouth is intense, his muscles visibly coiled.

And yet, he doesn't leap into the fight.

His choice is confusing to say the least. Particularly when he has the power to end this woman.

I can't spend another second trying to figure out his motivations.

I guess it's just me and the Commander now.

Her weapon ripples in her hands, the gold it's made of resuming the shape of a sword. I've remained crouched on the floor and my mind is working through the scenarios. I could leap up at her, try to rip out her throat or her heart, but I've tried that already and failed...

My heart hardens.

Maybe failure is my best option.

I plant my feet, pressing my body weight down into my legs where I crouch. Then I force myself to glance wildly at the fallen panthers, allow my eyes to widen as if in fear, making it look like I'm cowering and a little frozen.

She's only two paces away from me and the sheer hatred in her eyes, the twist of her lips, tells me she won't question my subterfuge. She'll see only the kill.

I exhale a long, slow breath, counting out the heartbeats.

Her sword slices through the air toward my neck. A perfect arc.

Everything around me becomes silent as the blade glints, the soft light reflecting off it onto the myriad of glass shards, all twinkling.

At the last moment, my right hand shoots up into the blade's path.

The sword's trajectory will carry its blade right through my upraised claws, a blow certain to slice them clean off before it reaches my neck.

The muscles in my arm tense.

I turn my face away and brace for the impact.

CHAPTER ELEVEN

*T*he sword hits my claws.

Metal shrieks and shatters. Razor-sharp shards of gold fly to either side of me.

One of the shards spins right into the angel's own leg, ripping through her dress and impaling her thigh. Another shoots into her foot.

The remaining pieces of her shattered blade soar through the air, hit the ground, and scrape across it, the force of impact leaving scratches in their wake.

The panthers are luckily all clear of the spiraling metal—the angel saw to that.

The Commander screams and propels herself backward across the floor, her hands fluttering around the gold impaled in her thigh. Still crying, she drops to a crouch and wrenches the shard out of her foot, but she leaves the one in her thigh where it is.

Smart. Since it may have pierced a major artery.

I check my claws where my arm has remained upturned.

They're perfectly unharmed. Perfectly smooth. Not even notched where the blade struck.

Unbreakable.

I return my attention to the angel where she crouches opposite me. Tears of pain streak her cheeks and her blood is very slowly soaking her dress across her thigh and the top of her boot, along with both of her shoulders and her stomach.

I, on the other hand, have only sustained the injuries I chose.

"Your sword is broken," I say matter-of-factly. "I could end you now."

"No," she whimpers, her focus flying from one broken piece to the next, her eyes narrowed in concentration, and I sense a tingle in the air.

Is she trying to call the pieces to her? I suppose she must have that sort of control since she commanded her weapon to transform at will.

The damaged pieces don't move and her eyes widen.

I reach for one, noting the blackened edges where my claws tore it, and I hold it up for her to see. "Your weapon is dead."

As I speak, the panthers gather around me once more. One of the males limps a little, but his wobble eases quickly, and I hope that means he has accelerated healing.

To the angel, I say, "With a single command from me, these beasts will tear you apart. Why should I stop?"

I don't intend to kill her. The keeper was right about leaving a trail of blood. I don't need more angry angels coming after me. All I want is a way to leave.

But the Commander doesn't know that.

I expect her to have some angry response, some righteous rebuke, but she seems fixated on my legs now. I follow her focus to the inky blood sliding across my knees and down my shins. It's from the cuts I sustained when I slid through the broken glass.

Actually, now that I'm paying attention, I discover that there's a fucking glass shard still sticking out of my right calf.

I pull it out as she watches, hiding my grimace since I won't give her the satisfaction of seeing my pain.

"You have black blood," she whispers, her face very pale. "What *are* you?"

A myth. A nightmare.

A rare combination of my father's and mother's disparate genes.

I'm not a hellhound like my mother and according to her, I'm not like my father, so the fact is… I don't know what I am.

Fucking whatever.

I'm simply me.

I answer the Commander by baring my teeth at her and allowing them to grow sharp before her eyes.

Her focus darts to the keeper, as if she's re-evaluating him now too. The strain around her eyes only increases.

"What are *you*?" she asks him.

He finally steps forward, and I note that the tension has left his body. "What aren't I?" he replies.

The Commander's scowl returns and her pure scent is muddied with anger.

"Angel," I say softly, demanding that her attention return to me. "You haven't answered my question. Why should I let you live?"

The panthers edge toward her, punctuating the threat.

Her mouth works over her words. "Because I can grant you amnesty. On my command, no other angel in this city will stop you from leaving. You wished to pass, did you not?"

It's what I hoped she would offer me, but the breadth of her promise gives me more hope than I anticipated.

No other angel...?

I dare to step closer to her, but I stop several paces away. A safe enough distance. She's still gripping the hilt of her sword in her left hand. The blade is mostly a useless stub, but it has some sharp edges. My claws are indestructible, but the rest of my body isn't.

"What about a Sentinel?" I ask. "Can you command one of those?"

Shadows grow around her eyes, unexpectedly dark for such a pure being. "This city is mine. No Sentinel acts here without my permission."

I've struck a nerve, but I don't know why. Her claim was emphatic, but there's an edge to her voice that makes me wonder if she's lying. It sounds more like a prideful statement than an accurate one.

I speak cautiously, testing her. "There's a Sentinel named Zadkiel. If you can guarantee he won't follow us, then we will leave you in peace."

More than anything, I want to kill Zadkiel, but taking revenge on him is second to punishing the man who hired him. I can't do that if I don't make it out of this city. Once I reach my destination, Zadkiel won't be able to touch me. Even a Sentinel wouldn't dare step into the stronghold I plan to conquer.

For some reason, the Commander flinches at the mention of Zadkiel's name, but she tips her chin up. "I can guarantee it."

I consider her for another second before I untie the black sash from around my waist and use it to wipe some of the blood from my legs, as if I'm taking my time to consider her offer.

I'm happy to see that my skin is healing.

The Commander's eyes narrow briefly at the material, as if she, like the angels in the kitchen, recognizes the sash, but her lips quickly press together. She seems to be working hard to stop herself from commenting on it.

I re-tie the material around my waist, ignoring the damp of my blood, using the seconds to think through her claim and the high chance that she's lying.

With a loud scoff, I shake my head at her. "What am I

thinking? You don't have that sort of power. Even as Serene Commander, you can't control the movements of Sentinels—"

"I can guarantee it!" Her voice is sharp, spoken through gritted teeth.

I narrow my eyes at her. "How?"

She swipes at the smudge on her cheek. "Because right at this very moment, my sisters will be preparing to lower his body into the ground."

CHAPTER TWELVE

y eyes widen. I can't stop myself from recoiling.
I was not expecting the Serene Commander to tell me that her angels are putting Zadkiel into the dirt.

My breathing is faster than it should be. My voice is a stifled snarl. "He's dead?"

Decades of hatred rise up within me. Earlier, I wondered if Zadkiel was called to join whatever battle was fought here and the Serene Commander's claim would support it. What's more, the keeper said earlier that he could smell a legion of angels outside this building and hear the clanking of metal and scraping of soil.

It would certainly explain why there are so few angels within this building and why others haven't converged on us yet.

"Shovels and dirt," I murmur. "They're busy digging graves."

My distrust of any angel's word runs deep. Sure, the Commander's sisters might be burying the dead, but that doesn't mean Zadkiel is one of the deceased.

"Why should I believe you?"

The Commander's eyes gleam. "Go and see for yourself."

I don't try to hide my disgust at the way she's trying to lure me into danger. She wants me to step outside this building and expose myself to a whole legion of angels. Zadkiel could be overseeing the burials and the Serene Commander wants me to walk right into his arms. Especially given that she's discovered she can't beat me herself.

"Fuck you," I whisper before I call the panthers to me with a soft, "Come. We're leaving."

The keeper has edged closer to me, and a brief glance at him gives me the chance to see his firm nod, as if he agrees with my decision. Although I'm not sure if it's because I'm letting the Commander live or because I'm taking my chance to run.

"You have another way out?" I ask him, remembering his earlier shout.

"I do." He surprises me by scooping his arm around my waist and practically lifting me off my feet. He seems now to be in an even greater rush to get me out of here. "This way."

Instead of heading toward the arched passageway that I'm sure is the quickest exit, he pulls me back toward the doorway we first came through.

His arms become painfully tight across my chest and stomach, but the pain is weirdly reassuring. It reminds me that I'm still breathing, that I survived Zadkiel, and I'll survive this Cathedral too.

The panthers stay close to the keeper's sides, their footfalls silent.

In the distance, I can now sense a flurry of movement and I inhale the sickly scent of flowers, which is growing stronger with every breath I take.

No wonder the keeper is in a hurry.

Some, if not all, of the other angels must be coming back into the building.

As much as I'm enjoying my body's press against his hard

chest and thighs, I whisper, "We'll go faster if you put me back on my feet."

He places me back on the ground, but he doesn't let go of my hand. His grip is so tight that there's no hope of escaping it—not that I want to right now. The aftereffects of the fight are starting to hit me, a combination of elation at beating the Commander with emptiness that I had to leave her alive. The keeper's grip is keeping me balanced between the two emotions.

His face is filled with concentration as he leads me, not back toward the underground cage, but in the opposite direction. The farther we get from the atrium with the broken roof, the less damage appears on the walls and ceiling.

"I need space," he mumbles. "To try what I'm going to try."

My eyes widen. I don't like the sound of that. Before I can ask him what he plans, he speaks.

"You made a good choice."

The corners of my mouth turn down. "Leaving her alive?"

"No." He casts a shadowed glance my way. "Refusing to fall for her trap."

The anger I've been suppressing surfaces in a rush. "Don't praise me for that!" I snap. "Leaving her alive was hard, but walking away without knowing if Zadkiel is really alive or dead? That was nearly fucking impossible. Even now, I want to turn back and make sure of it."

As I speak, my heels are digging in, my hand is tugging in his, my body defying my logic. I allow a groan to expel from my chest. "I need to see his dead face."

More than anything, I need a release from the decades-old fury within me.

The keeper's hold on me doesn't loosen and it's suddenly clear to me why he's gripping me so tightly. He knew I'd change my mind. And he's smart enough to bring it up now so that it won't come up tomorrow, or the day after, or in a month's time, only to have my anger derail me then.

"Who was he?" the keeper asks, a question that must have been burning at him.

"He was my mother's jailer. The one who lured her into a cage. He tormented me for twenty-three years." My voice is tight with wrath. "I need to spit on his grave. I need to scream at it. I need to stomp on his dead body and break his brittle bones. I need to carve my mother's name into his decaying flesh and curse his soul. I need to drag him to the gates of hell and watch him burn."

Tears are gathering on my cheeks and I let them fall. "I *need* to know that he's dead."

"No," the keeper says, more softly now. "You don't."

I drag at the air, swiping angrily at my wet cheeks. "You're fucking heartless."

"I'm only reinforcing the decision you already made," he says. "As for being heartless, I wish I were. Unfortunately, I now have a heart. *Your* heart. And through it, I can feel your pain. It's bloody and raw and screams for justice."

"Then you must understand that I need closure."

He shakes his head. "What you *need* is to not to risk your life further in this place and to conserve your anger for the man who was responsible for imprisoning your mother in the first place."

It's exactly the decision I made when the Serene Commander tempted me to go outside. The keeper's speech simply echoes back to me the choice I know to be right. The choice that will keep me alive.

I grit my teeth and squeeze my eyes closed beneath the blindfold.

"I know it," I say, my agitated breaths rattling from my chest. "That's why I'm going to deny what I want and choose to leave instead."

When I open my eyes, I find the keeper smiling at me. Well, not so much a smile as a dark glimmer in his eyes and a curve to his lips that has the power to make my heart cease beating.

He's fucking gorgeous in all his smiling darkness.

At some point, we've stopped walking. The panthers are milling around us and beyond the sound of their soft paws, I sense the movement of angels. I left the Serene Commander alive so she'll either be true to her word and command the angels to leave me be, or she'll break her word and have them searching for us.

What confuses me right at this moment is that, while we've been talking, the keeper has brought me back along a corridor I was sure we already passed through.

I recognize the ornate mirror on the wall opposite us, the fissures through the plaster on either side of it, and the way the slim, wooden console sitting in front of it has bumped away from the wall.

"We're going in circles." I tilt my head at the keeper, confused as he continues to gleam at me. "You said you needed space to try something, but we've walked down this corridor before. What are you doing? Why are you risking keeping us here?"

He can't be lost, can he?

Or worse, betraying me?

I tug away from him, distrust rising within me, but again, his hold on me is like iron.

His lips press firmly together, his smile vanishes, and he sighs. "We're here because you have resolved to deny your wants for your needs."

My brow furrows. "I don't understand what you mean."

He considers me with eyes that are surprisingly soft. "For the very reason that you have the strength to stay the course, I will give you the closure you seek."

Now I consider him warily, my lips pursed.

He gives me a small smile. "You proved your determination to me by denying your fury. It takes deep strength to reject what you could take in the present because you're resolved to achieve a greater purpose in the future. Because of that, I will give you what you want."

I'm stiff as he turns me toward the mirror and pulls me back against his chest.

His right arm rises at my side, hand turned palm up.

Energy crackles around his fingertips, but not sapphire light like the dark warlock's power he uses to create the illusion of clothing. This is emerald green. The tendrils grow in strength and waft across to the mirror.

When the light spreads across the reflective surface, it becomes molten like a pool of silver, swirling at the edges.

Our reflections disappear and within it, a new image forms.

We're looking down at a scene, our view closing in on a body lying on the overturned earth. It's wrapped in a white cloth. Angels surround the body, one of them dropping a shovel to the earth beside it before she stretches out her back and rubs her forehead, smearing dirt across her face.

The body is Zadkiel's. His eyes are closed, but there's no mistaking the shape of his face or the color of his hair.

His skin is gray. Lifeless.

In the next moment, the angel who was holding the shovel adjusts the cloth, pulling it over his head. She gestures to her sisters and then they lower him into the grave beside him.

"He's really dead." My whisper is bleak. A part of me wants to rage at fate for stealing his death from me.

It was *my* right to kill him, not anyone else's.

"Something powerful ended him." The keeper growls at my ear. "The angels within this Cathedral are a danger, but it is that *something* that we should evade now."

"Yes," I whisper. I have enough battles ahead of me. I don't need another enemy.

I have my closure. Zadkiel is dead. I'm alive.

And I want to stay that way. The growing brightness within

the vision that the keeper's showing me indicates dawn is on the horizon. Soon, I'll have to contend with sunlight. Traveling in the shadows will become much harder.

The keeper points at the solid wall behind us. "Our exit is here."

My brow creases. "That's a wall."

He releases me but tugs me toward the solid surface. "Come."

I cast my gaze to either side of us along the corridor, my mind refusing to believe that he's walking toward the solid structure. "Come... where?"

He throws me a reassuring look over his shoulder, but his focus shifts to our right.

Fuck. I guess the Commander is a liar after all.

My senses tell me that a group of angels is hurrying toward us, the intensifying floral scent in the air indicating that they're now far too close for comfort.

I'm also aware of a haze building around me, the keeper, and the panthers—a haze that's quickly enveloping the keeper one step ahead of me and the panthers all around us. Then me, too.

The fog is thickening so fast that I can't breathe.

It's as if the air is being sucked out of my lungs and my chest is imploding.

What the fuck?

A scream builds inside me, but I can't cry out, can't move, as the fog suddenly swirls and a tornado of mist forms in front of me. The keeper's dark form blurs, swept into the tornado like streams of black blood in churning water.

My body seems to disintegrate and the scream in my mind fades as everything goes dark.

CHAPTER THIRTEEN

I land heavily on all fours, my knees thwacking the hard surface that appears suddenly beneath me.

I'm grateful that I can breathe again, but my limbs are refusing to obey me, keeping me on the ground as if my instincts are telling me to never let go of the earth again. "What the fuck?"

I don't know where I am, certainly not in the Cathedral anymore. A rush of air brings a maelstrom of scents that makes my head swim. Old food. New food. Oily scents I've never smelled before. On top of that, the air is intensely salty and feels heavy with moisture, a phenomenon I can't explain.

The surface beneath me is rough and gray like gravel. *A road, maybe?* If so, I need to move quickly. Mom warned me about stepping onto roads. Moving vehicles are to be avoided.

A quick glance from side to side tells me there are only three vehicles nearby and they're all stationary, sitting within white lines that mark the surface at regular intervals. I try to look up, but bright lights shine in my eyes from multiple spots high around the space, obscuring the sky and making it impossible for me to keep looking skyward.

The darkness I glimpse beyond the lights is confusing, since only moments ago, it seemed that dawn was on the way.

Still, I've seen enough to decipher what sort of place I've arrived at.

This must be a parking lot.

Low-lying buildings squat around the parking lot on the three sides I can see. They have glass fronts, but all are dark inside except for one to my left. Inside that one, I make out a few tables and chairs and a counter in the background, along with several humanoid shapes moving around within it.

Then a groan sounds behind me and I twist to find the keeper also resting on his hands and knees. His cheeks are tinged green, and he appears to be trying to hold on to the contents of his stomach. The panthers are scattered on either side of him, all lying on their sides, their chests heaving and tongues out.

"What the fuck was that?" I ask the keeper.

"I translocated us to a safe place," he explains, visibly swallowing as he wobbles upright, slowly making it up onto his knees, where he remains for a long moment. "I'll admit, my skills need some work."

I raise my eyebrows at him. "You think?" I also make it up onto my knees, trying to make sense of the distant rushing sound. It's strong and constant. "Where are we?"

The keeper's chest fills out as he takes a deep breath and then seems somehow to exhale his nausea. His cheeks regain their color and his eyes brighten. "A little town off the northeastern coast of Australia." He brushes his hands off. "It's on the other side of the world, which means night is only beginning."

Well, that's something positive at least.

"Nobody will find us here," he says.

I narrow my eyes at the rundown buildings, the chipping paint and peeling flyers plastered to their sides. I can now make out the signs in the fronts of some of the stores: *For Lease.*

"That's because nobody lives here," I say, surmising what I can from the empty buildings.

It's probably just as well because I'm nearly naked and surrounded by four savage panthers, who are finally rising back to their feet.

The keeper gives me a devilish grin. "Granted, the population isn't the highest, but there are burgers."

He gestures to the lone shopfront that's lit up. It seems to be the source of the oily food smells I've been inhaling. The glass door is slightly ajar and my head is now swimming with the scent of food, or more accurately, the scent of *meat.*

"I smell meat," I say, salivating as I speak. "Burgers are meat. So *yes*, burgers please."

Before I can take a step toward the building, the keeper's hand wraps around my arm.

"Probably best to leave this interaction to me," he says. "You should keep the panthers out of sight." He casts around and points to the vehicle that's parked farthest back in the parking lot, although it will still be visible from the building. "Stay with that truck. Make sure the panthers hide behind it."

As he speaks, he rolls his shoulders as if he's shaking himself off and, in that moment, his visage changes again.

His skin becomes white but tanned, his hair becomes blond and windswept, and sunglasses appear on his face, except that they sit on his nose without frames in sight. I'm not sure why he'd want sunglasses in the middle of the night until I catch a glimpse of his very black eyes behind them. I guess he wants to conceal whatever power he intends to use next. His clothing transitions into low-slung jeans and a loose tank top that reveals the muscles across his biceps and forearms.

"What about my clothing?" I ask before he can turn away.

He tilts his head and considers me over the top of the dark glasses. "Do you want warmer clothes?"

I rethink my request. The air is muggy and warm. Clothing would only cling to me. My thought was more for blending in, but like the keeper said, there's nobody around. "Actually, I'm comfortable."

"Then you're perfect as you are."

He saunters away, his hair continuing to grow as he walks until its tangled strands meet his shoulders.

When he disappears into the building, I retreat to the truck. It's dark blue and has a tray on the back, inside of which rests a narrow board. The board is mostly white but with a wavy pattern on it and it's shaped sort of like a rectangle except that each end is tapered.

I don't know what it is, but when I tap its surface, I ascertain that it's solid. Confident that the back of the truck is safe for the panthers, I urge them up into it, where the sides will conceal them. They spring into it and seem happy enough to settle there.

Returning to the front of the vehicle, I fold my arms across my chest and lean against the hood while I wait for the keeper to return. I make out his shape inside the shop where he appears to be speaking to one of the humans, who is standing behind the counter.

Studying my surroundings, I catalog the things I recognize and the things I don't.

Most of it, I'm fine with. Parking lot, vehicles, shops with old signs in the windows. Trees at the open end of the parking lot and the vague outline of houses behind them.

But there are certainly things in the outside world I don't yet know about. Like the object in the back of this truck. *What the fuck could it be? Some sort of portable table, maybe?*

The problem is it's the small mistakes that could get me killed.

85

Once I reach my enemy, I'll have to pretend I know everything about all things, even if I don't.

A few minutes later, the keeper emerges from the shop with packages in hand.

I lean forward in anticipation when he reaches me, ready to rip open the bags and reveal the food inside, but he places them out of my reach on the far side of the truck's hood, wraps his hands around my waist, and hoists me up onto it—even as I'm grasping for the food.

"We can eat here," he says, joining me on the makeshift seat.

Finally, he passes me one of the bags.

I unwrap it quickly and assess its contents: a bread roll with meat inside. Looks like cheese and lettuce next to the meat.

Quickly unraveling Mom's shirt from around my left hand, I push the material beneath my bra strap to keep it safe.

The first bite of food makes me groan. "Fuck me. That's good."

He grins at me, tucks his newly blond hair behind his ear, and takes a bite of his own burger.

"What are these?" I ask, poking at the other package inside the bag, which contains long sticks that smell like oil and goodness.

"Fries," he says.

Okay, yes, I know about fries. These are just much thicker than the ones Mom described.

I smash several into my mouth on top of another bite of burger, not caring that the sauce is dripping down my chin. "Fuck me twice."

Within minutes, I've devoured the first burger, only to find a second one hiding beneath the now-empty fries holder. Wiping my chin, I give the keeper a happy smile.

His lips draw back from his teeth in a snarl-like grin. Whatever windswept visage he's maintaining right now, he can't seem to subdue his dark power.

Before I can take a bite of the second burger, there's a flurry of movement from within the shop. Some sort of minor commotion.

A human figure has lurched up from their seat, which was previously hidden behind the peeling posters plastered against the glass, and now hurries toward the door.

I pause, the burger raised to my mouth.

A moment later, a man bursts from the shop into the parking lot. He's definitely human. Maybe early thirties. I don't detect any magical power emanating from his body and he doesn't appear to be armed except for a paper napkin scrunched in his fist.

He storms toward us, his cheeks flushed red.

"Oi, mate!" he shouts at the keeper, pointing at the vehicle we're sitting on. "That's my ute."

Ute? He must mean the truck.

The keeper calmly extends his hand toward the man, at which dark light shoots through the air. The human is breathing so hard that he sucks the darkness right up into his nostrils.

"This is not your ute," the keeper says.

The man pulls up short, now only five paces away. He blinks at us. "Mate, that's not my ute."

The man peers around the parking lot, his face flushing again, his hands lowering. "Why am I out here?"

"I don't know," the keeper says. "Why don't you go back inside?"

"Yeah." The man nods. "I'll go back inside."

The human pauses mid-turn and casts a glance back at the keeper. "Nice sunnies."

"Thanks," the keeper replies, tapping his glasses.

Sunnies. It must be a colloquial term for sunglasses.

The man disappears into the shop, muttering something about "bloody drongo wearing sunnies at night."

I let out my held breath, my forehead creasing. "What did he call you?"

The keeper shrugs. "Australian slang escapes me."

Now that the interruption is over, I bite into the second burger.

The keeper's attention returns immediately to me, no longer quite so nonchalant. "Tell me about the man you seek."

The burger instantly sours on my tongue. "Dammit," I mutter. "I was enjoying my food."

The keeper side-eyes me, giving me an unfeeling look over the top of his sunglasses that turns quickly into a piercing stare. "It's important to have a plan."

"Oh, I have a plan," I say. "Of course I have a fucking plan. I've had years to think about it."

Years to think about all the things I *don't* know and all the ways I *can't* plan.

"Okay," I say on a heavy sigh as the keeper's gaze continues to pierce my bravado. "I maybe have part of a plan. The *beginning* of a plan. Fuck it, I *wish* I had a plan."

I meet his eyes and explain. "Mom told me everything she knew about my father's empire and the supernaturals within it, but that knowledge is over twenty years old now. I have no way of knowing what or who has stayed the same and what's changed."

The keeper's expression softens. "That's fair. So tell me what you know and we can take it from there." He takes off his sunglasses and winks at me. "After all, you have me now. So your plan would have to change anyway. A blank slate isn't a bad thing."

It's a very reassuring response in the face of the fact that I have twenty-year-old information and no clear path ahead.

I proceed to summarize as much of my knowledge as I can in as short a time as possible, but the keeper doesn't seem to have any trouble keeping up.

"The main headquarters is in New York," I say. "I know the location and layout of every building that forms part of the network, including the underground levels. I also know the locations and layouts of the back streets and tunnels that connect the buildings. I know the names and powers of the supernaturals who stood at my father's right and left hands at the time, along with the mercenaries who served him. And I know all about the business operations they conducted." I pause. "All of which could have changed."

The keeper purses his lips. "The best place to start is with family. That's more likely to have stayed constant. Other than your mother, who else are you aware of?"

"I have an uncle," I say, my lips twisting a little. Mom didn't like him and he's my most likely suspect, as far as the one behind her imprisonment is concerned.

I quickly clarify, "He's my father's brother, not my mother's. My grandparents on both sides are dead. I have no other aunts or uncles that I'm aware of."

"What about siblings? Yours, I mean."

I shake my head. "Mom said I was my father's first child and he was killed before she was imprisoned. She was running for her life when that angel entrapped her."

"Hmm." The keeper seems to chew on that for a moment. "You mentioned there were certain supernaturals who stood at your father's side. What do you know of them?"

"Aside from the mercenaries, there were two powerful generals," I say. "A man and a woman. Brother and sister. The woman was a witch and the man was a snake shifter—cobra, to be exact. Apparently, they have an older brother, who is a wolf shifter, but he wasn't sworn to serve my father. Mom spoke about them with a kind of reverence I always found surprising."

"A witch, a snake, and a wolf," the keeper muses, a crease appearing in his forehead. "Siblings with such different powers is unusual."

I'm nodding. "I thought it was strange, but whenever I questioned Mom about it, she would give me this smile and tell me that the gods make mysterious moves that are not for us to question." I sigh as I continue. "She wouldn't tell me who betrayed her: my uncle, the male general, one of the mercenaries, or someone else." My hand clenches around my food. "My real challenge is figuring that out."

"What if you can't?" the keeper asks. "Or what if the one responsible is already dead?"

"If I can't figure out who it was—or even if it comes to light that they're dead—the fact remains that whoever subsequently took over the empire knowingly stole it from me."

The keeper tilts his head. "Knowingly? How so?"

I growl at him. "Every supernatural who is aware of the existence of the empire is taught unbending loyalty to the family that controls it—the family I was born into. Control of the empire is the birthright of the first-born child. Always. Of course there are contingencies if there is no child, but my mother knew the rules. She proclaimed her pregnancy and staked my claim. Once there is a child, only proof of death can nullify their claim. I have the black blood and my father's golden eyes to prove my identity. If the empire still exists, then whoever rules it knows they don't have that right."

"Well," the keeper says, eyeing me cautiously. "Then you must tell me the name of this family because surely, I've heard of it."

"It's the most powerful supernatural family in New York," I say, returning his bright gaze. "Oh, not the families who live in the limelight and make a show of their power. No, my family stands in the shadows behind them all. It's my family that has stood behind some of the most notorious human gangsters in history."

The keeper's eyebrows rise. "The human mafia. I'm aware of it. Some dark creatures whose power I tethered had memories of working with human gangsters, or of being killed by them, but those supernaturals were all ruled by—"

He takes a quick breath and his eyes widen at me.

I can't help my cold smile as I watch his thoughts click over. I let him speak first.

"Well," he says, his eyes glittering and dark. "No wonder you want what's yours."

My lips stretch into a snarl. "I want what's *owed* to me."

The keeper inclines his head at me, as if he's greeting me for the first time.

A murmur passes his lips, speaking a title I haven't heard since my mother passed.

My title.

His eyes gleam as he says, "Well met, *Ultima Nostra*."

CHAPTER FOURTEEN

*M*y title's meaning is layered. The empire was started by the Family Nostra, so at first, the title was simply connected to their surname, but it evolved over time to take on a greater meaning.

Literally translated into modern English from the old tongue, it means *Our Ultimate*, or *Our Last*. To those who are part of the empire, it gives a sense of belonging and complete loyalty to the Ultima Nostra, who stands at the end of all things and to whom they owe their lives. No matter what other debts they may owe, and no matter what other allegiances they might carry, the Ultima Nostra's demands can override it all. If the Ultima Nostra commands them, they obey.

The keeper's gaze darkens until I imagine his blue eyes are the color of a stormy sea—not that I've ever seen the sea in person.

"That is truly a title worth killing for," he says.

I acknowledge that truth with a nod. "The empire controlled by the Family Nostra is vast and powerful. I have no doubt it still exists. It survived through centuries of changes in the human world, through medieval wars and the Industrial

Revolution, and it evolved with technological advancements. There's no way it would have crumbled in the last two decades." My lips rise in a snarl. "Whoever controls it now is living off my mother's blood."

The tips of my claws extend as I speak. I fight to pull them back before they slice up my beautiful burger. Nothing and nobody will ruin this food, not even me.

My voice is quieter as I continue. "She watched my father die and then she was forced to flee or she would have been next," I say. "But she wouldn't tell me the name of the man responsible."

Wait...

I suddenly sit bolt upright. "Fuck! I've been so stupid!" I spin to the keeper. "If you can see the memories of dark creatures whose magic you tethered, then you would have seen my father's death and his final memories." My eyes are wide. "You can tell me who killed him."

The keeper withdraws a little, a wary light growing in his eyes.

"I don't want your hopes to rise," he says. "I've tethered the magic of countless creatures since my creation. Thousands in the last century alone. Murder is a common occurrence. I rarely take note of it. And I don't bother with a creature's identity, only their power."

I won't give up so easily, not when something—*anything*—he remembers could help me. "My father's name was Taiven Nostra. He was a powerful being. More powerful than others. He would have stood out."

The keeper's brow furrows. "Well, what kind of supernatural was he?"

"He was a fallen angel, but fallen by birth, not choice."

The keeper's eyebrows rise. "That is rare. And also dangerous. Creatures born into dark magic can take on the power of their ancestors."

"Making each generation stronger than the one before." I incline my head since my ancestors' power was also born in me, the accumulation of a thousand years of chosen darkness.

"My father's grandfather was a Sentinel," I say, "who turned to the dark when he bathed himself in the blood of his enemies in an act of personal vengeance. His name was Cormorant Nostra. He founded the family and ruled for centuries until he passed control to his son, who finally passed it to *his* son—my father."

The keeper's eyes are narrowed. "Yes, I would remember them."

His gaze becomes distant and I wait for him to sift through his memories, trying not to hold my breath as the silence stretches.

His forehead is fiercely creased as he says, "I do recall the death of a dark angel..."

I lean forward, my tension rising.

"But that was near the end of medieval times," the keeper says.

My shoulders hunch a little. "That would have been my father's grandfather."

The keeper's eyes remain narrowed as if in deep concentration. "I remember another dark angel during the Industrial Revolution."

I nod. "My father's father. He died before the beginning of the human war known as World War II."

But my hopes are rising again because it seems the keeper is searching his memories from the oldest to the newest, so he should recall my father's death next.

The keeper folds his arms across his chest and lets out a deep breath. "That is all," he says.

I stare at him. "That's all? No, that can't be all." I can't keep the tension from my voice. "If you remember my father's ancestors, then you must remember him, too."

"I don't," the keeper says, returning my stare without a hint of a lie in his expression.

I don't doubt his sincerity, but I'm struggling to understand how it could be so. "How the fuck can you not remember him?"

The keeper casts a sharp glance my way as if he's about to rebuke me—I expect him to—but his expression quickly softens as his gaze flows across my face from my compressed lips to my desperate eyes.

"There are two explanations why I might not have tethered his magic," he says, "but I doubt either will be welcome news."

I lean back a little. "I can handle it."

"One is that he was killed for his power and whoever killed him siphoned all of his power as he died, leaving nothing for me to collect."

"Fuck," I whisper, fighting a shiver of apprehension. "That's very possible. Mom said my uncle—my father's brother—was born with only a fraction of his power. That happens with the second-born. He was envious of my father's strength. He, or any of the other men close to my father, would have coveted his power. And they would need that level of authority to hold on to the empire."

The keeper exhales heavily. "It will make your opponent even more dangerous."

"True," I whisper. The keeper said there were two possible explanations and now I ask, "What's the other reason?"

"The other is that the keeper of light magic may have tethered your father's magic."

I'm glad I wasn't trying to eat as he spoke because I would have choked on my food. "How the fuck could that happen?"

The keeper gives me a glance, full of deep pity. "You're aware of the four magics?"

"Of course," I say, not liking the hint of compassion he's aiming at me. "Dark magic, light magic, elemental magic, and the rarest: old magic."

"Then I'm sure you're fully aware that angels are creatures of light magic. Even an angel born into darkness will carry a spark of light somewhere within them." The keeper gives me a hard stare. "It's almost impossible to completely snuff out light magic." His nose wrinkles. "It keeps popping up. If your father committed a noble act before he died, an act of redemption, then his magic could have reverted to light magic at the end."

My eyes widen at this awful possibility. "Which means his magic wouldn't have come to you."

The keeper arches an eyebrow at me and my shoulders sink further.

"I guess that's possible." I sigh. "Mom said he died in front of her. She always choked up when she tried to speak about his final moments. If he gave his life for her... and for me... he may have redeemed his soul."

At the keeper's nod, my hope of gaining knowledge about my father's final moments fades.

"Fuck," I whisper. "Then I'm back to square one." I cast the keeper a pained glance. "Remind me never to commit an act of mercy or compassion. There's no fucking way I want my magic to be collected by the keeper of light magic when I die."

The keeper purses his lips, his piercing gaze now dissecting me. "But you are not a dark angel," he muses, his gaze running from my face to my toes, a long, slow look that feels like he's pulling me apart piece by piece.

He leans forward, his voice low. "If your father was a dark angel, how do you have claws?" Just like the Serene Commander back at the Cathedral, he asks, "What are you?"

Except that the way he speaks indicates he's intrigued, unafraid, as if he's anticipating the answer with great relish.

I grin at him, a smile that implies I know the answer, even though I don't.

Before I can reply, movement in the distance catches my eye. Another commotion from within the shop.

I arch an eyebrow, grateful for the interruption when the same human male as before bursts through the shop's front door and rushes toward us.

His scruffy hair flies around his face as he storms across the pavement. "Hey, get the fuck off my ute!"

The keeper rolls his eyes before flicking his fingers at the man. "Not your ute."

Dark light whacks the man's chest and splashes up across his face, bringing him to an immediate halt.

He blinks at us for a moment before he scratches his head. "It isn't?" He takes another look at the vehicle, peering at it and then us for a long, confused moment before he turns back to the shop. "I don't know why I came out here."

"Go back to your food," the keeper says, his eyes glittering. "Unless you'd like to stay and eat with us?"

The man blinks at the keeper, who returns the stranger's look with a gleaming smile so full of malice that it makes the hairs on the back of my neck stand up. Nobody in their right mind would accept his offer of hospitality.

I can't help but reach across the distance and run my fingertip around the edges of the shadows playing across the keeper's jaw. There's a hint of stubble there now and I can't be sure if it's part of his façade or if a real beard is trying to grow.

"Yeah, nah. Thanks anyway, mate." The human backs away and within seconds, he's hurrying back into the shop. A smart move.

I arch my eyebrows at the keeper, my fingers lingering on his chin. "How many more times are you going to compel that human?"

"Until I no longer find it amusing." He turns his wicked grin on me. Somehow, his smile seems to make the shadows darken around his face and the artificial lights around us dim. It's a comforting effect.

He returns his attention to the retreating man. "It's

intriguing to me that human males are so possessive of their vehicles," he muses. "Why is that?"

I shake my head and shove the final piece of burger into my mouth, speaking as I chew. "How the fuck would I know?"

The keeper shrugs, as if it doesn't matter. He watches me swallow. His own food was gone minutes ago.

"I didn't bring you to this deserted town on the coast of Australia only for the burgers," he says.

I fold the empty paper bag up into neat squares. "Oh?"

"Come with me." He slides off the truck's hood and calls for the panthers as he heads toward them and pulls a blanket from the back of the vehicle.

Then he holds out his hand for me. "There's something I want to show you."

"Oh-kay?" I slip my left hand into his before I slide off the hood and pitch my trash into the nearest trash can several feet away, making the shot perfectly.

The panthers leap from the vehicle and find the most shadowed spot in the parking lot a few feet away, waiting with their heads raised.

"But first I want you to close your eyes," the keeper says.

His wicked grin hasn't faded. If anything, it's grown stronger.

"Why?"

"Trust me."

I snort. "Trust you? Never."

He leans in close and I'm forced to tip my head back to keep him in my sights. He's only inches away from me and the power visible on the surface of his skin, the dark shadows flickering with sapphire light, draws me even closer.

Oh, to give in to the comfort I find in his dark presence.

But I shake myself.

If there's one thing Mom drilled into me, it's that sex is

about power and control, not pleasure. This man already has my heart and owes me revenge in return.

To give him the power of pleasure over me would be a dangerous move.

He gives a soft chuckle as I continue to glare up at him. "Okay, don't trust me. Just believe that you'll like what I'm going to show you."

Now that we've dispensed with any notion of trust, I'm intrigued enough to take a chance.

"Fine." I inhale deeply and lower my eyelids. "My eyes are closed."

CHAPTER FIFTEEN

*T*he keeper tugs on my hand. "This way. We'll go as slowly as you like."

It's not so difficult to navigate with my eyes closed. My animal senses pick up a lot within my environment: the soft hum of vehicles in the far distance; the quiet screeches of some sort of animal in the tall trees at the end of the parking lot, and the swish of our feet and the panthers' paws against the pavement. I have a sense of where the sound is muffled and where it flows freely, which tells me when objects are near.

Of course, the keeper's presence is like a dark void next to me, powerful beyond measure, even more so with my eyes closed.

When I can see him, I can keep him contained within the limits of his form, but now that my eyes are closed, his power feels...

Massive.

As if it stretches well beyond the limits of this parking lot. Seemingly held together only by his will and the intense flow of dark magic from the ring around his finger. Which is itself like a beacon behind my eyelids.

"Around a corner now," he says, tugging me to the left. "And another corner."

The moment we complete the second turn, a gust of wind hits me, even saltier on my tongue than the stifled breeze within the parking lot.

"Straight ahead now," the keeper whispers at my ear. "And across a street."

A deserted street, it seems, since I can't hear any sounds of people or machinery that could indicate vehicles are near. The keeper said the population in this coastal town is low, but it must also be approaching the darker part of night now. Creatures like me come out at night, but humans need to sleep.

"Through this park," the keeper murmurs. "Not far now."

He steers me on a curving path across a soft surface that makes my toes curl. "Are we walking on grass?" I ask, nearly opening my eyes to see it.

"We are, but wait. Don't open your eyes yet," he says. "You'll spoil the surprise."

I give a soft growl that I'm giving up the chance to see grass in favor of whatever surprise the keeper has in store for me. It had better be fucking good.

My feet finally leave the soft ground and then I'm walking on a surface that feels like pavement again. It's a descending path that makes me wobble for a second before I regain my balance.

My next footfall crunches on a rough, powdery substance.

"What is that?" My softly whispered question is snatched away by the wind, which has become intense, gusting against my hair and chest. If I were wearing loose clothing, it would be plastered against my body. As it is, the cold makes goosebumps rise on my skin and my nipples tighten unpleasantly.

I wrap my free arm across my chest and I'm on the verge of asking the keeper for an illusion jacket when he makes a growly sound, his lips close to my ear. The tension in the sound tells me he isn't happy with something. Emerald light flares beyond my eyelids. And then, suddenly, the wind dies down, leaving only a peaceful quiet and a comfortable warmth.

"Better," he says. "Only two more steps now."

Now that the ferocious wind has died down, I can more easily sense the panthers milling around me, the brush of their fur against my thighs and the soft purring sounds they're making. It's as if they're supremely happy and now my level of anticipation increases.

If the panthers like what they're seeing, then maybe I will too.

The keeper lets go of my hand but doesn't stop touching me, gliding his palm along my forearm and up to my shoulder.

He whispers in my ear, "We're here, but don't open your eyes yet."

Then I feel the tug of his hands at the back of my head.

"You need to see this with your eyes, unfettered by a blindfold."

My reaction is defensive and not entirely rational. My hands snap up behind my head to stop him from untying the material. "Stop. I need this blindfold."

It's my guard against the world. My safety net. Without it, I'll feel exposed. Worse, I'll feel like I'm putting this piece of my mother away from me.

The keeper doesn't rise to my anger or react to my fear.

"Not right now you don't." His compelling whisper sends a tingle through my body. "If you won't trust me, then trust the darkness that lives within me."

Trust the dark.

When the light has only ever brought me pain and torment, the dark is my solitude. My constant.

His lips brush against my earlobe, and it feels like a spark. A burst of heat that soothes my tension.

A moment later, he steps away from me. He may have loosened the blindfold, but my own hands are keeping it in place. It's now my choice to remove it.

"Take off your blindfold and open your eyes," he says.

My heart is pounding because his voice is layered with tones that speak to anticipation, the same kind he exhibited when he asked me what I am.

My hands drop away from the back of my head and with them comes the blindfold, gripped between my fingers.

Slowly, I open my eyes.

The breath stops in my lungs. I try to breathe, but I can't.

Hell, breath isn't important right now.

In front of me, a dark sea churns, its waves rushing forward and drawing back, the fierce water becoming nothing more than a gentle flow at the edge of the beach I'm standing on. Sparkling sand stretches out far into the distance on either side of us, gently glimmering in the darkness all the way to a peak at each end of the beach. In the far distance, the waves crash against rocky outcrops.

Trees sway and bend in the force of the wind that the keeper has somehow stilled where we stand. *Palm trees.* I think that's what they're called.

But above us... *Oh, above us...*

The night sky glistens with a thousand stars, a deep dark that is more magnificent than I ever imagined.

"Beautiful darkness," I whisper.

The panthers have gathered around me, each one looking upward, their purrs like a melody in the salty air.

The keeper has stepped away from me and, when I drag my gaze from the night sky for the briefest glance at him, I find that his countenance has changed once again.

His hair is now as inky black as the panther's fur. His eyes are the darkest blue like the sea that churns in front of me. His body is leaner, but no less muscled. Less like a bear and more like the sleek and deadly panthers.

His voice is as low as the hum of beating wings as he looks right back at me. "Yes, you are a beautiful darkness," he says, his gaze devouring me, his lips curving upward. "And I can't wait for you to unleash your rage on the world."

CHAPTER SIXTEEN

$\mathcal{I}$ stay like that for a long time, taking in the beauty of the night sky. Allowing my mind to be consumed by the darkness above me, mesmerized by the way the light of the stars breaks through the ink so that the two exist harmoniously: light and dark. Somehow strengthening each other.

The gods make mysterious moves, my mother said. I can't imagine what deadly threats lie within the beautiful landscape above me.

At least I'm aware of the ones that walk this Earth.

Eventually, the keeper takes himself quietly off to the nearest palm trees, an arched cluster of them dense enough to provide a cave-like shelter, leaving me standing with the panthers.

He spreads out the blanket he took from the truck and sits on it, contemplating the ocean from that position.

Even though I don't want to tear my eyes away from the night sky, I have no doubt that once the sun rises, my senses will be overloaded. I'm forced to acknowledge that I need to sleep and here is as good a place as any to get some rest.

"Come on," I say quietly to the panthers, inclining my head at the secluded trees.

They follow me to the space where the branches overshadow the sky and then they lay themselves down on one side of the blanket, where they can nestle together.

They haven't stopped purring, although it's a much softer sound now, blending with the gentle breeze. As I sit next to the keeper on the blanket, I notice a faint, emerald glow across the tree branches, which indicates that his magic is continuing to keep the wind at bay.

In the far distance, lightning cracks across the horizon. A storm that sizzles through the sky and lights up the crashing waves. Part of me wishes I was out there in it. My first real storm.

"Thank you for showing me this," I say.

The keeper has remained in his black-haired, blue-eyed form, and somehow, he seems most peaceful in it. Which is a strange thing since I also sense that the face he currently wears may be his darkest façade. Darker even than the devil's form he took on at the Cathedral to scare the shit out of the angels.

"There's a world beyond vengeance," he says as he continues to contemplate the horizon.

He spoke so softly that I'm uncertain if his comment was directed at me or if he's trying to convince himself of it. My forehead creases as I contemplate the possibility that he, too, may carry grievances that require vengeance.

He may not know everything about me, but I know hardly anything about him.

Whether or not his statement was directed at me, I exhale a heavy sigh. "Not for me, there isn't."

He doesn't respond, although I don't miss the tightening of his lips and the tension in his shoulders. In the distance, sapphire-blue lightning spears across the sky, piercing the quiet dome around us.

It suddenly occurs to me that the storm may not be a natural one. Indeed, the keeper may have created it; a manifestation of his power and his peacefully dark mood.

Despite his striking features, he's dressed in a simple T-shirt and sweatpants. His feet are bare and his legs are long enough that his toes scrunch in the sand beyond the edge of the blanket.

"Do you have a name?" I ask him.

"Do you?" he retorts, flashing me a sharp glance.

My hands fly upward. "Whoa, touchy."

"Is that your name?"

"No, I was describing your reaction."

He scowls at me before he returns his attention to the horizon. "I don't remember my name. My memories of my life before I became the keeper are sparse and, try as I might, I can't recall my identity. The other keepers may have retained parts of their former selves, knowledge of their former lives, but dark magic is not like other kinds of magic. Over time, it destroys and consumes, eating away at life."

I nod. "That's how dark magic works. It feeds on life." I grimace, suddenly realizing something. "Is that why you said you can only create illusions of clothing and food, and not the real thing."

He nods. "Illusions involve simply rearranging what's already there. If I want to draw power to create something from nothing, then dark magic demands I take life. The more significant the outcome I desire, the more life I must take. That is the cost of dark magic."

I speak carefully. "I thought there would be enough power stored in your crown to do whatever you want."

He holds up his left hand. "This crown allows me to access every kind of dark magic there is: sorcery, witchcraft, shapeshifting. It gives me the knowledge to use that magic and it allows me to harness the energy in the environment around me, similar to how elemental magic works. But there are limits to what I can achieve without taking life from those around me."

I constrain my shiver as my focus shifts rapidly to the panthers, then to the trees, and finally to my own self. All of us are living beings that could feed the keeper's dark magic.

"Yes," he says, as darkness grows across his face. "The trees, the panthers." He pauses. "You."

This time, I don't bother hiding my shudder.

"Cold?" he asks.

"Fuck, yes." I wrap my arms around myself. As much as there's a part of me that doesn't want the details, I can't stop myself from seeking answers. "Did you drain life when you translocated us here?"

"No," he says. "I harnessed the energy in the crown to move us around."

I relax a little. "What about using your compulsion power on the angels and humans?"

"I merely rearranged their thoughts. No life taken."

"And illusions work the same way, yes? You're just... rearranging something that's already there. So if you wanted to change your shape into, say, a bear, that would be fine?"

"Yes."

I relax even further, since there seems to be a lot that the keeper can do with the energy in the crown alone. "What about the lightning out on the horizon?"

He sighs and takes longer to answer this time.

Finally, he says, "There's a palm tree farther down the beach that's about to fall. Listen..."

Sure enough, a *crack* sounds in the distance. It's followed by a soft groan and a *thud*. I picture the tree now lying on the sand, its trunk rotten.

My brow furrows. It's not that I'm overly concerned about him draining life from a tree, but it has confused my understanding of how he uses his magic.

"But... if I understood you correctly before, you only need to take life if you're creating something from nothing. Surely, the crown allows you to harness the energy in the air to create lightning?"

He nods. "It does."

I blink at him. "Then... why?"

His jaw clenches. "Because I'm a dark creature and I have the power to choose."

"Well, fuck me," I whisper. I'm not sure if I should be terrified or excited that he chooses not to limit himself.

His dark-blue eyes raze across my face. "Don't worry, I promised you revenge. That means not taking a shred of your life." He inclines his head at the panthers. "Or theirs."

His voice lowers. "But you should know, beyond my deal with you, my choices are my own. If I want something badly enough, maybe I won't care what life I take in the process."

An incredibly dangerous truth.

Beneath it, I sense an even greater darkness. He may warn me about taking what he wants, but the tension around his eyes and lips speaks to me of a lingering shadow. A deep rage. The kind that can only have simmered for millennia. Maybe since the time of his creation.

He told me he doesn't remember his name, but I push a little further, selecting my words carefully.

"Do you think it's possible that you chose to become a keeper or is it more likely that you were forced into it?"

His lips twist and he answers me with a question. "You know why we were created, yes?"

"My mother told me the story, which basically boils down to: Untethered magic was destroying the world. The keepers were created to absorb the excess magic and stop such a thing from ever happening again."

He nods. "So when you ask me if I might have chosen to be a keeper, the only true answer I can give you is this: Is there truly a choice when the world you know will be consumed if you don't act?"

I don't have an answer for that. Mostly because speaking the truth is too fucking bleak.

Sometimes choice is an illusion.

CHAPTER SEVENTEEN

I'm not afraid of the keeper's anger, the simmering rage that seems to beat in time with the crashing lightning out on the ocean.

Leaning back on my hands, I say, "Well, since you don't remember your name, why not choose a new one?"

He casts me a hard stare and I return it with wide-eyed anticipation. "A real choice for once," I say. "Completely your own."

Some of the tension leaves his body and his countenance flickers, shifting a little. For a few seconds, I glimpse the blond-haired, tanned, and laid-back façade he wore when we were eating burgers.

Then he returns to his darker countenance. He folds his arms across his chest with a moody huff. "I don't know where to start."

I shrug. "Start with… Greg."

I peer at him, gauging his reaction.

He stares back at me in all his dark glory. No matter how brightly the lightning flashes, it doesn't lessen the depths of the shadows that live across his skin.

I grimace. "Nope, you're not a Greg. How about... Dave?"

His glare increases.

I give him a wide grin. "Look, you'll have to come up some ideas of your own if you don't like mine. I can keep going forever. I've got all the names I've ever read in books. Bob, Brandon, Brady... B names are great. Why don't we start with Brett and take it from there?"

He screws up his nose. "No, not Brett."

"What's wrong with Brett?"

"I'm not a Brett."

I narrow my eyes at him and take another stab, this one closer to a name I suspect he might enjoy. "What about Diavolo?"

His lips stretch into a smile that should make me worried.

"Devil," he says, the dark light in his eyes growing.

I arch an eyebrow at him. "Well?"

"I don't hate it."

I give him a victorious smile. "Good." And then a solemn nod. "Well met, Diavolo."

His gaze passes over my face. "And you? What is your name?"

My grin rapidly fades. "I don't have a name."

His eyebrows rise.

"Mom taught me that names have power," I explain. "She said I would need to make a name for myself."

"Names do have power," the keeper murmurs. "But what did *she* call you?"

"Daughter."

"And what did you call her?"

"Mother."

The keeper—whom I now need to think of as Diavolo—acknowledges my reply with a brief nod. "Family roles have power, too."

He appears to think for a moment. "Does that mean I should

call you... Traveling Companion? Wild-Haired Woman?" He pauses, and it seems he's holding his breath before he speaks again. "Friend?"

I screw up my face in disgust. "Don't you fucking dare call me 'friend.' Friends are *nice*."

"Well, you need some sort of name in the interim before you choose your own." He leans back on his elbows and stretches out his legs. "Just keep in mind that Diavolo is taken."

I shake my head and roll my eyes, scoffing. "Wild-Haired Woman."

It's not inaccurate. My tresses are bunched across my chest, irrevocably knotted. The thick strands are so heavy and long that they extend all the way to my waist. I tug at the matted knots as I consider whether or not the keeper *should* call me "Wild-Haired."

There are worse names.

His voice breaks my thoughts. "I can unravel those knots if you like?"

I purse my lips at him, dubious of his offer. "Another illusion?"

"No, an unwinding spell. And don't worry, I won't have to kill a tree to do it." A hint of emerald light plays around his fingertips. My doubt only increases. I'm coming to associate the emerald light with witch-like powers. He's using that power to keep the wind at bay, but his translocation effort wasn't quite so successful. I'm wary of the calamities that could befall my tresses if I let his magic near them.

Diavolo casts me a baleful expression and I can only imagine he's sensing my feelings on the matter.

"It's your choice," he says.

"Fine. Okay. Do it."

I try not to hold my breath as I turn my back on him to give him full access to my hair. He doesn't waste time getting started and I'm immediately aware of the growing emerald glimmers, then a sense of weightlessness as the clumps lift off my back without tugging against my scalp.

A few seconds later, the mass of hair nearest to my left cheek unravels before my eyes, the strands neatly separating and then falling softly to my chest, where they float a little around my body.

The strands appear so light. So free.

I'm startled by the sudden burn of tears behind my eyes.

Mom's hair was beautiful, lush, and golden. When she was alive, she would comb my tresses with her fingers, gently unraveling any knots that might have formed. But after she died, I couldn't undo the knots at the back of my head by myself, so I let them clump.

A moment later, every twisted bunch of hair lifts away from my shoulders and sides. Every knotted strand seems to unwind at the same time, and then all of them float around my face.

My head feels lighter than it has in years and my hair appears much longer than before as it falls softly around my body, all the way to the blanket.

"All done," Diavolo says.

I collect myself before I turn back to him, wanting to thank him.

But he's all business. "We'll sleep here for the night and head to New York before the sun rises. It will be early evening there, so you won't be exposed to the sun at its brightest on either side of the world."

"Good," I say, keeping my voice neutral.

Inside, I'm hugely relieved. My eyes are slowly adjusting, but I couldn't handle the bright light back in the veil and I imagine witnessing the sun at its peak will be a similarly challenging experience. I'm sure I'd attract too much attention walking around in public with a blindfold on, although sunglasses are certainly an option. Real sunglasses, that is. Not the illusionary kind.

My next challenge is going to be my sensitive hearing. I'm not unaware that the keeper may well have brought me to a near-deserted town for that reason, among others. Since we arrived, the roar of the ocean is the loudest sound I've encountered, but it's what Mom would have called 'white noise.' Far more bearable than sudden bangs and clangs or the roars of vehicles I'm sure I'll encounter in the city.

Diavolo gestures at the panthers as if they pose a greater problem. "However, the panthers will need camouflage."

All four of them appear half-asleep where they lie at the edge of the blanket, but the moment he speaks about them, their ears prick up and their silver eyes flash open in the shadows.

Diavolo is right. I know enough about human life to understand that panthers aren't household pets that could blend in on the streets.

But that isn't my greatest concern.

My voice becomes hard as I speak. "These panthers are legends. Even people who don't know what they are will view them as a threat—and so they should. Any supernatural who *does* know what they are will want to trap them and use them for their own purposes."

His gaze is chillingly icy. "They will try to kill the panthers and sell their body parts," he says bluntly. "Their claws and teeth would be priceless."

A growl rises to my lips. "I will never allow that to happen. I will kill anyone who tries to imprison them or who harms them in any way."

The male panther nearest to me edges closer, rounding the blanket to settle down beside me. His head nudges my side before he snarls up at me, as if to voice his own determination to protect the pack.

I nod down at him, guessing at his state of mind. "You don't belong to anyone but yourselves," I say to him before I turn to the other panthers. "But as long as you stand at my side, I will protect you like family."

Across from me, Diavolo's eyes have crinkled at the corners. "Well, better that it doesn't come to bloodshed, then."

Sapphire light flares around his fingertips, the same light he used when he gave me clothing. He inclines his head pointedly toward his magic as if that's the solution.

"An illusion?" I ask.

He gives a single nod in reply.

The panthers all side-eye me, especially the female, who has lifted her head. She looks from the keeper to me as if to say, *Don't you dare.*

I suppose pretty jackets were bad enough, let alone changing their entire appearance.

My only response is an apologetic grimace.

"What animal should they be?" Diavolo asks me.

The grimace is frozen on my face. The panthers seem to understand everything we say, and I know they won't like my answer.

I choose to speak in a whisper—as if that will make my suggestion more palatable to them. "Some kind of dog, I think. So they can blend in to human society."

The panthers' eyes widen, and the males lower their heads in an aggressive stance, their lips drawing back from their teeth. The female hisses at us like the big cat she is, her teeth gnashing and catching at the shadows.

I quickly follow up with a hopeful: "Some kind of attack dog, of course. Big and scary as fuck."

The female stops hissing, but her eyes narrow dangerously at me.

Diavolo studies his fingernails, the light playing around his hands. "If they don't want to be dogs, we could make them cats. But they'd have to be housecats." He watches them from beneath his eyelashes. "I wonder if they'd prefer to be housecats?"

The panthers yelp and recoil and the female hisses again, a threatening sound that would make most supernaturals run for their lives.

"Dogs, then," Diavolo announces, sitting completely upright while the coils of energy grow thicker around his fingertips. "But what kind?"

I run through the list of big-dog breeds Mom warned me about and discover it's quite short. "German Shepherd? Rottweiler?" Then I snap my fingers. "Doberman Pinscher. They're sleek, black, fast, and around the same size as the panthers are now."

"Good," Diavolo replies. "The closer the illusion is to their natural form, the longer it should hold. After all, we don't want it wearing off while we're out in public."

Without waiting for the panthers' reaction—not that it would matter now since they seem resigned to accepting their fate—Diavolo extends his hands toward them and closes his eyes.

"Sleek. Black. Fast," he murmurs beneath his breath as sapphire light wafts gently across the air and coils around the panthers' bodies.

The light flows over their forms from their tails to their heads. Their tails shorten, but their black fur remains much the same, shortening only slightly. Their bodies elongate a little but are no less muscular-looking, while the biggest change is to their faces.

Their snouts become longer, their heads narrower, and they lose their whiskers. Finally, their eyes turn from silver to the darkest brown, practically black.

The final change is the addition of a patch of russet fur on each of them. One of the males has russet fur across his front right paw. Another has a patch across his right shoulder. The third male wears a russet patch on his chest. And the female has a russet snout.

They stare at each other as they rise to their feet and then turn their heads to consider their own bodies as best they can. The female panther finally looks up at me. She growls in the back of her throat.

It's a distinctly *canine* growl instead of a feline snarl.

She coughs, growls again, and then shrugs her shoulders before she settles back onto the sand with her pack.

"Not as bad as it could be, huh?" I ask, grinning at her.

They look fearsome but entirely normal. They'll be protected this way.

"I've poured as much staying power into the magic as I think is safe," Diavolo says. "Let's see how long the illusion holds."

He settles back onto the blanket, lying down and folding his hands behind his head.

In the distance, the lightning has died down, but not completely. It flickers at the corner of my eye, reminding me of the immense power Diavolo controls.

He lifts his left hand toward me and beckons me to come to him. "Come. Sleep while you can."

He gestures to his side, as if he wants me to lie there. A tempting position. It's been a long time since I could snuggle against another living creature. My pack instincts are growing stronger by the second, but logic tells me that huddling up against a being like the keeper is a dangerous move to make.

"It's winter on this side of the hemisphere," he says, the corners of his lips twitching upward as if he reads my mind. "It's warm right now, but the temperature is bound to plummet during the night. Don't stay over there, where you'll freeze in your underwear. Come over here, where it's warm."

Said the predator to his prey.

I'm sure there's a human nursery rhyme warning of these situations.

I grin right back at him because I'm also certain there would be nursery rhymes warning of creatures like me.

CHAPTER EIGHTEEN

*S*lipping across the blanket, I curl up against Diavolo's side.

He immediately catches the edge of the blanket behind me and pulls it over us both. A second later, the male panther behind me relocates even closer to me, plunking himself down at my back and pushing me even closer to Diavolo's side within the blanket.

He's lying on his back and I catch my breath as my head ends up on his shoulder, my thighs pressed against his left side, my upper leg sliding a little across his hip. My left arm curves across his chest. If I were to adjust my position a little—move my upper arm and leg across him—I could be said to have captured him within the blanket instead of the other way around.

His blue eyes glimmer with sapphire light, a cold, glittering expression as he peers down at me from beneath his lashes. The longer I hold his gaze, the darker the light in his eyes becomes, a dilation of his pupils, and I sense the twitch of his fingers before he reaches beneath the blanket to wrap his hand around my upper arm.

His fingers are warm and his hold is light. Soft enough to be interpreted as a caress if I wanted to believe that was his intention.

I allow a small smile to creep across my face as we lie like that for a long moment.

Then I speak. Quietly. But I choose my words carefully. "The name I want for myself means *Conqueror*. But I haven't earned that name yet."

He seems to chew over this for a second. "Conqueror," he murmurs, his eyes darkening even further. "It will be a fitting name for you."

For the first time since he wrapped the blanket around us, he releases my gaze, his focus dropping to my lips. "What makes you think you haven't already earned it?"

My jaw clenches. "I will deserve that name when I avenge my mother."

He makes a humming sound in the back of his throat as if he disagrees, his hand softening even further around my arm, his thumb brushing slowly back and forth across my skin. I fight the tingling sensation and the way I'm suddenly acutely conscious of the delicious press of his thigh against my pelvis.

"You conquered your cage," he says. "You conquered the Serene Commander at the Cathedral—"

I growl at him. "With no help from you."

It's unsettling to me that he didn't step into that fight.

"It wasn't my battle," he replies calmly, seeming unmoved by my indignation. "You didn't need my help."

I narrow my eyes at him. "You'd never seen me in a fight before then, so you couldn't have known that at the time."

The play of his fingers is now like a dance down my arm to my elbow, where it rests near my hip. "I wanted to see what you could do. It's important for me to know when to step in and when to let you fight your own battles."

I recall the way he twitched when it had looked like the

Serene Commander's blade was going to cleave my head from my shoulders. "So you *would have* stepped in if I'd really been in trouble."

He gives me a disarming smile. "Maybe."

I huff at him. "That's a yes."

"Well, of course it's a yes." His lips are suddenly very close to mine. "You can't take your revenge if you're dead."

"No, I can't," I say, studying him closely. "Which is why it's even more curious to me that you hesitated to help me."

His lips part, as if he's about to say something. Then they press together. "I knew she wasn't going to kill you."

My brow slowly furrows. He is so very close to me now that the curve of his lips is blurring in my vision. "You sound awfully fucking sure about that."

"You saw an enemy, but I saw more," he says. "There was soot on her face. Her energy was low. Her home had sustained considerable damage." The keeper pierces me with his now very-black eyes. "She only fought us because she was frightened by our presence."

My scowl fades a little. *Was she frightened?*

Well, if she was, her fear was warranted. But even so, I disagree with the conclusion the keeper drew from the angel's fear.

My upper arm snakes forward so I can catch his arm even as he holds mine. My small hand barely makes it around his forearm, but I hold on tightly as my voice becomes a growl once more. "Fear and desperation make creatures *more* dangerous, not less."

He doesn't deny it, his black eyes glowing down at me with a brightness that feels like he's tearing at my soul.

It fucking hurts.

Or... it would... if I had a soul.

He nods slowly. "I made you a promise," he says, his voice low. "For which you paid the ultimate price."

His hand slides up to my chest, his palm pressing at the location of my heart while his fingers extend across my shoulder.

His touch reminds me of what I've already sacrificed in pursuit of the revenge I seek.

The love in my heart. A beating organ with feelings that only ever caused me pain.

His features smooth out, becoming blank, and somehow, he's fucking scarier this way. "I promised you revenge and I promised you would live to have it," he says as the shadows grow around us and, in the distance, another streak of lightning cuts across the night sky. "But beyond that, I am not yours to command."

I draw a sharp breath, but if I push through the mire inside my mind, there's a message I believe he's trying to give me that I probably should have understood already:

He is not mine to cage, no matter what he promised me.

And yet...

He is destined to walk this path to revenge with me.

As I plunder the depths of his eyes, I'm reminded that I made a dangerous deal.

His fate may be bound to mine, but by giving him my heart, I have bound myself to him.

I dare to close the gap between us and whisper against his lips. "I know what I want you to call me."

Heat flares in his eyes, but the only move he makes is to capture my hand and press it to his chest. "You don't have to tell me. I already know because it's in your heart."

I exhale quietly, accepting how vulnerable my feelings are to him.

Another streak of lightning crashes across the sky, this one flickering right above us, licking the darkness like a snake's tongue as the keeper says, "I will call you 'Veda.'"

I can't stop my smile—a smile that must betray my approval of the name he's given me. "As you like."

Dark energy flashes across the air above us and the keeper's gaze passes across my face, once again focusing briefly on my lips before he pulls back even further.

"I like," he says.

He settles back onto the blanket and I allow my head to rest on his shoulder.

Above me, the palm tree branches partially obscure the night sky, but its beauty is even more alluring now that I can only catch brief glimpses of it through the branches.

I speak carefully. "Thank you for showing me the night sky. I'm grateful to have a name and to try burgers for the first time. It's nice to have hair that isn't clumped anymore."

His voice rumbles at my ear. "But?"

"But tomorrow, my only plan of attack is to bust down the doors of one of the empire's strongholds and announce my claim. They'll kill me on the spot. And if they don't succeed right then, they won't stop until I'm dead."

The keeper's arms tighten across my back before his right hand rises to my face, tipping my chin so that he can see my eyes.

There's a fresh glow across his face as another streak of lightning bursts through the air above us.

"What if you don't go as yourself?" he asks.

I stare back at him. "What are you talking about?"

"What if you don't return to New York as yourself?" Sapphire-blue energy crackles around his fingertips, licking dangerously at my skin. "Just like the panthers, I can give you any appearance you like."

The crackling energy grows as he sweeps a few strands of my straightened hair forward and allows them to rest across his palm.

"Red hair, brown hair, blonde if you like." His focus switches to my face. Releasing my hair so that it falls across my chin and chest, he traces the edge of my jaw. "Blue eyes, green eyes, brown eyes…"

As his focus lowers to my lips, his fingertips pause at the edge of my mouth. "But, even if you ask me to, I won't change your lips."

"Why not?" I ask, my voice a hoarse whisper. The longer he studies me, the more strongly the dark energy within him calls to me in ways I need to quantify. Ways I need to put aside and keep in their place because otherwise, I'll move my hands and explore the rising sensations that are heating my thoughts and warming the space between my thighs.

"Because this mouth should not be messed with," he says.

I arch an eyebrow at him, trying to lighten the intensity in his expression. "Is it my sharp wit?"

A slow smile tugs at the edges of his lips, but he doesn't reply for a long moment.

"Possibly," he finally says.

I swallow and focus on what he's offering. "If I can conceal my identity, it changes everything. I can infiltrate the empire."

"You can break it from the inside," he says, his fingers resting on my chin as a hint of challenge enters his eyes. "The best way to take your revenge: When your enemies won't see it coming."

Rapidly thinking it through, I say, "We can pose as mercenaries. Offer to become servants of the empire. But I'll need weapons and clothing—real clothing—as well as a base of operations."

"I can give you all of those," he replies. "I have a place in mind."

I consider him carefully. "Where?"

"You'll see."

My eyes narrow.

"You'll like it as much as you like burgers," he promises,

widening his eyes at me innocently, but he can't conceal the darkness lurking at the back of his expression.

Choosing not to push him, I say, "You could make me look like the Serene Commander. All blue-eyed and blonde-haired and stunningly beautiful."

"Bad idea," he immediately replies. "Someone might recognize her."

"True." I shrug as best I can where I'm lying all pushed up against him. "Oh, well."

He brushes the hair back from my jaw before his fingers slip across my upper shoulder. His voice resonates with the darkest magic as he says, "You're already stunning."

I shouldn't believe him. Flattery comes easily to the tongues of dark creatures. Or so my mother warned me.

The corner of his mouth twitches as he lifts his hand one last time to press it over mine, which has remained on his heart.

"Your distrust is warranted," he murmurs, reminding me once again that my feelings are open to him. "You should expect me to betray you eventually."

My eyes widen at how openly he has acknowledged the basic nature of all dark creatures.

"But for now," he continues, "we are allies, both of us playing out our roles to the inevitable end."

"Whatever that end may be," I whisper.

He keeps my hand over his heart—but really, it's *my* heart I'm pressing my hand against—a connection I didn't know I needed until this moment when exhaustion finally pushes into my consciousness.

It's been a long day and tomorrow will be harder.

The path before me is uncertain. All I know for sure right now is that I will return to the place of my conception, despite the danger that waits for me there.

CHAPTER NINETEEN

I return to wakefulness, aware of one of the panthers licking my face. It seems a very dog-like thing to do, assuming the illustrations in books of dogs licking their humans is anything to go by.

I crack open my eyes while the male panther with the blaze on his paw nudges my face, growling softly in my ear.

"Okay, okay." I push gently at his face. "I'm awake."

The sky above me is shadowed but carries a tinge of light that tells me dawn is on its way. Reaching for my blindfold, which has remained tucked into my bra strap, I prepare to wrap it around my face if I need it.

Opening my eyes fully, I find myself able to cope with the light without the blindfold for now, but I have no doubt that will change.

The air is colder and crisper than it was last night, while the last stars dot the dissipating darkness above.

Diavolo stands at the bottom edge of the blanket with his back to me, but I don't miss the claws that have extended from his fingers and the sharpness of his teeth as he half-turns toward me.

He's still wearing his dark-haired, blue-eyed persona.

Remaining where I'm sitting on the blanket, I speak softly, knowing he can hear me over the swell of the nearby water.

"What's wrong?" I ask, studying him closely.

He shakes his head and is silent for so long that I'm surprised when I get a response.

"Your heart was hurting," he says.

I press my hand to my chest, even though I know it's *his* chest that will have hurt in the night.

"I should have warned you," I say. "I have nightmares."

He snorts. "Nightmares. Is that what you call them?"

"Okay, then. Let's say they're vivid dreams." I glide to my feet and pull my hair back from my face. I quickly take stock of my current state of health. Alive. Breathing. Dusted with sand. It's enough.

"You dream of a glittering home and the mother you lost," Diavolo says, turning his back fully on me once more.

"Yes." I check for the other panthers, finding them standing guard a short distance away on either side of Diavolo. "Constantly."

"You need to learn to guard your dreams," he says as he continues to survey the beach. "Or they could be used against you by a supernatural who knows how to read them."

I let out a soft sigh. *Easier said than done.* I don't hold much control over my dreams.

As I step off the blanket and toward Diavolo, the crunch of my feet on the sand is overly loud in my hearing.

He finally turns fully toward me. His claws retract, his teeth even out, and his features change. He morphs back into his more muscular persona with the pale-brown skin and brown eyes.

"If you need to pee, there's a private spot behind the tree there." He points. "Once you're done, we should leave. I sense humans are not far off."

I have no objections since I sense the humans too—a group of them approaching the opposite end of the beach. At least they're far away for now.

I disappear behind the trees and then quickly return to wash my hands in the salty water. By the time I'm done, the first rays of light are threatening to break the horizon.

Tying the blindfold across my eyes, I breathe easily again. Although I'm not so happy about the freezing-cold water that trickles down my back since I splashed it everywhere when I tied the material around my head.

It makes me even more surprised to see that the group of humans who have appeared at the other end of the beach are all stripping off their clothing. Then they pull on tight, black suits instead.

Narrowing my eyes and using my strong eyesight to focus in on them, I recognize the human male from last night. The strange, rectangular object from the back of his truck is lying on the sand beside him.

I'm startled when he and the other humans run toward the water, each with a rectangle tucked under their arm. They splash through the shallows and launch themselves onto their rectangles in the surf.

What the fuck are they doing?

My eyes widen when they ride the rectangles smoothly over the first wave and into the next.

"Huh," I mutter. "Water-riding." I glance down at the panther with the russet paw who has remained at my side. "Looks like fun. If you want to freeze your pants off."

I shiver a little since I'm not exactly warmly dressed myself. Collecting the other panthers on the way back to Diavolo, I plant myself before him. "I'm ready."

I take a deep breath, preparing to have my stomach flipped and to land on my hands and knees on the other side.

Emerald light glimmers around his hands and a haze builds around us.

"To New York," he says as the fog thickens, forming a tornado of mist that sucks the breath out of me. "And your new base of operations."

I come back to myself with a *thump*, but this time, I find myself wedged between Diavolo at my back and the four panthers at my front, as if we all switched places and got plastered up against each other along the way.

A rapid glance at my surroundings tells me we're in a small room with walls that reach the ceiling on three sides. The walls to my left and right are covered with open shelves and hanging racks holding everything from clothing to shoes to belts, all of it messily shoved in, material dripping over the edges of the drawers.

While we seemed to be all piled up against the narrower wall behind us, the fourth side, which is directly ahead of me, is wide open and looks into a bedroom like something out of a fairy tale.

It's dark in this room, but I'm glad I'm wearing my blindfold, because late-afternoon sunlight gleams behind sheer curtains on the far side of the bedroom.

Most importantly, I don't sense another creature anywhere nearby, certainly not in the bedroom opposite us.

The panthers peel off me one by one, silently dropping back to the floor and shaking out their dog bodies. Their lips draw back as they turn their snarls on Diavolo, who has remained behind me.

I guess they didn't appreciate becoming pancakes, either.

Although I have to admit it's not entirely unpleasant being smooshed up against him.

Able to take a deep breath now that my chest isn't being crushed, I ease away from the keeper with a whisper. "Where are we?"

His voice sounds at my ear. "This is a dressing room in an apartment belonging to a recently deceased witch. She was assassinated. Poison, so there wasn't any blood. She managed to make it all the way home before she died. Right there, actually."

His arm moves at my side, brushing my hip as he points to the floor at my feet.

"The assassin followed her in, took away her body, and locked up after himself," he says.

"An assassin," I mutter, digging into my memory as I scrutinize the shelves. "Mom warned me about them. She said the Assassin's Legion has a base hidden in Boston, and I should avoid them at all costs."

Their base isn't far enough from New York for comfort and my chances of staying off their radar could be slim.

"Well, conveniently for us, this witch's memories indicated she had no family and she lived alone. What's more, the human authorities won't be aware that she's dead, so we shouldn't be disturbed."

The shelves may be messy, but the material protruding from them is so soft that it slithers through my hands when I reach for it. The keeper said he could solve my clothing problem and I'm assuming this is how.

"I suppose you're hoping these will fit me?" As I turn to him, unexpected movement flickers directly behind him.

My claws snap down as I make out the shape of a woman standing directly behind the keeper.

I leap back, narrowly avoiding bumping into the panthers, who quickly scatter to either side.

The woman is only partially visible. I can't see much more than the side of her body and her arm, but she has claws.

Deadly, black ones like mine.

CHAPTER TWENTY

"*D*iavolo," I whisper urgently. "Step toward me slowly."

I'm shocked that he hasn't sensed the woman's presence already. And that the panthers haven't reacted to the threat she clearly poses. *And* that I didn't sense her presence myself before this moment.

The keeper's brown eyes have flown wide. Despite my warning, he takes quick glances behind himself before he lifts both of his hands warily in my direction.

"Easy, Veda." He moves aside so that more of the woman comes into view before he gestures at the wall and the large, reflective surface resting flush against it. "It's a mirror."

A mirror?

I peer at the shiny surface and the silhouette within it that's visible in the dark. My hands slowly lower as I stare back at the woman who stands before me.

I thought I would be happy to see myself for the first time. I thought, or rather hoped, that looking at myself would be like looking at the mother I'd lost. That I'd see parts of her in the shape of my face, my physique, but instead, it feels like I'm staring at a complete stranger.

"That's… me?"

I barely know myself.

I've seen my arms and legs and torso before, simply by looking down at them, but never in connection with my shoulders, neck, head, and face. Never as a whole person standing tall in front of me.

A ragged bra and underpants cling to a slender, muscular frame. My legs are longer than I thought they were, proportionate to my torso. My bust is curvier and my waist narrower, cinched in even more tightly by the sash I took from the Cathedral. My mother's shirt has remained safely tucked under my bra strap, the shirt's material so threadbare that it fits neatly there.

Slowly retracting my claws, I approach the mirror so I'm standing only two paces away from it.

I reach up to touch my face, tracing the shape of my jaw and lips, then my earlobes up to the bottom edge of the blindfold.

Finally, I run my hands down the mess of hair that falls past my waist, the gray strands framing my face, the rest of my hair black to my shoulders before it turns blonde.

Trusting that it's dark enough in this room, I reach up to untie the blindfold, needing to see my full face, if only once.

The panthers have quietly gathered around me now and Diavolo remains at the side of the room, his expression shuttered.

I'm sure I'll only get a glance before the light filtering in from the bedroom gets the better of me, so I take a deep breath, open my eyes, and then close them again.

In that single look, I see the golden eyes my mother spoke of.

Unnatural. Predatory. The look of a fierce, dark thing.

My father's eyes. Along with my black blood, proof that I'm his daughter.

Holding my head high, my eyes now firmly closed, I re-tie the blindfold before opening them again.

Then I fold up my feelings, even though I know full well that the keeper will have experienced my turmoil at meeting myself for the first time.

My lips are dry, but I manage to speak, sounding wooden. "You should check if there's any food we can eat. I'll look through the clothing for what might fit me. Then I'll decide what illusion you should place around my appearance. As soon as night falls, I want to head out to one of the empire's strongholds and let it be known we're looking for work."

The keeper gives me a nod before he ushers the panthers out of the room. "Take your time. I'll see what I can do about the windows and sunlight."

I rally a little before he reaches the end of the dressing room. "You could have at least brought me to a dead vampire's lair."

He sticks out his tongue in a gagging gesture. "Too many blood stains on their clothing." But he quickly smirks at the overly-stuffed shelves. "This witch liked to shop."

He saunters away but pauses again. "By the way, there's a bathroom around the corner. You might like to take a shower."

The suggestion of a shower startles me a little. I've only ever cleaned myself with a makeshift sponge and water in a bucket.

I'm affronted. "I don't stink."

Diavolo makes a scoffing sound as he disappears into the bedroom.

Or do I?

Meh. Who can tell?

Mom spoke of this stuff called deodorant and maybe the witch has some somewhere, but it's not my first priority.

Quickly opening drawers and rifling through the clothing options, I discover that the keeper was eerily precise in choosing this particular witch.

Her clothing is exactly my size. Even the underwear fits,

although the bras are slightly too small and push my breasts upward. But it's nothing too uncomfortable.

By the time I've gathered a pair of black jeans, a black shirt, and clean underwear, the keeper has pinned blankets over the windows and it's dark enough that I can comfortably remove my blindfold.

I fold it up carefully and leave it, the sash, and my mother's shirt safely in one of the few spare spaces I find in a drawer. I won't be able to wear this old material out in public. Better that I find something else with which to shield my eyes.

I make a quiet promise that I'll only retrieve the material from the shelf once I've avenged my mother.

An hour later, I've showered for the first time. It's an unpleasant experience that initially involves scalding myself, leaping clear of the hot spray, slipping on the wet floor, and landing on my backside.

Diavolo calls through the door to ask if I'm okay. "Lots of supernaturals die in showers." There's a dark chuckle in his voice. "Maybe I should come in there and help you."

What a tempting thought.

After declining his offer and finally figuring out how to turn the faucet to make the water run warm instead of hot, I manage to scrub myself clean. It's a small mercy that I already know how to use the cake of soap.

Drying myself is the best part of the whole experience.

Damn, these towels are like... Well, I don't have a comparison yet. Mom used to say things like 'smooth as silk' and 'fluffy as clouds,' but for now, these towels are my 'soft as' comparison.

"Soft as towels." I sigh happily as I rummage through the tubes and canisters sitting on the sink, under the sink, and in the little cupboard on the wall.

I find a bottle labeled *deodorant*, but it has a strange, rolling-ball thing on the top of it that makes no sense to me. Besides, Mom said deodorant was some sort of spray...

I spy a canister, also labeled *deodorant*, which I accidentally spray in my face before I get it anywhere near my armpits.

Dark saints, I'm hairy.

I grimace at my underarms and legs.

Wild-haired, indeed.

Continuing my rummage, I come across a razor. Now *this* I know how to work, because Mom once tried to convince our jailor to get her a razor 'for her legs,' which she showed me how to use—right before she also tried to use the blade on our jailor. It earned her a burn across her cheek and that was the end of smooth legs.

I'm also happy to recognize a hairbrush, toothbrush, and hair ties, all of which I put to good use.

Finally, I stand once more in front of the mirror, dressed in a dead witch's clothing, my armpits and legs smoother than they've been since I hit puberty, and my hair resting in a single, long braid across my left shoulder.

I look like a real person.

Except for my eyes. And my claws, which I choose to extend at that moment. And my teeth that I can sharpen at will—

Wait, what the fuck?

I lean forward, staring at my sharpening teeth, startled to see my canines for the first time.

Before my eyes, my canines turn as black as my claws and appear just as sharp.

I've run my tongue over them countless times and never been the wiser as to their color.

Dark saints. Mom didn't have teeth like these.

I remember the way she'd gleam at me and tell me I could rip someone's throat out with my teeth. I didn't realize how true that could be.

The surprised crease in my forehead smooths out as I come to terms with this new aspect of myself.

Well, maybe this is what you get when you combine a dark angel with a hellhound. A whole bunch of dark fuckery.

Of course... there's one other aspect of myself that I don't examine right now because it was always fucking useless to me, so I leave it be.

When I emerge from the bathroom, I find Diavolo leaning over the table in the kitchen, a large piece of paper spread out across the wooden surface. A bowl rests to the left of the paper and an old tome sits on the right.

He's stayed in his brown-eyed form, but his sleeves are rolled up and his shirt is now unbuttoned at the top.

The panthers have found themselves places on the plush lounge chairs nearby. I take note of the fact that they've retained their dog-like forms for nearly twenty-four hours, so the longevity of the keeper's illusion magic seems strong.

"I found a map of New York city," he says without looking up. On the next beat, he points to the bowl. "That's cereal for you to eat." And then the tome. "This is the witch's grimoire. But the assassins must have cleaned out all of her supplies because I can't find a wand or any potions anywhere. I'll have to fashion some sort of illusion wand to mask how I'm really creating magic."

He taps the map. "Now. Show me all the places you know."

Scooping up the bowl and trying not to get distracted by the first mouthful of puffy squares of sugary deliciousness, I lean in close to Diavolo and take quick stock of the map.

It's elaborate and detailed, but Mom made me memorize all the landmarks and it appears that most of the structures have remained the same as what she described.

"Here," I say, balancing the bowl in one hand while I point at the corner of a block that sits three blocks east of the Hudson River. "There's a tavern called the White Wing. It's one of the more public places where the empire conducts business. The front is a regular restaurant, but Mom told me there's a green door on the far side that will let us in to the space behind it. The empire exists behind doors and in dark places, but this tavern won't be as difficult to enter as some of the other places and, at the very least, we can gather information while we're there."

I'm suddenly aware that the keeper isn't looking at the map anymore.

"Are you paying attention?" I ask, glancing up at him.

"Very much so," he says, his focus lingering on my face. "You clean up nicely."

I purse my lips at him before I put the bowl back on the table. "Flattery is a tool," I say. "I'm not sure why you're trying to use it on me."

In fact, he's tried it a few times now. Implying that he likes the shape of my lips. Calling me 'stunning.' Talking about beautiful darkness.

He steps closer and his features flicker a little, a brief hint of those powerful, blue eyes shining through. "Maybe I'm simply speaking the truth."

I consider him carefully. "Truth is never simple."

His eyebrows arch. "Isn't it?"

I dismiss his question because debating the nature of truth will only sidetrack us.

Turning my attention back to the map, I trace my fingertip along the roads leading away from the White Wing Tavern. "There are underground tunnels through here and here, so we need to be careful we don't make too much of a splash or they'll very quickly call in reinforcements."

"Okay, then," Diavolo says, stepping back again. "Choose your appearance and I'll take you straight there."

Now, I allow myself to smile because I've decided how I want to look.

CHAPTER TWENTY-ONE

I step from the emerald mist, this time landing neatly on my feet with the four panthers at my side and Diavolo behind me.

I cast him a quick, backward glance, and he responds with a smirk. He's getting better at translocating us without mishaps.

Quickly ascertaining that we're alone in the service alley at the side of the tavern, I take a moment to orient myself. The space is dark enough to be comfortable, but it isn't the brightness so much as sounds and smells that are likely to become a problem for me.

Luckily, I found all sorts of solutions to my sensory issues among the witch's belongings. A masquerade mask has provided me with a more acceptable blindfold to wear in public —not that I knew what to call it until Diavolo told me—and he obliged me by using his power to fuse gauzy cloth over the eye holes.

For my ears, I made earplugs out of one of the witch's beeswax candles. My hearing is sensitive enough for me to pick up the sounds around me without being overwhelmed by what will be an inevitable mash of music, voices, footfalls, vehicles, and… sex? Assuming that's what I'm hearing from the building up and to my right. Who knows, I could be wrong, but Mom didn't hold back on telling me all the things in that regard.

Carefully, I take my first steps along the alley.

Diavolo follows at my back, his agreed-upon persona firmly in place: the tall, muscular one with the brown hair, brown eyes, and light-brown skin. I considered asking him to wear his blue-eyed, black-haired persona, but he only seems to shift into that form when his mood is at its darkest. I need him to be completely in control of his emotions for the path ahead.

He's dressed in a suit and carries a black wand in a holster beneath his jacket—it's an illusion, but he'll be able to pretend it's the conduit for his magic.

For myself, I chose an appearance close to my real coloring to ensure the magic of the illusion lasts as long as possible. My hair is now all black and my eyes, if they could be seen behind the gauze, are slate gray. My chin is delicate, my cheekbones softer, and my neck slightly more slender. I've combined my appearance with a low-cut, black top and black pants, finishing off the look with sandals I'll be able to slip off quickly if I need to run.

With this cute face, I'd look like a sweet, little pixie from a children's book, except that I asked Diavolo to give me a tattoo down my right arm.

As much as I like the contrast with my otherwise cute appearance, the tattoo isn't for show. Rather, it's my warning system. I can easily see if the ink is vanishing, which will help me keep track of my illusion.

For all intents and purposes from this moment on, Diavolo is a warlock and I am a pixie. Of course, if I need to use my claws, I'll look like a wolf shifter, but the visual confusion can only be to my advantage and I'll deal with that if or when it happens.

I prowl to the end of the alley, grateful for the gauze over my eyes when I'm confronted with the streetlights. Sadly, there isn't much I can do to dampen my sense of smell, which is currently being assaulted by all kinds of sweet and cloying scents—primarily coming from the flowering vines crawling across the alley wall on my left.

The keeper is a shadow at my back as we round the corner. Music filters from the tavern a short walk up ahead, the front wall of which sports more vines and flowers above the windows.

As we walk, Diavolo murmurs the names of objects all around us. I don't stop him because as much as it sounds like he's listing things off for his own benefit, it's helping me confirm my knowledge of the world.

Lamppost. Streetlight. Pavement. Curb. Fire hydrant. Sports car. Tow truck. Crosswalk...

I'm distracted from his murmurings when a human passerby jumps at the appearance of the four Dobermans.

I bare my teeth at the stranger in what I'm sure is a sweet smile. Here I am, all pixie-like, taking my vicious doggies out for a walk. Just for fun.

When we reach the tavern door, my focus is quickly on the vines and flowers that continue to curl across the front of the building. My senses tingle a second before the female panther gives a soft growl and the keeper leans in at the same time.

"The flowers reek of magic," he says.

"I can smell it." I'm not sure how or when those innocent-looking vines or flowers might attack, but they could be capable of anything—sprouting poisonous thorns or spraying deadly mist. I'd rather not find out.

Through the glass windows, the tavern appears completely normal inside: soft lighting, neat tables, a bar at the side. It's full of human patrons.

The green door in the far shadowed corner makes me smile. Mostly because Mom's information was correct.

It's not that I doubted her. Rather, I doubted my ability to apply what she taught me. Seeing the door, exactly where she said it would be—exactly where I *remembered* her saying it would be—is the validation I need to feel confident proceeding inside.

Carefully pushing open the tavern's front door, I hold it open for the panthers to slide in ahead of me.

The human, who stands at a little counter near the entrance, splutters at me. "Uh, miss? Excuse me? You can't bring those dogs in here. Miss?"

I keep on walking, gratified when ribbons of dark light waft around the restaurant, reaching every human in the place, and the keeper's voice sounds clearly in the sudden silence. "You don't see any dogs. You don't see us. We were never here. Now, carry on."

The human returns to the list in front of him and the chatter around us resumes as if we don't exist.

As I head straight for the far door, movement above me catches my attention. I glance up from beneath my lashes to see that the ceiling, and a portion of the wall directly above the green door, is painted with a pattern of the same kind of vines and flowers that grow outside.

Strange.

Stranger still is that the painted flowers seem to turn to follow our movements as we approach the door.

"Careful," the keeper warns at my back, indicating he's noticed the painted flowers too. "It could be some kind of security system."

I'm not about to back out because of it.

When my hand lands on the door's handle, I focus on what I can sense beyond it. There's a hollow, which could indicate a corridor of some sort, and the sounds are fuzzy, but I sense a much larger space beyond the corridor.

"We should prepare for a welcome party," I whisper to the

keeper before I push open the green door and step into the corridor.

The female panther and the male with the blaze on his paw immediately surge forward, acting like guard dogs ahead of me. The other two males remain close at my sides while the keeper stays at my back, his shadow casting ahead of me now that the light from the tavern is behind us.

The door slips closed, leaving us in darkness.

The corridor is only short and I can see the room beyond it. It's large and filled with tables, maybe ten or twelve, with men sitting around all of them. Some of the men are holding glasses that undoubtedly contain liquor. Others are flipping coins and nursing squares of paper close to their chests—some kind of game, maybe.

I expected to be able to hear their conversations.

In fact, I anticipated them all turning toward us at once, and my body is tense with that possibility. But strangely, the men don't give any indication they've seen or heard us.

What's more, the space around us is weirdly echoey and the sounds ahead of us are muted. Sort of like when I put my head under the shower and the falling water muffled all other sounds.

"Cards," the keeper rumbles behind me when I slow my pace. "In case you were wondering what they're playing."

"Of course," I mutter. "Gambling."

Ten more careful steps take us to the end of the corridor and still the men don't seem to be aware of our presence.

It's odd, to say the least. Fucking unsettling, actually.

"Why haven't they noticed us?" I whisper to Diavolo.

A deep crease has formed in his forehead, and he shakes his head. "I don't know."

"Well." I exhale. "There's nothing for it but to make an entrance."

I step into the room with the keeper and panthers close behind me.

As soon as we move beyond the corridor, the nearest man jumps so suddenly that he nearly topples his chair. With a shout of alarm, he points at us.

Within seconds, all of the men have whirled in our direction, jumped to their feet, and pulled out guns of varying sizes and shapes with a chorus of metallic clicks.

Fuck. The walk through the corridor was so peaceful, I was hoping we might just slide on into the room.

Looks like that's now out of the question.

CHAPTER TWENTY-TWO

*E*very single one of the thirty men points a weapon in our direction. There are so many barrels filling my view that for a moment, I can't focus on the men themselves.

My hands fly up into the air. "Easy, gentlemen. No need to rush to violence."

The energy around the men indicates they're all supernaturals. I can tell from the auras around their bodies. Some are shifters, some are warlocks, some are mages. There are even a couple of vampires. At least, I think they are. Given it's the first time I'm seeing these auras, I can only hope I'm identifying their species correctly.

Regardless, I have no doubt their weapons are magically powered, since the air around the guns is filled with glimmering energy that makes the hairs on the back of my neck stand up.

My panthers have taken up position in front of me, their Doberman heads held high and alert so that they stand nearly as tall as my waist.

Diavolo is a tower of muscles where he remains a step behind me and to my right, and I sense he's two seconds away from lashing out with more power than a regular warlock should control.

"Where the fuck did you come from?" one of the men demands to know, his rifle aimed at my stomach. He's taller than many of the others, broad in the shoulders, and he sports a skull tattoo on the side of his neck, which is concealed slightly by his collar. Like the other men, he's wearing a suit.

It's not the question I was expecting. More like: *Who are you? What do you want?* Not: *Where did you come from?*

I raise my eyebrows as I hook my thumb back toward the corridor. "We walked through the door."

"What door?" he snarls.

"Uh… that door." Again, I jab my thumb in the door's direction. But I'm suddenly filled with uncertainty. Maybe there's something about doors that I'm missing.

I whisper to the keeper, "Doors are for walking through. Right?"

"Uh-huh," he says with a firm nod.

Opposite me, the man's lips twist. "Oh, you think you're funny, don't you? Let's all walk through a fucking door that doesn't exist, shall we?"

Doesn't exist?

I eye the man, noting the way he isn't looking at the corridor. I suddenly consider the possibility that he might not be able to see the door.

I'm not sure how or why that might be, but it would explain why our appearance startled the men so much. If they can't see a door, then I imagine it looked like we appeared out of nowhere. Or walked through a wall.

With that thought, I relax, because I seem to have the upper hand.

"You don't see a door?" Keeping the man in my sights, I turn to Diavolo. "Do you see a door? Because I see a door."

"Uh-huh." Very slowly, he sweeps aside his jacket to reveal his illusion wand.

"A completely visible, clearly there, door?"

"Uh-huh." Now his hand very slowly closes over the hilt of his weapon, although it's his fingers that glimmer with sapphire light.

"A green door," I finish with a smile.

"Very green," Diavolo replies.

The man's face has turned red and he splutters so hard that he spits as far as my feet. "Stop talking about a fucking door!" he roars, launching himself at me. "There's no fucking—"

There are flashes of black and then—

Thud.

It happens so fast that Diavolo doesn't even get a shot of magic off.

The female panther leaps, her muscular body flying through the air and into the big guy, knocking him down.

In unison with her, the male panther with the russet paw also leaps, but at the man's weapon hand.

All three hit the floor. The female's jaw is locked around the man's neck while the male panther has his wrist.

I expect to see blood, but neither of the beasts rips or tears, and the man has frozen beneath them. His eyes are wide with apparent shock, and he appears a little dazed, no doubt from the knock to his head when he landed.

The moment he hits the floor, there's a collective gasp from the other men.

Half of them adjust their aim, their weapons clicking as they train their guns on the panthers.

The other half take a quick step back as if they'd like nothing more than to get the fuck out of here.

Diavolo removes his hand from his wand and tips his chin at the panthers, both of whom are now looking to me as if for instructions.

"Step back," I murmur to the panthers. "I think we've shown our new friends enough for now."

The panthers open their jaws, revealing the tiniest pinpricks of blood on the man's neck and wrist, before they step back toward me.

To the man on the floor, I say, "If you value your life, I'd advise you to move very slowly. My pan—uh, dogs—are due for a meal and I'd rather they didn't eat my new friends."

Despite my warning, the man with the skull tattoo scrambles to his feet and hurries away, finding himself a table at the back of the room.

It's then that the sound of a chair scraping back reaches me. A man, much taller than the others, moves at the table on my far right. He wasn't visible to me before. It seems he remained sitting when we first arrived and now that the others have stepped back, they've revealed his presence.

This man rises slowly to his feet. Like the others, he's dressed in a suit, but otherwise, he stands out from all of them.

He has ice-blond hair with startlingly amber eyes, a combination of coloring that I don't see on any other man in the room. His skin is fair and the breadth of his shoulders beneath his jacket and thickness of his neck behind his collar indicate a muscular frame rivaled only by the keeper.

He's holding a small, golden object in his right hand, sort of like a cube but slimmer and more rectangular. His thumb moves at the side of it and a lid flips open. There's a soft *click* as a flame appears.

I'm sure I have a name for this object. Some sort of fire creator... or fire lighter... *A lighter!* That's it, I'm certain of it.

He flips the lid closed with a *clack* and the flame disappears.

His gaze finally clashes with mine and it's like that little flame has licked across the distance and sent a burn through my entire body. Surprisingly... it's not entirely unpleasant.

Where the keeper is all darkness, this man is like light. But not a pure, angelic sort of light. More like a blinding-hot flash that could kill me if I get too close.

"Friends, huh?" he drawls, referring to the way I addressed them all. "I guess we'll see about that."

I mutter a response beneath my breath. "Well, the fact that my dogs didn't eat that guy should count for something."

If this new man hears me, he doesn't react. While the others remain in apparently wary silence, he speaks to the man standing beside him—a lean guy with a shaved head. "Get Vanguard. Tell him we've got a problem."

"Sure thing, Jonah." The man with the shaved head doesn't hover, quickly weaving through the room and disappearing through the far door.

As he rushes away, my mind is whirling. Jonah asked him to get someone called "Vanguard." Which happens to be the surname of both of my father's generals: the brother and sister. The snake shifter and the witch. Although it's unclear which of them is being summoned right now.

I edge closer to Diavolo while Jonah—since that seems to be his name—approaches us with a calm confidence that contrasts sharply with the demeanor of the men around him.

As he steps closer, his height becomes more apparent, and I'm glad Diavolo chose his taller, bulkier form.

"Beautiful dogs," Jonah says, inclining his head at the panthers.

"I appreciate you giving them space," I reply, a grudging acknowledgement of Jonah's intelligence when he stops a sensible five paces away from them.

Now positioned directly in front of us, he peers at all of us, but his focus is more intently on Diavolo. Unsettlingly, Jonah's gaze falls nearly immediately to the crown on the keeper's hand.

I know what the crown is because I know what the keeper is. I do hope Jonah doesn't know what he's looking at or we could be in trouble. After all, the keeper is supposed to be in his realm. Not gallivanting around New York city.

Of course, it might be helpful if Jonah knew what he's really up against, but there's no way that the keeper would be allowed anywhere near the Nostra empire. The Ultima Nostra would see him as a direct threat.

"I'm Jonah Hartvigsen," Jonah says, politely introducing himself in a way that tells me he intends to keep things civil while we wait for the big guns. "And you are?"

"Veda," I say, deciding to play the politeness game for now. "This is Diavolo."

Jonah gives Diavolo a short nod, not combative, exactly, but not welcoming, either.

"What about your beasts?" Jonah asks. "What do you call them?"

Panthers. I call them 'panthers.'

Inwardly, I sigh. *Well, fuck, it would have helped if I'd given them names already.*

"I call them 'hunters,'" I say, while mentally adding naming these gorgeous creatures to my to-do list after surviving this encounter.

Jonah gives me a smile that shows his perfect, white teeth. He clicks open his lighter and the little flame appears before disappearing again with another *clack*.

Since he's standing closer now, I can make out some sort of inscription on the front of the lighter, maybe a rune. Definitely not in a modern language. I may struggle to name every single object I come across, but Mom did her absolute best to teach me about the existence of magical runes and of other languages.

There's a stir on the far side of the room and finally another man looms in the doorway.

It has to be Vanguard. James Vanguard. The male general.

An unwelcome shot of fear strikes through me as I take him in. It's not so much his physical appearance but the energy around him that seems to drag the air out of my lungs and squeeze my chest.

He's tall and lean. His hair is dark brown and long enough to fall across his brown eyes, which, even from this distance glimmer visibly with a crimson hue. A short, neatly sculpted beard shadows his strong jaw. I'm surprised to see a scar running down the left side of his forehead and the upper curve of his cheekbone—a wound that would have come awfully close to destroying his left eye.

On his back, he carries what looks like a sword, its braided handle visible over his right shoulder. I haven't come into contact with many swords—really only the angel's sword back at the Cathedral—but the handle appears finely crafted. I'm sure the blade will be nothing less than superior.

Everything and everyone else in the room—except for the keeper and Jonah—seems somehow smaller and insignificant in his presence.

Every other man moves out of his way as Vanguard steps into the room and approaches us at a dangerously stealthy glide, his footfalls practically silent. Despite keeping their sights on us, the other men also manage to incline their heads as if they would normally bow to him.

It makes me wonder: Could *he* be the new Ultima Nostra?

But no. If that were the case, Jonah wouldn't have referred to him as "Vanguard." Once anointed, the Ultima Nostra is only referred to by that title. If that reasoning holds true, then my father's brother—my uncle—is still my most likely suspect.

It doesn't mean Vanguard wasn't complicit in my father's death, and I don't know for sure if Vanguard willingly stood— or stands—at the side of my father's murderer. There are still so many questions, but none of them are my biggest problem right now.

At Vanguard's appearance, the other men seem to have

relaxed, including Jonah, as if they feel they have nothing to fear now that he's here.

It's unsettling.

Worse, Diavolo's jaw has tightened, tension builds in his shoulders, and darkness grows across his features. Sapphire light glimmers around his fingertips and he seems to have forgotten to use the wand as a decoy.

My mother told me that James Vanguard was a snake shifter, but the man I'm looking at is certainly far more than that.

Well, now I'm worried.

CHAPTER TWENTY-THREE

"General Vanguard." Jonah greets the newcomer, but it seems he doesn't need to say more.

"I see the problem." Vanguard's voice is low and sends a chill down my spine.

He keeps his eyes on us as he stops at Jonah's side.

It doesn't feel far enough away.

I fight the urge to glance at the door behind us, plotting our exit if we need it.

"They claim to have come through a green door," Jonah says.

Vanguard barely reacts, but his focus flickers from us to the door at the end of the corridor behind us.

I'm not imagining it. He sees it. I'm sure he does.

Despite that, he says, "They're lying. There is no such door. Only a wall."

What little tension remained in the room seems to lift.

"Jonah and I will deal with them," Vanguard says calmly. "The rest of you, get the fuck out."

He doesn't raise his voice, but the other men scatter, pouring from the room. Only Jonah remains at Vanguard's side.

The last man closes the far door behind him.

Diavolo sends me a sharp glance, and I appreciate that he hasn't lashed out yet. Or spoken up, for that matter. The darkness on his face tells me he won't have pleasant things to say.

As it turns out, *I* might not have pleasant things to say, either. This man was one of my father's generals. If he's still part of the empire, then he either betrayed and killed my father himself or turned a blind eye to that betrayal. Neither makes me like him very much.

Of course, I can't let on about that at all.

I remind myself that I'm nothing more than a mercenary looking for work.

"General James Vanguard." I incline my head without taking my eyes off him. "We were hoping we might meet you."

He arches an eyebrow at me. It's his left eyebrow and it accentuates the scar. It's strange that he has a scar at all. The most powerful supernaturals usually heal completely due to their considerable powers. I can't help but wonder how he got it.

Still, I think my comment has genuinely surprised him. I imagine nobody looks forward to meeting this man.

"Okay," he says. "I'll bite. Why were you hoping to meet me?"

"Because we want in," I say. "We need work and we have skills to offer. It's our understanding you're the person to speak with about that."

I try to not to cringe at my own response. Hell, I have no idea how a mercenary applies for a job. *Please, sir, let me infiltrate your empire?*

But Vanguard nods as if my response is somewhat expected. "We've had many like you over the last few years. Since new management took over Draven Industries, many skilled supernaturals have needed a new master."

I'm not sure how I feel about the concept of having a 'master' and if the way Diavolo has bristled is anything to go by, he doesn't like it much, either, but my focus now is more on the mention of that other organization.

Draven Industries. Mom described it as a major arms dealer that provides weaponry to the underground throughout many eastern states. Or it was. It sounds like it's had some upheavals.

I decide not to confirm or deny Vanguard's assumption. Let him think what he wants.

"We're willing to swear allegiance to the Ultima Nostra." I choose my speech carefully, since I only have the assumption that Vanguard, Jonah, and the men who left the room work for the Ultima Nostra.

When Vanguard doesn't give a hint that I've spoken incorrectly, I add: "For the right price, of course."

"Yes, of course," Vanguard replies, as if this is completely reasonable. "The Ultima Nostra is always looking for new soldiers. But what is the right price?"

His speech sounds casual, but I'm not so comfortable with the way he begins a stealthy pace across the floor. It's a gliding movement, back and forth, back and forth, slowly and carefully like a snake that's trying to mesmerize me.

His focus darts to the corridor behind me. Instead of haggling over money, he asks, "Do you know what that green door is?"

I don't react to his admission that he can see it.

Instead, I shrug and take my best guess. "A concealed entrance." I glance at Diavolo. "Which we shouldn't have been able to find."

Vanguard shakes his head. "It's far more than that."

I try to quell the new wave of worry rising within me, since Vanguard is now gleaming at me. He looks utterly delighted that I have no idea about the nature of the door.

"Well, then enlighten me," I say, "because it looks like an ordinary door to me." I turn to the keeper. "Looks ordinary to you, too, Diavolo?"

"It does, Veda," he replies without taking his eyes off Vanguard.

Vanguard breaks into a grin and it chills me to my fucking bones.

"Not a door," he says. "It's a death trap designed to kill any supernatural who steps through it. Yet, somehow, you survived."

Oh, this conversation is about to go bad.

My instincts scream at me to either attack or run. But I can't be certain which would be wise. I'm not sure now that I'd prefer to take my chances escaping through a death trap door or if I'd rather fight my way past Vanguard and Jonah and try to make it to the exit on the other side of the room.

It's Diavolo's reaction that keeps me standing where I am.

Unexpectedly, his tension is gone and he's smiling as broadly as Vanguard. A fucking scary grin that reminds me I have a pretty nasty smile myself.

"Well, as you say, here we are," he says. "We walked through your death trap without a scratch."

I follow up the keeper's response by blowing a raspberry. "Death trap? That's fucking nothing. We've survived worse."

Not a lie as far as I'm concerned.

Diavolo continues. "So it seems you either have a very big, fucking problem. Or you have two very powerful supernaturals who are willing to work for you. Which will it be? Enemies or allies?"

Vanguard narrows his eyes at me, and again, it chills me.

I take a moment to appreciate just how fucking scary all three of these men are. I haven't even seen Vanguard in action and I already believe he's strong enough to have murdered my father, or to have been complicit in his death.

Truth be told, I'm a little in awe.

As for Jonah, who has remained a step behind Vanguard and has kept both the panthers and us in his sights... Every time I look at him, it's like reaching out across the distance and taking hold of pure energy. Where the keeper's power is vast and massive, Jonah's is compact and intense.

The female panther looks up at me at that very moment and licks her lips as if she would relish tasting both Vanguard's and Jonah's blood.

I remind myself who I am and every ounce of uncertainty leaves my body.

After all, what delightful adversaries now stand opposite me.

Vanguard's response is soft. "But you see, there's a flaw in your understanding of this situation."

"What's that?" I ask.

"I didn't create the death trap. My sister did. Right after we had a disagreement."

That little tidbit of information piques my interest. Maybe his sister—my father's second general—had a problem with what happened to my father.

Vanguard takes a step forward, only to be met by multiple growls. I'm a little impressed when he doesn't appear remotely alarmed by the panthers.

He gestures to the corridor behind us. "My sister originally created that door and passageway for her and me to use whenever we liked. It provided quick and easy access into this room. I would regularly pass through it—not when others could see me, of course, so as not to give its existence away. But then, one day, I made a mistake that hurt her very badly."

He takes another step forward and meets more growls—and again ignores them.

"To punish me, she poured all of her power into a spell she cast over the door and the corridor, so that the next time I stepped through it, I'd be killed."

He points to the scar on his face. "This is a reminder that family will always try to end you."

"Ouch," I whisper dramatically. "She must really hate you."

"She did," he says. "Maybe she still does. I honestly don't know since I haven't seen her since."

I'm suddenly a little concerned that Vanguard is telling us all about his family troubles. To a point, I guess he wants us to be aware of how much he distrusts us, but this extra information feels... too personal.

"Why do I get the feeling you wouldn't tell us any of this if you thought we were going to walk away from this encounter alive?" I ask.

Vanguard arches his eyebrows at me, and as if to disprove my suspicion, he holds up his left hand while very slowly removing the sword from his back, pulling the strap and scabbard over his head and placing the sheathed weapon on the nearest table.

His gesture has the appearance of a sign of peace, but somehow, it feels like an act of war.

My claws are two seconds away from emerging and my teeth are aching to sharpen. Beside me, Diavolo has once again reached for his fake wand.

I watch carefully as, opposite us, Vanguard calmly proceeds to remove his jacket, which he drops over the back of a chair. Followed by his shirt.

Meanwhile, Jonah flips open his lighter, triggers the flame, and then clacks it shut again.

Vanguard looks up between undoing shirt buttons to shake his head at me. He may as well be waggling his finger. "The fact that you can see the door is concern enough. The additional fact that you survived passing through it is much more worrisome."

Well, fuck. I imagine he'd really worry if he knew we breezed on through the corridor without any problems at all.

But right now, it's what's under his shirt that concerns me.

His chest and arms are covered in tattoos from his collarbone to his waist. Countless snakes appear to swarm across his skin, all of them inked in black. I recognize some as cobras from the distinctive scales stretching out on either side of their heads, but I don't know what species the other snake tattoos may replicate. Nothing harmless, that's for sure.

They look so fucking real that I could swear they're moving.

"Of course, I take your point," Vanguard says as he turns back to us. "Why be enemies when we can be allies?"

Damn, what is it with that smile he's wearing?

I suck in a breath through my teeth. "See, you say that and yet, I get the feeling you'd rather be enemies."

Vanguard gives me a slow nod. "Your feeling is correct."

I exhale a sigh and flash a final, resigned glance at Diavolo, who doesn't look terribly sad about Vanguard's response. I'm not sure exactly why, but I get the sense the keeper's spoiling for a fight with these guys.

I guess infiltrating the empire isn't going to work, after all.

My claws snap down.

The panthers bare their doggy canines, and Diavolo's hands glimmer with energy that feels so sharp, it could take my skin off.

"Okay, then," I say to Vanguard, my lips drawing back from my sharpening teeth. "Enough talk. Let's get on with it."

Vanguard's expression hardens a second before energy sizzles around his body.

My eyes widen and my heart stops when every snake tattooed on his body suddenly springs to life.

CHAPTER TWENTY-FOUR

I don't have the chance to blink before the snakes rise off Vanguard's chest and arms in a swarm of gleaming light.

Three of them shoot through the air straight at each of the panthers, while five streak toward me, and eight fly toward Diavolo.

If I had even a heartbeat to think, I'd probably be offended that Vanguard thought he had to send a greater force into battle with the keeper, but hell, I can barely take a breath before the snakes are on me.

Their bodies are pure energy and transparent, other than their glowing outlines. They dart toward me as fast as if the air were solid ground, their fangs bared.

The first one reaches me, and I brace for it to either take solid form and bite me or to simply sail through me without damage, given its translucent form.

My hands fly up, my claws out, ready to defend myself.

The moment the snake makes contact with my chest, I prepare to slash through it.

I freeze in shock when its luminous body disappears into my chest, but at the same time, its fangs tear through my torso as sharply as if they're made of bone, not energy.

Before I can scream, two more snakes hit my chest and the final two wrap around my arms, each of them ripping through me without drawing a drop of blood.

Now, a scream of pain rises to my lips, my legs buckle, and I feel like my insides have been torn to shreds.

How the fuck do I defend myself against translucent creatures like these?

But the ripping agony doesn't drive me to the floor.

No, it makes me angry.

Around me, the room is filled with fury and chaos. Diavolo's sapphire magic explodes around his body but doesn't seem to make a dint on the snakes.

The panthers aren't faring much better. Two of the males already appear immobilized, lying on the floor, whimpering as they attempt to snap their jaws at the snakes, but the reptiles are relentless. The female panther and the male with the blaze on his paw leap into the air, trying to catch the snakes, which shoot out of their reach before circling back toward the other panther's hind legs, tearing through them back and forth while the panthers try to turn and defend themselves.

The fucking reptiles are doing the same to me, sending my body into shock as they rage through me.

Across the way, Vanguard's face is creased with concentration, his focus darting back and forth, his hands moving across the air, seeming to direct the snakes as they attack us.

That's all I see before a cobra soars right at my face.

If its energy tears through my mind...

Oh, no, you fucking don't.

With a scream, I slash at the snake's head, my reflexes defying the paralyzing pain that's controlling my body.

My eyes shoot wide when my claws cut right through the snake's transparent form and, where the sharp, black edges of my claws meet the reptile's body, the snake takes form.

Real, tangible, killable form.

My action is so wild that my claws nick my left forearm as they arc down through the air, but I don't care.

The cobra's bloody head falls to the floor, along with its body, both writing at my feet. Cut apart.

I can't help but feel pleased despite the onslaught from the other snakes.

It turns out my claws really can cut through anything.

Across the room, Vanguard gives a shout, stumbling back a step and clutching his chest.

His wide eyes fly to me, his focus darting to the broken snake at my feet.

His face is pale with apparent shock.

It looks like this pain may be a new experience for him.

Across from him, Jonah has stiffened and the energy around him seems to blaze as his eyes widen, appearing alarmed for the first time.

It seems they may not have the upper hand after all.

I can't stop the smile breaking across my face even as the other snakes drive their bodies through my arms and legs, sending blinding pain through me.

Fuck the pain.

Cutting the snake apart made Vanguard vulnerable, even if it was only for a few seconds.

Now, he's in my sights, and I'm determined to make him feel as much agony as possible so I can cut him down, too.

I launch myself toward the panthers with a scream. "Cut the snakes! Make them bleed!"

I have no idea if the panthers' teeth will have the same effect on the shadow snakes, but the panthers are ancient creatures, so anything is possible.

At my cry, the female panther abandons her attempts to defend herself, leaping at a snake attacking one of the male panthers instead. That serpent is a much easier target since she can leap right at it, rather than trying to contort herself to bite it.

It's moving so fast that her teeth only catch its tail, but it's enough.

Chomp.

She spits the tail to the floor. The rest of the snake's body writhes in the air for a second. It falls to the floor before it can reach the other panther.

All of the panthers rally and suddenly, they're a team, leaping and biting at the reptiles that attempt to attack each other.

Vanguard gives another shout, although it's muffled when he clamps his teeth together. The alarm in his eyes now tells me that pain like this is definitely a rare experience for him.

I don't know why my claws and the panther's teeth can make such a difference to these snakes when they simply sail through other parts of our bodies, but we have the upper hand right now and I don't intend to squander it.

Satisfied that the panthers can defend each other, I grit my teeth, snarls forming in the back of my throat as I pitch myself toward Diavolo, intending to defend him from the snakes attacking his body.

I pull up sharply as I take full stock of him.

His eyes have turned completely white, but the color within them is swirling like...

Smoke?

An acidic scent rises off his body such as I've never smelled before, but it feels both hot and freezing at the same time, burning my lungs when I inhale.

His skin where it's visible has turned gray, but not a sickly gray. It's a deep, dark color. Like the scorching burn that I once wore across my cheek after my jailer torched me with his light magic.

Diavolo's form expands before my eyes, growing taller, his muscles expanding so quickly that he tears through his shirt and pants. And yet everything about him is suddenly smoke and darkness. A contradiction between ripping his clothing while appearing insubstantial.

It isn't exactly a warlock kind of power, but who am I to say?

The snakes that were passing through him as his form changed sail on through, seemingly without making any impact now.

They arc across the air, turning and driving through him again, but they merely float through his body, pulling smoke with them. It's hard to tell, but I imagine they appear a little dazed and disoriented when they emerge.

Vanguard certainly does. He has dropped to one knee and when he lifts his head, he can't seem to focus on us. He blinks rapidly and gives his head a shake, as if he's trying to clear his thoughts.

Jonah darts in front of him, a snarl on his lips, the lighter gripped so tightly in his hand that it's only partially visible. Whatever magic Jonah controls, I imagine we're about to see it.

Without a word, Diavolo inclines his head at our opponents.

I don't need any further invitation.

As we pass the panthers, they leap up at the remaining snakes. They'll keep the snakes busy and watch our backs.

Diavolo and I prowl toward Jonah and Vanguard.

I veer to the right, Jonah firmly in my sights, while Diavolo focuses on Vanguard. Not that I don't want to fight Vanguard, but Diavolo seems awfully tunnel-visioned right now.

I catch a flash of steel as Vanguard reaches for his sword and unsheathes it, revealing a gorgeously crafted, curved blade. I don't exactly have time to admire it, but it's etched with letters that are similar to the inscription on Jonah's lighter.

Speaking of...

With a final clack, Jonah closes the lighter, places it on the table behind him, turns back to me and then—

A ball of flames explodes around his body and suddenly, he's a mass of molten heat like a fucking volcano.

CHAPTER TWENTY-FIVE

ell, fuck me.
I jolt to a stop, my claws extended and my teeth bared.

Jonah's amber eyes blaze at me as the fire encompassing his body settles down into a simmering blaze, but I don't imagine for a moment it's a good thing. Every inch of his visible skin is striated with lava lines. A crisscross of molten threads. Unlike the Sentinel's light, which could burn the flesh from my bones, this man's power is the darkest amber. Deeply dark. Nothing light about it.

It doesn't look like he's inclined to give me a chance to catch my breath, storming straight for me.

I have three seconds before he'll make contact, and I should probably be worried, but my face seems to have other ideas, my lips tugging up at the corners.

"Neat trick," I whisper as his fist flies at my smiling mouth.

I duck the blow, making the most of my smaller size to dart to the side.

He follows me faster than I thought he would, more agile

than I expected—*damn him*—and takes another shot at my face. Except that this time, his fist is unclenched.

Again, I evade him. As I move, my claws make contact with the side of his bare chest, scraping across his scorching skin. I feel the heat all the way through my hand, as burning hot as whatever magic broke the seal on my cage in the veil.

As fucking hot as dragon's breath. Not that I've ever been breathed on by a dragon. But I'd bet it feels something like this. In fact, it's awfully similar to the heat that broke the magical seal on my cage. Different, but just as hot.

Despite the claw marks I leave across his side, he doesn't flinch. In fact, his fist flies so close to the side of my face that the heat sizzling across his hand is in danger of burning my mask right off me.

I dart sideways once again, ducking under his arm, and driving my claws upward, scratching all the way around his bicep.

He could have easily punched his fist into my exposed back, but he doesn't aim any hits at my body, reaching for my face yet again, his fingers once more narrowly missing the side of my mask.

It dawns on me that his primary intention might be to un-mask me, rather than to bludgeon me to death.

Hell, I wouldn't care if he saw my face, but, dammit, the brightness of his body would be fucking unbearable for my sensitive eyes.

I leap backward, trying to put some space between us, baring my teeth at him.

Off to the side, Diavolo casts me an alarmed glance. He's holding his own against Vanguard, who wields his sword expertly but ineffectively, since the blade simply sails through Diavolo's body.

Maybe Diavolo thinks he should have fought Jonah, since

he's taken on a smoky form and all, but I shoot him a *don't-you-fucking-dare-get-involved-in-my-fight* glare.

I can handle Jonah.

After all, the cuts I've left on his body have yet to heal. Molten lava bleeds from them. Although he doesn't seem the least bit worried about the wounds.

I leap toward him again, ready to fight dirty, preparing to deliver a series of cuts to his stomach, chest, and shoulders.

He moves as fast as I do, switching tactics so quickly that my head spins. Taking the cuts I inflict first on his chest, his hands wrap around my shoulders, his touch searing my skin.

He wrenches me off my feet and shoves me down onto the surface of the nearest table. I smack into it, my thoughts whirling, since it's fucking unpleasant to be thrown down like that.

The moment I hit the surface, he lets go of me. His hands fly back from me, a confusing move, but my damn instincts drive me upward, telling me to get off the table as fast as I can.

He uses my upward momentum against me.

His hand closes over the front of my face and the mask tears away from me.

A scream wrenches out of me. Not because of the heat that burned across my shoulders when he threw me down or across my face when he snatched my mask, but because of the bright light now filling my eyes.

I squeeze them shut, hoping my other senses will save me from being incinerated. I'm surprised he didn't burn me to a crisp when he dumped me on the table.

I sense the movement of air above me a split second before his hands close around my shoulders again. I push back, but damn, he's strong.

He shoves me back to the table, and I brace for burning pain and death.

I'm surprised when neither happens.

His voice snarls close to my ear. "Who are you?"

I'm aware that he's leaning over me and the volume of his voice means his face must be inches from mine. My legs are on either side of his hips and he's taking a real risk that I won't drive my claws into his sides since he hasn't immobilized my arms, other than to pin my shoulders.

Maybe he thinks I won't risk burning myself.

I crack open my eyes the barest slit, side-eyeing his hands, which have returned to normal where he holds me. No more burning flames around them, and on top of that, the brightness of his body has decreased. All of which would explain why I'm not burning to a crisp and screaming in agony right now. Even so, every other part of him that hovers only inches from my body remains scorching hot and faint lines of lava threaten to ignite again.

If I make contact, I'm sure I'll risk some nasty burns.

"Give me back my mask," I growl. "It's too fucking bright without it."

His forehead creases. Just the tiniest. I suppose he thought I would worry about my identity, not my eyesight.

A gleaming smile forms on his lips. "Too late. It's ashes now."

I curse beneath my breath, but his smile only grows.

"I seem to have an unfair advantage now," he says.

"Good for you," I snap. "It won't last long."

I may not be able to see much through the slits of my eyelids, but in the background, the panthers appear to have nearly finished dealing with all of Vanguard's snakes. It will only be seconds before they launch themselves at Jonah's back.

"Give me your real name and we can call a truce," Jonah says.

"I told you. I'm Veda."

He shakes his head. "That's a powerful name for any supernatural, let alone a pixie. Or are you a wolf shifter?"

My eyes are adjusting faster than I thought they would,

although that really only means I'm not in intense pain anymore. I still can't focus well. "Are you saying it's too powerful for a woman like me? That's fucking insulting."

He leans a little closer. So close that his amber eyes fill my vision. "I'm saying that names have power. If Veda truly is your name, then whoever named you knew what they were doing."

I want to snarl at him, let my lips curl, tell him I fucking named myself and yes, I knew what I was doing, but suddenly, my mother's voice is in my head.

Sex is control.

My legs are inches away from wrapping around his hips—if I dare risk the burns. It wouldn't take much to lift my hands, retract my claws, and let my fingers play across his sides.

He's leaning in to me, his face is close to mine, and there's a curiosity in his eyes that seems stronger than his distrust. At least, I hope it is.

I allow my lips to soften and force my eyes to open the slightest bit more so that I'm looking directly at him from beneath my lashes.

"I wasn't given a name when I was born," I say softly, speaking the truth. "I named myself. Veda." I roll my name around on my tongue. "Maybe I'll conquer you, too."

Dark saints, I'd love to bury my teeth in Jonah's flaming neck right now. Whether or not I'd tear flesh or enjoy playing with fire is another matter.

His expression softens. "Maybe you will."

His guard is down. His hold on me has relaxed.

Well, thank you, Mom.

I reach upward, preparing to release my claws and drive them toward his ribs on either side of me. I don't want to puncture his lungs or kill him—that won't make me his friend, assuming by some miracle I can salvage this situation—just wound him enough for me to dominate this fight.

It's at that moment that Diavolo's furious shout reaches me. He's a blur of darkness as he rages toward us and launches himself at Jonah.

The impact of his big body hitting Jonah's equally large frame creates such a *thud* that it jars through me.

Despite my shock, I have a split-second awareness that I'm about to be free and I'm not going to waste my chance.

I launch myself up and off the table, my claws extended.

But Vanguard has followed close behind the keeper and swings his sword at Diavolo's moving back, a blow so quick that the blade is a mere glimmer in the air.

The sword sails on through the keeper's smoky form, barely upsetting the white smoke behind him, and arcs toward me instead.

Fuck!

I'm halfway up off the table and my neck is directly in line with the blade. There's no time to defend myself.

Vanguard's sword meets the side of my neck at the exact same moment that the tips of my outstretched claws impale the front of his throat. Shallowly.

We both freeze.

Across the room, Diavolo and Jonah hit the floor, rolling away from each other and nimbly back to their feet.

Diavolo is snarling at Jonah. "Lay a hand on Veda again, and I will end you."

Jonah's reply is sharp. "It's not me you have to worry about."

Diavolo's focus flies immediately to me and Vanguard, and he stops very still. Even the panthers have fallen silent.

Opposite me, droplets of blood slide down Vanguard's clavicle from the puncture wounds created by the tips of my claws.

As for my own neck, I sense the warmth of blood from the cut of the blade pooling gently at the base of my throat.

With a single slice, Vanguard could kill me.

With a single push, I could kill *him*.

My eyes are suddenly wide open, but it doesn't do me any good. I can't see a way out of this.

CHAPTER TWENTY-SIX

I try to still the heaving of my chest. Can't do anything about the sweat dripping down my face. I'm struggling to ignore the pain in my eyes and the sharpness of the wound at my neck. But I defy the fury of battle that tempts me to throw caution to the wind and try to subdue Vanguard without getting myself killed.

Across from us, Jonah and Diavolo are keeping clear of each other, Jonah inching toward Vanguard while Diavolo veers toward me.

Neither of them comes too close. Which is wise. Any sudden moves could be a trigger for this situation to go very badly.

"It's a rare day that I meet my match," Vanguard says to me in a grudging tone.

"You're the one who wanted to be enemies," I snap, trying very hard not to move my neck when I speak. Also trying not to squint.

My eyes are watering and I'm sure Vanguard thinks it's from the pain of the cut at my neck.

His response is slower, and it sounds as if there's a shrug in his voice. "Well, there's enemies and then there's *enemies*."

I narrow my eyes at him. "What kind of enemies are we?"

"The kind who could be of use to one another," he says. "Now that I've tested your powers and abilities."

I don't trust him one bit. I try to assess his expression, but I can't glean anything about his true thoughts.

Through gritted teeth, I say, "I'm still feeling the pain of those fucking snakes and the burn of your lackey's hands. I'm not sure I feel like being a useful enemy to you."

At the side, Jonah's brow draws down at my reference to him as a 'lackey' and I can't let the moment pass. After all, my shoulders are still smarting. I'm sure my skin is burned, although it's the least of my worries right now.

"Oh, you're offended?" I shoot at Jonah, again without moving anything other my mouth. "No more than I was insulted when you questioned my name. What sort of name is Jonah, anyway?"

"It's a homophone," he grumbles. The lines of lava crisscrossing his chest have all but died down now and there are dark rings forming under his eyes.

I wasn't expecting him to give me a response, let alone such an analytical one. "A what?"

"A word that sounds like another word," he says.

When I continue to stare at him blankly, he continues in the next breath. "It's one of the closest modern names pronounced in the English language that sounds like my species."

I narrow my eyes at him, wondering what species sounds like 'Jonah.' Certainly not 'volcano man.'

I should probably be paying more attention to Vanguard and my current predicament, but identifying what Jonah is is important too. Seeing as he could burst into flames again at any point. "What is your species?"

"What's yours?" he retorts. "No ordinary wolf shifter has claws like that."

I allow myself to smile. "Claws that could have been working for you, not against you." My gaze returns to Vanguard. "If only you'd taken us up on our offer."

A gleam has grown in Vanguard's eyes that contradicts the blood continuing to slip down his chest.

"Maybe I still will," he says. "But for now, the choice is yours: Would you like to die or call a truce?"

I give a growl of frustration that he's only now offering me what I came here for.

"Truce," I snarl.

"Good." He begins to nod, but it only serves to bring his neck closer to my claws and he immediately stops.

"I'm going to withdraw my claws," I say. "You're going to withdraw your sword. And then we're going to back away from each other." As his blade moves at the corner of my eye, I warn, "*Slowly.*"

The blade barely shifts, moving in the most infinitesimal increments, while I carefully lift my claws at the same excruciatingly slow pace.

As soon as the sword lifts clear of my throat and I can be as sure as possible that he won't flick it into me, I jump backward, landing deftly several paces away. Checking my neck wound and finding that it's healing already, I edge toward Diavolo, who is stepping carefully toward me.

He pauses on the way past the chair where Jonah flung his jacket and shirt, scoops up the shirt, and rips a strip off the bottom of it.

"Hey," Jonah growls.

Diavolo snaps back. "It's the least you can fucking do."

He reaches for me, extending the strip of material with a quiet, "For your eyes."

I quickly wrap the material around my face, breathing a sigh of relief as the pain in my head abates.

I catch both Vanguard and Jonah watching with creases in their foreheads and curiosity in their eyes. I imagine they thought Diavolo was going to wrap the cloth around the wound on my neck.

The keeper's own clothing is torn and blackened with soot where his form expanded and, whereas he towered over me before, now his presence engulfs me. I don't mind. The scent of smoke and ash wafting off him overpowers the scent of fire on Jonah's shirt material.

I keep my claws extended and my teeth bared when the panthers join us only moments later. I'm glad they didn't try to get involved in my fight with Jonah or the interaction with Vanguard.

On the floor in the background, the writhing snakes finally stop moving. Luminous energy glimmers across their skin as every one of them becomes translucent again, the pieces of their bodies rise off the floor, and their transparent forms meld together.

I'm a little disappointed when their newly healed forms glide across the distance toward Vanguard.

I was hoping we'd permanently ended those fuckers.

They fit themselves back to his chest and arms, where they reform tattoos across his skin, a seething mass of ink once more.

Vanguard rolls his shoulders, closes his eyes briefly, and when he opens them, his expression is brighter, as if some of his energy has returned.

Daring to turn away from us, he crosses to the other table, reaches for his shirt, and begins to pull it on. "Well, now I understand how you survived my sister's traps."

I want to ask him about her power and tease out more information about her, but it could be unwise. After all, he thinks we conquered her magic, so we should have some knowledge of it already.

Vanguard pulls up a chair and takes a seat.

Jonah, on the other hand, collects several bowls off the

nearest tables, empties what looks like nuts out of them, and pours clear liquid into them. I have no idea what he's doing until he places the bowls on the floor a good distance away from all of us and says, "Water. For your dogs. They'll be thirsty after that fight." He exhales before muttering, "Least I can fucking do."

The panthers are quick to avail themselves of hydration and the fact that they don't hesitate eases my mind that this volcano man isn't trying to poison my beasts.

I give Jonah a grudging nod before he returns to Vanguard's side.

After folding his arms across his chest, Vanguard turns his attention to Diavolo. "You're an enenra masquerading as a warlock."

A what-ra? My forehead creases as I rummage through my memories of all the supernatural species my mother told me about. I'm perplexed that I don't know what an enenra is. I try to hide my confusion, but Diavolo seems to understand exactly what Vanguard is talking about.

"I'm a demon of smoke and ash," he says, as if he's acknowledging Vanguard's proclamation, but I'm certain he's only spelling it out for my benefit. He's too perceptive not to have caught the press of my lips and my flash of confusion.

He continues to Vanguard. "I'm sure you can understand why I like to keep that to myself."

Vanguard nods. "Indeed. Enenra are rare and dangerous enough to be a target for those wishing to make names for themselves."

Diavolo tips his chin up, as if this is exactly the reason he pretends to be a warlock.

"As for you." Vanguard points at me. "You're not a pixie and you're not a wolf shifter."

I remind myself that he can't identify me from my powers, only from my blood and my real eyes. He won't associate my claws or teeth with my late father since there's nothing angelic about them, and I was careful to hide my other attribute that might raise eyebrows.

The furrow in Vanguard's brow deepens as he continues to scrutinize me.

"I am what I am," I say.

His lips part, as if he's going to ask more, but he presses them closed again.

"Very well." He leans back in his chair while the snake tattoos seem to darken across his chest. "I hope you can forgive the reception I gave you, but I needed to uncover your true powers, since I sensed you were concealing them."

I screw up my nose, pretending his comment doesn't unsettle me. "Eh, I'm not really inclined toward forgiveness, no."

He gives a sudden laugh, his brown eyes filling with crimson swirls. "That's fair."

His smile quickly fades. "Now that I've verified your skills, I believe you're both in a position to be of use to me." He unfolds his arms as he continues. "But you can't simply waltz in here and expect me to trust you. Trust has to be earned."

Grudgingly, I say, "Well, I suppose that's also fair."

"The Ultima Nostra demands complete loyalty," Vanguard continues. "Until you prove yourselves, you won't be welcome into the outer circle of his soldiers."

"Fuck the outer circle," I snap, speaking without filtering my thoughts, but there's no way I want to fuck around in the outer circle for years. "We want to be in the inner circle. Serving the Ultima Nostra himself. You've ascertained that we're strong enough. We can be useful in ways that others can't."

Vanguard raises his eyebrows at me.

My jaw clenches as I realize I've potentially made one small mistake: I described the Ultima Nostra as 'himself.' I have no idea if leadership has changed hands multiple times. If the current leader is female, then I'm fucked…

"You're ambitious," Vanguard says, and I inwardly breathe a sigh of relief.

"Ambitious *and* proud," I say, again speaking without a filter. "I don't want to grovel for scraps. I want a place where our skills are recognized."

I take a few steps forward, daring to narrow the distance between us.

"I promise you," I growl, speaking another truth, "in return for such a place, I would give my life."

CHAPTER TWENTY-SEVEN

*V*anguard's lips part at my promise. He considers me quietly for a long moment.

Jonah, too, surveys me with a resurging curiosity in his eyes. Again, I'm aware of the heat he controls, once more like a burn from my hair to my toes.

For the entirety of that long moment, I worry that I pushed too hard, was too truthful, too vulnerable in speaking my truths. I've stepped past Diavolo and I can't see his reaction, but I sense his growing tension. But there's no taking my words back now.

Finally, Vanguard breaks the silence. "Every dark creature who comes to me wants a place in the inner circle, but very few make it there. Most come to understand that their place is in the *outer* circle, and they accept whatever is given to them. However, I will acknowledge that very few can challenge me or Jonah. Your skills may well put you in a different position."

He folds his arms across his chest again, the fingers of his right hand tapping his left bicep. He casts the quickest look at Jonah, an unspoken communication, at which Jonah nonchalantly picks up his lighter and plays with the lid, the *click-clack* filling another silence.

I want to break the moment, to argue our case further, but Diavolo's hand slips across my lower back, his presence now at my side, and it feels like a warning to stay quiet.

Around me, the panthers have raised their heads from their bowls of water and are also waiting quietly.

"Okay." Vanguard leans forward. "I have a delicate task that can only be completed by the most skilled supernaturals. If you succeed, I will give you a path into the inner circle."

He's not exactly opening the door directly to the Ultima Nostra, but it's a start.

I speak without hesitation. "Tell us what the task is, and we'll get it done."

Vanguard takes a deep breath. "A package needs to be delivered by train from New York to Boston."

I try to hide my immediate grimace. Boston is headquarters to assassins. I really don't want to stir up a hornet's nest there.

Vanguard is still speaking. "It's an extremely valuable package. Multiple parties will do anything to get their hands on it. Put simply: Many supernaturals want to use it while others will be determined to destroy it."

Diavolo's forehead is creased. "Sending it by train doesn't seem like the best idea. Surely, you'd do better with, say, a helicopter."

Vanguard shakes his head. "Too easy to shoot down."

"What about translocating it?" Diavolo asks, and I'm sure he was building up to this with his helicopter comment.

Vanguard's jaw clenches. "There is not a single warlock I trust enough with this package to leave it alone with them. If Jonah had that skill, I'd choose translocation in a heartbeat. But I trust nobody else to that extent."

Jonah speaks up. "A warlock with ulterior motives could move the package anywhere and we'd never find it again."

Diavolo shakes his head. "But a train—"

"Is filled with human passengers who will make a

supernatural attack more difficult. Also large enough that I can have a whole team scattered throughout the relevant car. One member of the team will be a warlock who will ensure the humans who step on board can't be mind-controlled."

I don't love the idea of a team any more than I love the idea of a train, but I hold my tongue. It also seems that Diavolo's compulsion power will be no use to us.

"Our team will control the entrances and exits, and we'll have supernaturals following in the sky to ward off any attack from there," Jonah says. "Any overt magical combat will expose the supernatural community to humans. Even our enemies won't risk that."

"I assume you'll both be there, too," I say.

"I will be," Jonah replies. He continues more slowly. "Vanguard will be at the station when we leave, but he won't travel with us."

I'm surprised by this. "Surely, you would be best placed to protect the package, whatever it is?" I say to Vanguard.

He gives a heavy exhale. "This package is being sent to a powerful supernatural who, despite their agreement to secure the package where it can't be found again, will try to kill me on the spot should I attend in person. In addition..."

He swallows and if I didn't know better, I'd say his voice is filled with sadness. "Once the package is on the train, it's better if I have no further association with it."

His sudden show of emotion throws me, especially since it feels genuine. I consider Vanguard carefully, wondering about his personal investment in the outcome of this undertaking.

I ask a question I'm not sure I want the answer to. "Is this job for the Ultima Nostra, or is it for *you?*"

Vanguard's jaw clenches. "It's for me. But if you get the package to its destination, I will give you a direct path into the inner circle."

I continue to consider him warily. "We're complete

strangers. If this mission is so important to you, why would you risk trusting us?"

"Because you survived my sister's spell," he says.

I'm even more cautious now. "Why is that important?"

He rises to his feet and the snake tattoos appear to shift across his chest. "My sister wants to destroy this package. Make no mistake: She will come after it. You have the powers needed to stop her."

Hmm. Twice now, Vanguard has indicated that he and his sister are enemies.

Which means she could be my ally. It will be a shame to fight her and put her offside. But that's a problem I can deal with later.

For now, gaining an understanding of all the current players in the empire—and outside of it—can only benefit me.

I look to the keeper, a final check that he's willing to go along with the mission. He doesn't object. Merely inclines his head.

"We're in," I say to Vanguard.

"Good," he replies. "Meet us the night after tomorrow, 6 P.M. sharp, at the Moynihan Train Hall, Penn Station."

I quickly commit our destination to memory. "How will we find you once we get there?"

"We'll find you," Jonah says. His focus falls to the panthers and his expression becomes rueful. "Unfortunately, you'll need to leave your dogs behind. One of them might pass as a mobility assistance dog, but not all four."

The female immediately growls.

"Looks like you're it," I say to her.

"You'll have to put her on a leash." Jonah grimaces. "Make sure she's okay with that."

The panther growls at that suggestion—not a happy sound this time—but I stare her down. An illusion leash can't be that bad. "It's either that or you stay behind."

She makes a huffing noise that sounds alarmingly like her panther voice before she turns her back on me. As my gaze flows across her, I'm suddenly aware that her fur appears darker than before. When I cast a glance at her paws, it looks like the tips of her claws are silver again.

Fuck. Her canine appearance is wearing off.

"We'll be there," I say to Vanguard. "Now, would you rather we exit via the death trap or is there another way out of here?"

I want nothing more than to turn tail and get the fuck out of here before the panthers lose their canine appearances altogether, but I can't appear too keen to walk through the green door again.

"This way," Jonah says, gesturing to the far door. "I'll show you."

I quickly gather up the panthers and take Diavolo's arm, facing away from both Vanguard and Jonah when I mouth *panthers*.

Diavolo's expression remains neutral, but I hope he understands what I meant. It seems that he does when, in the next moment, he strides ahead of me, saying to Jonah, "Lead the way."

Vanguard watches us go as we follow Jonah out into a dimly lit corridor.

The walls appear sturdily built, although the paint is peeling. We pass two doors, each one marked with a different symbol, but Jonah doesn't offer any explanation about them. Within a few minutes, we approach a door marked with a symbol that looks roughly like a tree.

"This door lets out into a children's playground," Jonah says. "There aren't usually many kids there at night, but you'll want to keep your Dobermans close or the human parents could get anxious. Many humans don't know how loyal and brave these dogs can be." He lifts his focus from the panthers. "Once you're in the playground, I trust you'll know your way from there."

"Sure," I reply. If the panthers weren't in danger of losing their canine illusions, I might hesitate at this point, try to find out more from Jonah about the mission ahead of us.

It's not like we even know what 'the package' is, but then, if Vanguard wanted to give us advance notice, he wouldn't have described it so vaguely. I imagine we'll find out tomorrow.

As it turns out, Jonah compels me to pause another moment when his now-cool hand snakes out to cup my forearm. "You can keep my shirt."

He must mean the strip of it that's covering my eyes.

"Don't worry. I was going to."

I'm aware of Diavolo bristling at my back, a menacing form, and the eerie, white smoke filling his eyes as he glares Jonah down. After all, he warned Jonah not to lay a hand on me again.

One corner of Jonah's mouth tugs into a smile and I'm not sure if it's for my benefit or Diavolo's, but he lets go of my arm.

Pushing open the door, I step into a very small clearing, around which is a dense semi-circle of closely-packed trees. The foliage hides from view what lies beyond them, but the city sounds rush back in.

Thank the dark saints my earplugs weren't dislodged during the fight.

The door closes behind the keeper and the panthers, and then we're alone in the clearing.

He promptly waves his hand, a soft, green glow forming before he says, "I've cast a protection spell around us in case they're somehow watching us. It will mask our actual movements and create an illusion that we're stepping away from this clearing already."

Just in the nick of time, too.

One of the male panthers' heads suddenly expands, popping back into its rounded, feline shape. Another one's butt transforms, its tail lengthening and its back claws turning silver. Both animals hiss with displeasure, their voices audibly catlike while their bodies are suddenly an eye-widening mix of big dog and big cat.

"Oh my." I turn to the keeper. "You need to do something about that."

"Well," he says, with a wicked gleam in his eyes. "Since we're about to step out into a children's playground..."

His magic glows.

Each of the panthers hisses-growls-yelps as their bodies shrink dramatically in size.

I blink at the four fluffy, little dogs staring up at me. They're like shoe-sized puffs of black fur with startled, brown eyes peeking out of the middle.

"Now, they're cute," the keeper announces.

I clap my hand over my mouth, muffling my outrage. "Cute? You made my panthers *cute?*"

At that moment, the panthers seem to find their voices, breaking out into a chorus of indignant yaps. They express their displeasure by jumping up at the keeper, but they're so little and he's so tall, they barely make it up his shins.

He pays them no attention, his magic glowing once more as he adjusts the illusion around his body, returning from his smoke-demon shape to his brown-eyed form. His torn clothing mends itself until once again, he's dressed neatly in pants and a shirt. When the panthers give up trying to get his attention by barking and start biting his shoes instead, he simply waves his hand and his shoes morph into thick-soled boots.

Their tiny teeth don't stand a chance.

He looks up to find me glowering at him.

"I'm protecting them," he says. "We don't need anxious parents running around screaming about dangerous dogs."

"Granted, that's probably your intention." I give him a suddenly malicious grin. "But who will protect *you* from *them* when we get home?"

I breeze past him toward the nearby trees, slightly confused when his expression softens despite the impending threat.

"Wait," he says. "Let me fix your blindfold."

He's by my side in seconds, reaching for my face. "I'll make it invisible." His fingertips brush my forehead and his magic glows again. "So you can keep wearing it."

"You could have done that with my masquerade mask," I grumble.

He shrugs. "You looked good in it."

I narrow my eyes at him, even though he won't see the movement beneath the sash.

"There," he says. "All done."

I shake my head at him. "Don't think you can be all sweet to me and I'll ignore what you've done to my panthers."

His hands fall to my shoulders, but he doesn't make contact, his palms hovering. The sudden darkness in his eyes—the flash of blue irises—gives me pause. "What's wrong?"

"Your skin is burned."

I shrug. Which is a bad idea because it brings my shoulders up against his palm and that brief contact sends pain shooting through my chest.

I recoil a little, hunching away from him.

"You're not healing," he says, his lips pressing together in an angry line.

I study the wounds for the first time since Jonah touched me. I have a high pain tolerance when it comes to flesh wounds. I learned to deal with burns because they were inflicted so regularly. Actually, I remember one instance when Mom was hit with light repeatedly in the same spot on her back and afterward, she said she felt no pain at all. When I asked her why, she said that the nerves on that spot must have finally died.

Well, not so for me. Not yet, anyway. I definitely felt pain when I brushed my shoulders against Diavolo's palms.

The skin across both of my shoulders is red and raw, the flesh exposed.

I quickly look away with a whispered, "Fuck."

Around me, the panthers have become silent and now they gather around my feet, soft whines reaching my ears as they attempt to comfort me.

Diavolo reaches for me again. "Let me heal you."

"How?" I snap, my sudden awareness of my pain making me angry. "With an illusion that makes me think I'm healed when I'm not?"

"No," he says, and now his features morph into his blue-eyed persona, the strands of his hair casting shadows over his face. "With the oldest magic I control."

While his gaze pierces me, he lifts his right hand toward the nearest tree.

The color of the leaves is muted in the dark, but their surfaces gleam as if, in the daylight, they would be vibrant green.

When the keeper's fingertips twitch, the nearest leaves curl and blacken, falling softly to the ground.

Dark magic.

For which the cost is life.

I close my eyes as the keeper's hands lower to my shoulders again, accepting his power. Sensing the way my skin reforms. Breathing more easily when the pain subsides.

Finally, I sense him step back and when I open my eyes, he's morphing into his brown-eyed self, the darkness and shadows in his expression easing.

My voice is small, mostly because I'm again asking a question I'm not sure I want answered, and I'm not entirely sure it isn't rhetorical. "Why couldn't I heal myself?"

Diavolo's reply is grim. "Because of what Jonah is."

CHAPTER TWENTY-EIGHT

*T*he city lights twinkle beyond my blindfold as we pass through the playground and onto the footpath beside the street.

Diavolo didn't want to translocate us directly to the witch's apartment from within the clearing because a burst of magic so close to the door would have inevitably attracted attention.

Once we emerged into the playground, the night air was refreshing. Sort of. Minus the conglomeration of scents from humans, vehicles, and restaurants. But I wanted to both clear my head and acclimate myself to the city lights and sounds, so I opted for the walk.

The keeper has remained tight-lipped since his declaration about Jonah's nature and I don't want to push it. I will, eventually, if he doesn't offer up that information, but for now, I'm prepared to leave him with his scowling thoughts.

The panthers scamper around us, keeping close and veering clear of a group of teenagers who make 'Aww' sounds as soon as we step onto the footpath.

I'm on the front foot when one of the girls bends to the

nearest panther. I'm surprised when the male panther nuzzles up to her, licking her fingers and making her laugh.

Of course, he could be buttering her up before he chomps down on her digits.

I scoop him up before there's bloodshed.

"He's adorable," the girl gushes.

I paste a smile on my face, hoping my wolfish teeth aren't showing as I hold tightly to the panther and try to ignore the way he's salivating all over my hand.

"Uh-huh," I say. "Extremely adorable. And not at all hungry."

The girl's forehead creases slightly, but one of her friends grabs her arm and pulls her onward. I'm relieved when she and the other teens continue on their way.

"You said *home*," the keeper finally says.

I'm not sure what he's talking about. "Huh?"

"Before. You said *when we get home.*"

So I did. It was in the context of the panthers expressing their feelings about being turned into puppies. I'm not ready to reflect on why I called the place where I'll sleep later 'home.'

I bristle a little. "And?"

He taps his chest as if to remind me he knows what I'm feeling, and the way his lips tug up tell me he knows what a big deal having a 'home' would be to me.

But the topic of my thoughts isn't what he comments on.

"Jonah knows what I am."

I pull up sharply, glad there wasn't a human walking close behind me.

Diavolo continues. "I'm sure he recognized the crown."

I grimace. I thought that might have been the case when Jonah's focus had lingered on the ring.

I want to poke holes in Diavolo's theory, mostly because I don't want it to be true.

"Well, then why didn't he speak up when Vanguard called

you an en-en-en-en..." My forehead puckers. "How many *'en*'s are there?"

"Two," the keeper says. "En-en-rah. Like there are two *'na*'s in 'banana.'"

"Right. So why would Jonah go along with that? Unless they were playing..." I sigh as I roll my eyes at myself. "Well, of course, they were playing games with us."

Diavolo shrugs. "With which I played along."

Still, I persevere. "But how could he recognize your crown? Most supernaturals don't know the keepers of magic exist, let alone about the crown you wear. That knowledge has been lost over time."

Diavolo gives me a suddenly dark glare.

"Yes, yes," I say. "*I* knew. But that's because my mother told me."

"Who told her?"

My response is slower this time, because now that I think about, my knowledge is a little sketchy. "She said it was passed from mother to daughter. I assume her mother told her."

"Who was her mother?"

"I don't..." My forehead puckers. "Mom called her 'Mother.'"

"So you don't know your grandmother's name."

I sense Diavolo's frustration and it only accentuates my own.

"No, I don't know my grandmother's name or my mother's name, and yes, my mother was an expert at evading questions, and no, I wasn't old enough when she died to have found a way to wrangle the truth out of her. But at least I'm old enough now to know when to demand answers."

I glare at the keeper and the panthers oblige me by latching on to my mood and growling up at him too. "What is Jonah?"

"A creature that shouldn't exist."

"Which is?"

The keeper gives a heavy exhale. The color of his eyes flickers dangerously between brown and blue and even, unsettlingly, a fiery golden that I haven't seen before. It's different to the amber of Jonah's eyes. More animal somehow.

It wouldn't be a good idea for the keeper to transform in front of all these passersby, even if I'm a little curious about what his fiery-eyed form might be.

It's his reply that makes me miss a step.

"Jonah is a jotunn."

Mom may never have mentioned an enenra, but she sure as fuck mentioned the jotunns—or 'jotnar,' as she referred to their race.

My heart is as cold as ice. "The jotnar existed in the time of the old gods. Some of them walked beside the gods. Others fought against them. They all died in the old wars, along with the old gods. There's no fucking way one of them is still alive."

"This one is."

It would explain why I couldn't heal the burns on my own. A jotunn's power is the oldest of old magic. Nearly impossible to counteract. In fact, if the keeper weren't as powerful as he is, or as ancient as he is, he wouldn't have been able to heal me. Certainly, no modern witch could have helped me.

I shudder at the recollection that when Jonah's hands had closed around me, the burn was caused by the residual heat of his palms. He'd shut down his full power by then.

If he wanted to, he really could have incinerated me.

My voice wobbles, but I clear my throat and plow on. "If I accept for a moment—which I don't want to—that Jonah is a jotunn, then what does that make Vanguard?" I glare at Diavolo. "Or his sister, for that matter?"

The moment I ask my questions, I wish I hadn't.

Oh, fuck.

The gods make mysterious moves, my mother said.

"Dark saints," I whisper, trying not to stumble across the sidewalk as I reach for the nearest wall to lean against.

Thankfully, it's the corner of an alley and I can slip into the shadows within it.

Diavolo and the panthers follow me in.

I blow out my next breath, trying to calm my racing heart. "My mother always spoke about the Vanguard siblings with this reverence in her voice. But I never imagined that they could be..."

"Old gods."

If my heart felt like ice before, now I'm sure it isn't beating. Since its power belongs to Diavolo, I'm not surprised when he winces and presses his palm to his chest as if his insides are hurting.

"If this is true..." My voice is incredibly strained as I attempt to breathe. "Then which gods are they?"

Diavolo leans against the brick wall to my left. Somehow, he manages to choose the darkest, most shadowy patch, and his form practically disappears against it. "You told me your mother mentioned three siblings: a snake shifter, a witch, and a wolf shifter."

I give a short laugh. "And you told me that was highly unusual. Which I guess was the first fucking clue."

"A wolf, a snake, and a witch," he murmurs. "Unfortunately, I'm aware of three siblings with those powers."

"Well, fuck. So am I."

Oh, Mom.

Did she want me to make the connection? I guess I'll never know.

Suddenly, I'm laughing, a soft and dangerous sound as I verge on losing my mind. "Fenrir—the Wolf of War. Jormungandr—the World Serpent. And Hel—Goddess of Death and the Underworld."

"Three powerful and unpredictable gods."

My laughter dies as an eerie calm washes over me. An unsettling silence, during which I silently process the fact that my path to revenge just got so much harder. Even the city sounds seem muffled, but that's probably because there's now a roaring in my ears as my blood seems to begin pumping again.

Quietly, I say, "I'm glad I didn't know any of this when Vanguard—or rather Jormungandr—held his sword to my throat."

It would certainly explain why the other mercenaries had bowed to him when he first arrived. His quiet confidence. The way his tattoos had sprung to life.

"This might explain why each Ultima Nostra remained so powerful for as long as he did," I say, thinking it through. "Dark angels aren't weak, but if these gods stood at their sides for generations, what *couldn't* they conquer?"

Then I remember what Vanguard said about his sister and some of my anxiety lifts. "Except... they've had a falling out."

Diavolo leans toward me, and his silhouette becomes visible again. "Vanguard did something to make his sister hate him."

"Enough to want to kill him."

"We can use that," Diavolo says.

I nod. I'm not sure how yet. Not until I know the nature of the falling out and its reasons. "We can make them kill each other and destroy the empire's greatest protectors in the process."

"What about the older brother?" Diavolo asks. "Did your mother ever mention meeting him?"

I shake my head. "Mom said that the siblings parted ways when they were younger." But my voice becomes a growl. "If he makes an appearance, we'll find a way to destroy him too."

My hands form claws at my sides as I turn to the keeper. "If Jonah and Vanguard were playing games when they called you an enenra, do you think they know what I am?"

This time, Diavolo shakes his head. "Even I don't know what you are." His voice remains light as he continues. "Of course, you could simply tell me—"

"I don't know."

I hate making the admission, but I can't keep pretending.

He steps into the dim light, peering at me. "You don't know if you'll tell me or—"

"I don't know what I am."

He looks startled, his eyes widening. It appears that I've really surprised him.

After all, how could I not know?

I follow my admission with a heavy sigh. "My mother was a hellhound. My father was a dark angel. I have claws and teeth and..." I hesitate. "Things that don't fit together like they should. I'm not a hellhound. I'm not an angel. Even though I *can* fully shift into the shape of a wolf, I don't think I'm a wolf shifter—at least, not in the usual sense."

Diavolo's brow has furrowed. His focus drops to my claws, which have extended in the dark.

The very same claws that drew blood at Vanguard's throat. An achievement that seems like a fluke now.

Diavolo's expression clears as his eyes meet mine.

"You're you," he says quietly.

My own darkness lifts a little. It's not as though I suddenly feel like a unicorn floating on a rainbow, but some of my tension eases.

"Yeah," I whisper. "I'm me."

The keeper holds out his hand to me, his dark eyes moving across my face as he continues to speak softly. "Okay, *you*. Dawn is still a few hours away and we have time to kill and plans to make."

"Gods to kill," I correct him.

"That, too."

The puffy panthers follow us out of the alley, keeping close to my legs. I'm pleased to discover that most of the city's smells aren't bothering me so much anymore. The more time I spend out here amongst civilization, the faster I'm sure I'll settle into the world.

As we proceed along the footpath, I scoff a little. "Jonah said his name was a homophone for his race. But a homophone should sound exactly the same, no? At best, *Jonah* rhymes with *jotnar* and even then, you have to pronounce the 'J' differently."

Diavolo smirks. "The gods and those who stand beside them probably enjoy making up their own rules."

He draws to a stop beside a restaurant with a glowing, neon sign above the window.

"Pizza," he says, licking his lips as he reads the sign.

When I inhale the delicious scents wafting from the shop, more of my tension disappears. "Do you think pizza will taste as good as burgers?"

He grins. "Want to find out?"

"Hell, yes."

I follow him inside the store, relishing the moments when he compels the humans to look the other way and wrangles free pizzas for us and raw meat for the panthers. I discover that pizza is delightful—except for the ones that have little things called 'anchovies' on them. Salty fishes are not for me.

But even in these moments, I can't stop asking myself a question that is chewing up my insides.

If my claws can spill the blood of a god, what kind of creature am I?

CHAPTER TWENTY-NINE

*W*e take our time returning to the witch's apartment, which the keeper starts referring to as 'home,' and I decide not to correct him.

As the night grows deeper, we encounter fewer humans, and I want to continue exploring the city. I also take the opportunity to point out to the keeper more of the locations where the empire operates—or used to. It's gratifying that the buildings still exist, even if I can't yet verify that they're being used the same way.

By the time we return to the apartment, I'm full of food from late night takeout and exhausted from exploring, but it's really the approaching dawn that drives us inside. Or *me* inside.

Even the panthers no longer seem so cross about their current shapes, having elicited all sorts of cooing and head rubs from humans who were oblivious to the imminent danger to their fingers.

I guess even dark creatures like to be adored.

Once we're back inside the apartment, Diavolo lifts the illusions from me and the panthers. The panthers bare their teeth at him but plonk themselves down on the floor without delivering any sort of retribution.

"Traitors," I mutter as they stretch out on the soft floor—called carpet, I think—and rub their backs against the woven surface.

I pull the strip of Jonah's shirt off my face and add it to the row of makeshift blindfolds I'm accumulating. Removing the earplugs, I sigh with relief as I rub my face and roll out my shoulders.

As much as I need an illusion to conceal my identity, I'm looking forward to *not* needing it.

After using the bathroom, I give in to my sleepiness and drop to the floor beside the panthers, snuggling in beside them. They edge in closer, purring loudly as I close my eyes.

"You need names," I murmur, my voice muffled by a yawn. "Tomorrow. I promise."

A shadow falls over me and I crack one eye open to find Diavolo looming over us.

"There's a bed," he says, pointing to the bedroom.

"Too soft," I grumble, closing my eyes again. "I sat on it when I was choosing clothing and it nearly swallowed me. If you want to be devoured by a blanket, go right ahead."

I yelp when, in the next second, I'm being jostled around as Diavolo squeezes his big body between the nearest panther and my left side. He scoops me up and deposits me in the crook of his arm, my head resting on his shoulder. Somehow, he's made enough space between the panthers to lie on his back. When I crane my neck to see his face, his eyes are closed already.

I settle in and quickly fall asleep to the soft sounds of the panthers' purring and Diavolo's deep breathing.

I sleep all day and only wake once the sun has gone down. I find that the panthers have already woken and draped themselves over the lounge chairs. A thin blanket rests around me, thankfully not the one from the bed or I'd be smothered in it.

Rubbing my eyes and tugging at my unruly braid, I sit up and blink at Diavolo, who's clattering around in the kitchen, pouring cereal into two bowls.

"Hungry?" he asks.

I'm still full from last night—or, technically, this morning. I've never eaten so much food in the space of so few hours and my tummy is rounded out for the first time ever.

"Not yet," I say, conscious that the panthers have lifted their heads and are giving me their full attention. "I need to give the panthers names first."

He gives me a nod. "Food can wait."

I clear my throat as I turn back to the panthers, taking a beat to consider each one before I address them. "Names have power," I say, knowing they can understand me. "If I could interpret your snarls and purrs, I'd ask you to name yourselves, but as it is, this responsibility sits heavily on my shoulders."

Too heavily. What I call them is what they could become rather than what they are.

The female leaps off the nearby couch and approaches me with a snarl on her lips before she tilts her head at the males. I consider all four of them carefully. "I don't know how you came into existence or why there are only four of you in the world, but Mom was certain there were once more of you. If I could guess at your past, then maybe..."

I consider how close-knit these four are and the way they'd defended each other against the snakes. Also, the way the female is more vocal about her thoughts while the males are a little more chilled, but no less rebellious against the rules. If I had to guess, I'd say they'd done something incredibly unruly to have ended up in a prison in the veil.

My eyes suddenly widen. "You broke off from the others, didn't you? All four of you. Together. Something happened and you refused to go along."

It's a pure hypothesis on my part, but I know I'm close to the truth when the female panther's eyes gleam at me and the males all hop down off the lounge chairs to prowl toward me.

If only they could tell me their full history. How they came to be and what happened to the others. Why they rebelled.

But I have an idea what to call them now and I can only hope they approve of the names I'm about to give them.

My heart is up in my throat when, to the female panther, I say, "Anarchy."

Her eyes light up so brightly that it makes me squint. She draws her lips back from her teeth and snarls, a sound that quickly turns into a purr.

I turn to each of the males in turn. To the one that had the blaze on its paw when it was in its Doberman form, I say, "Riot."

Then to the other two: "Rumble. Strife."

Each of them gleams at me, their eyes lighting up before they lower their heads to me in a solemn bow.

"Well met," I whisper.

The weight lifts from my shoulders. I understand now why my mother called me 'Daughter.' I fear that if I were ever to have a child of my own, they'd remain nameless until they could name themselves.

I look up to find Diavolo sitting on one of the kitchen chairs, which he pulled out from the table.

I don't need his approval, but it looks like I have it when he tips his chin at me.

"Now, I'll eat," I say.

After quickly using the bathroom, I return to the table, scoop up the bowl of sweet, crunchy, wheat things, and head over to one of the windows. The blanket covering the panes has shifted a little to the side and we're high enough up that I can partially see across the streets around us.

I'm gratified to find that the sight of the city lights doesn't make me flinch. We have another night to kill before the mission and I'd like to test my eyesight without a blindfold.

I turn back to tell Diavolo so, only to find him gone from the room.

In the next moment, I hear rummaging from the bedroom.

He appears a second later, his arms full with beeswax candles.

I give him a quizzical look. "What are you doing?"

He pauses. "I'm going to take a shower."

"But you're perfectly clean." I envy the way dirt doesn't seem to stick to him at all. "Why would you take a shower?"

In contrast to Diavolo, I've got panther hair and soot and even a few spots of snake blood on various parts of my body. I gave my face a splash last night, but nothing more. Of the two of us, I'm the one who needs to wash.

Diavolo peers over the top of the mountain of candles to give himself a quick onceover. "Sure, there's no visible dirt. But I've never showered before. I think it might be fun."

I screw up my nose. "In my experience, showers aren't fun."

His eyebrows rise. "You must be doing them wrong."

I glower at him. "How would you know they're fun? Like you said, you haven't showered before."

"Plenty of dark creatures had fun in showers before they died. I saw it in their final memories." His lips curve in a wicked smile that warms my cheeks. "Mostly because they had company."

I splutter a little at his suggestion before I wonder if what he said is true. I spent my life in a cage, so how the fuck would I know? "Showers aren't meant to be taken alone?"

He shrugs. "It looked that way to me." He manages to approach me at a stealthy prowl, despite the precarious positioning of the uppermost candles. "Besides, I don't think it's possible to get completely clean unless someone else scrubs your back."

He towers over me even though he keeps a step away. I can't resist the challenge in his expression, all those shadows that pull me closer.

"Fine," I huff. "I'll scrub your back. Since you're so helpless."

He laughs as he heads toward the shower, and I'm stunned when his clothing peels itself off his body, somehow working its way around his arms to drop onto the floor.

I catch all the rippling muscles across his back before he turns the corner.

It dawns on me to wonder, if his clothing is an illusion, which it might well be... Is he actually walking around butt-naked all the time?

I give myself a hard shake. Best not to think too much about it.

Leaving the panthers in the bedroom, I follow the trail of discarded apparel, reaching the bathroom to find Diavolo in his underpants.

He has deposited the candles around the bathroom, lit each one of them—but only with the dimmest flame—and now he's standing in front of the shower, chewing on his bottom lip, his hands hovering over the water controls.

I lean against the doorframe, feeling vindicated when he continues to hesitate.

He reaches for the single faucet, turns it full hot, and my smile grows.

Then he side-eyes me, as if to check that I'm watching before he slowly pulls the faucet further toward the cold side, smirking at me before he turns the water on.

I roll my eyes. "Fine, but you've had the advantage of seeing how those things work."

There's an overly sympathetic glint in his eye. "You scalded yourself, didn't you?"

I send him a dark glower. "My soul is forever scarred."

The gentle steam from the apparently perfectly warm water rises around his near-naked body, white wisps that curl and curve across his thighs, chest, and biceps, fitting themselves to every hard contour.

His smile has softened. "Why don't you come on over here and heal those scars?"

CHAPTER THIRTY

y lips part as I consider Diavolo carefully, aware of the growing warmth in my body as he continues to appraise me. It's hard to know what he wants from me. At minimum, I'm here to scrub his back, but at most...

He existed in darkness just as I did. The difference is that he had a life before he became the keeper. In that life, he had the opportunity to do things I never could. Even if he can't remember doing them.

Despite my lack of experience functioning in this world, I'm not naïve about the heat in his expression or where the next hour could lead.

But I'm also clear about my boundaries.

My mother was blunt when it came to talking about sex. She said she would have waited until I was older to tell me all the things, but she already knew she didn't have long.

Her message was clear: Sex is not about pleasure.

It's about control and manipulation.

If I'm enjoying it, then I've lost control and I'm being manipulated.

I must never allow that to happen.

If I want pleasure, she told me: Give it to yourself.

She was matter-of-fact and descriptive about all things related to sex. All the ways it could be done. All the ways to touch a man—or a woman, for that matter. I have more than enough factual information, but putting any of it into practice with the keeper of dark magic could be a hazardous thing to do.

My lips twitch upward.

Hazards can be fun.

Without second-guessing myself, I step toward the shower, pulling my soot-smudged shirt up over my head and unclasping my bra, dropping both pieces of clothing to the floor. I pause to take off my long pants and my underpants, leaving myself entirely naked.

More naked than he is.

He becomes very still when my clothing meets the floor, his gaze running the length of my braid to my feet, skimming across my breasts, waist, and pelvis.

The heat in his eyes grows.

Right before I reach the shower, I pause again. This time to reach for soap and a small washcloth.

Holding one in each hand, I return to the shower. "I'm here to wash your back."

Dark light grows in his eyes, the edges of his mouth have relaxed, and his focus intensifies. "As you like."

He steps back into the spray, dousing himself in liquid before he emerges again, turns his back on me, and plants his hands on the tiles at the side of the shower.

I step right up to him, my left foot nudging up against the outer edge of his left foot, so close that my inner calf brushes the outside of his left leg. If I slipped farther to the side, I could straddle his leg, but for now, I make do with leaning my lower half lightly against him, skin brushing skin.

He casts a slow glance back at me while I take my time soaping up the washcloth.

The water and suds drip down my arm when I press the material to his back, starting with his left shoulder. Sweeping the cloth along the hard ridges, I follow the curve of his muscles to his spine and down to his lower back in long, slow strokes.

His muscles glisten with soapy suds. The gentle steam wafts around us as I work the cloth back up to his neck and across to his other side.

When I stretch out to reach his other shoulder, my breasts press up against his left side.

His breathing has increased. His hands press harder against the tiles. But he doesn't otherwise move.

I allow my body to press against him for another heartbeat before I plant my left hand on the side of his chest, my fingers splaying through the slippery suds, separating and closing.

I lean right into him as I finally reach across to his other shoulder, pulling the cloth all the way down his back to the top of his underpants.

I sense his muscles tense, as if he's about to move, and that's when I remove my leg, breaking the contact between us and slipping behind him.

Wrapping the soap up in the towel, I drop it to the shower floor on his right side, where he can see that I've abandoned it.

My hands close around his sides at his lower back and I sway against him, my breasts colliding with his back while my fingers slide all the way up to his shoulder blades and down again. As if I'm washing him with my hands now. Then back up again, traveling to his neck until my fingers disappear into his hair.

Still, he doesn't make a move, but I sense that the tension in his muscles is nearing a breaking point.

He'll move soon, and when he does, I'll need to be prepared.

Slipping my hands down his sides, I dare to dance my

fingertips around to his front, my right palm riding up his chest while my left makes it as far down as the top edge of his underpants.

He moves fast.

Spinning and pulling me hard up against his chest, he sweeps my legs around his hips and pushes me high up against the shower wall. His hand is cupping the back of my head. Not only cushioning it but controlling it.

Now, we're face to face. My body wrapped around him. My hands on his shoulders.

In the space of turning, he has transformed and I'm looking into the eyes of his darker self, the one with the black hair and deep-blue eyes who, despite his greater leanness, seems as physically strong as his bulkier form.

His lips hover near mine, the perfect curve of them a promise of tantalizing sensations if they were to touch mine.

Despite his restraint in kissing me, his dark eyes rage at me like a storm.

"Undo your braid," he says.

I'm surprised by his request, and I'm not afraid to show it, but my lips part in a soft smile. "No."

His jaw clenches. "Undo it."

I tip my head a little, testing how far this challenge will take us. "Only if you kiss me."

The darkness in his eyes increases. "As you like."

A thrill of anticipation fills me as he sways forward a little.

But his lips don't press to mine.

Using his lower half to continue holding me against the shower glass, he slides his right hand out from behind my head and, along with his left, closes his palms firmly around my sides beneath my breasts.

I gasp when his thumbs come to rest beneath my soft curves, but, even though I arch a little, he doesn't stroke higher.

His lips are curved upward now, a flash of his darkest smile as his biceps flex at the edge of my vision.

Then he's sliding slowly downward, holding me against the tiles with his hands while his head lowers to my neck. His lips trail across my skin, sending shivers through me, before he lowers himself even further, his mouth traveling slowly down toward the top of my right breast.

My eyes narrow at him when he skirts infuriatingly around my curves to reach my stomach.

Once there, he looks up at me before he plants a soft but deliberate kiss right above my belly button.

He growls against my skin. "Undo your braid."

"That wasn't a kiss."

His smile darkens and it only makes me want to push harder. "If you want my braid undone, kiss me properly."

"As you like."

Very slowly, he lowers himself further until he's kneeling on the tiles, his mouth at level with my pelvis. I can't stop the clench in my thighs or the tremble of pleasure that flows through me, a visible reaction I've been fighting since I first pressed my body up against his soapy skin.

Until now, my legs were wrapped around his waist above his hips, but now that he's lowered himself further, my feet are slowly sliding back to the floor.

I arch an eyebrow at him, waiting to see if he'll let my legs slide away from him. After all, I can't defy gravity.

But it seems *he* can.

My eyes fly wide when black light glows from the crown on his finger and a force I wasn't expecting presses up against my torso, holding me against the wall. It washes across me like a breeze, pressing from my shoulders to my hips, brushing lightly across my breasts. An unexpected caress.

His hands are now free to sweep my legs up over his shoulders, and he doesn't waste a moment to graze his mouth across my inner right thigh, moving through the water droplets toward my center.

"A proper kiss," he growls, his dark eyes devouring me as he nudges forward.

My arms and legs are completely free of the force that continues to press against my torso and I bury my hands in his hair, but my purpose is not to touch him.

My right hand closes around his head, gripping him and stopping his inward movement.

His lips are a mere half inch away from my center.

I want nothing more than to let him bury his head between my legs, to know what it feels like for his tongue to close over my clit, but I can't lose control.

I can't.

My jaw clenches as I fight my physical need, determined that my mind can overcome it.

He hasn't taken his eyes off my face and the darkness in his expression softens a little. Then, as if he's now testing me, he lifts his left hand and slides his own hand over mine at the back of his head.

"Hold on as tightly as you like," he says.

His tongue darts out, slips between my folds, and strokes across my clit.

Dark saints!

I should have seen it coming. I can't stifle the moan rising to my lips, even as I try to clamp down on the sound.

Warmth. Pleasure. A heady, needy ache burns through me like a shot of fire.

I want more, but is wanting more losing control?

Fuck it, where is the line?

My hold on his head loosens, but his hand tightens over mine, as if he's holding himself back for me, keeping his lips from me.

His tongue strokes against me again. An aching heat spills

through my pelvis, radiating out to my hips and rippling upward. At the same time, the force keeping me against the wall also moves across me as if it's tangible and not invisible, stroking and teasing my breasts.

I don't hold back my moan.

Can't stop my hand dragging him toward me.

I tip my head back when his mouth finally closes over my center, his tongue stroking hungrily over my clit.

His voice is muffled against me. "Undo your braid."

Ripping the hair tie off the end of the braid, I unfurl my tresses, allowing the strands to fall down that side of my body, spreading them out across my breast.

"There." My voice is throaty, but I manage to instill it with every ounce of independence when I continue. "Until I braid it again."

I sense him smile against me before his free hand rises to cup my visible breast, his fingers sending my body into a spin.

Groaning, I rock against him where he pushes his tongue against me. Every move of his hand and his warm mouth drives me toward a crash that defies my boundaries.

I'm so close to the edge that his question barely registers. "Do you know why so many dark creatures die in showers?"

I gasp. "No fucking idea."

"They slip and fall."

How fucking mundane.

His mouth pauses on me. "Are we going to fall, Veda?"

I drag in a breath as I open my eyes, aware of how tightly his hand is clamped over mine at the back of his head, as if he's expecting me to drag his head away at any second.

As if he believes I should.

The look in his eyes sends a shiver down my spine. It's the same darkness I saw on the beach when lightning struck the horizon.

It should scare me. So much about him should scare me. But

I won't hesitate to step into these dark waters. I'm not afraid to wade into the dark and let it lap at the hollow where my heart's love once was.

I pull my lower lip between my teeth as I look down at him from beneath my lashes.

He asked me if we were going to fall and all I do is challenge him. "Are *you*?"

CHAPTER THIRTY-ONE

*T*he shadows in his expression darken so suddenly that my head spins.

He shakes his head. His hand grips mine painfully as he removes my fingers from his hair. "Not today."

His tongue darts out, running the length of my clit before he eases my legs off his shoulders. The force that was keeping me against the wall lessens and I'm suddenly being lowered back to the floor.

My hand slips from his. My feet have barely touched ground, but he's already stepping away from me.

Wait... what?

He backs up while carefully navigating the edge of the shower, all without taking his eyes off me.

I remain where I am, my hair floating across one side of my body, aware of the blush across my breasts and the wetness between my legs. Fighting the ache he's leaving me with.

My gaze follows his features from his face to his chest and farther downward, lingering on the hard mound at the front of his pants.

My body isn't alone in its aching.

But, as surprised as I am, I understand why he's backing away from me. He asked me if we were going to fall. *We.* Together. I made it clear that if he falls, he'll do it on his own. Falling is not an option for me. My boundaries are built from bricks.

He takes another two steps away from me, and it seems he really is determined to walk away.

Well, fuck it. There's no way I can come down from this ache unless I do something about it myself.

If he wants to go, he can.

If he wants to stay, he can.

Either way, I'm in control of my pleasure now.

I give a soft sigh as my fingers slip between my legs, easing my need. My eyes flutter closed, my head tips back, and I don't hold back my moan.

His footfalls pause.

I listen to his silence, the hitch in his breathing, and then the footfalls that return to me.

Opening my eyes, I watch him return. All the hunkering darkness of him.

He plants his hands on either side of my head, his focus on my lips as I gasp and moan, holding nothing back.

"You need to be in control," he says without touching me.

I rock forward and brush my nipples across his chest. The contact nearly tips me over the edge, but even now, I control the release, willing my body to wait.

Just a little longer.

"Yes," I say.

His jaw clenches and I read the war in his eyes. He might know my feelings, but right now, *his* feelings are bared for me to see.

It's like looking into a mirror.

We are both dominant creatures and neither of us wants to bend.

I'm certain he's going to walk away and take care of the problem between his legs the same way I will. Alone and without giving any ground.

Or so I think.

Until the last second when he withdraws his hands from the wall, steps back, and slides his underpants to the floor.

"Then be in control," he says, standing in front of me like a dark god.

I take in the sight of him, the full length of his cock and all the hard planes around it from his hips up to his stomach and his chest.

There's nothing I want to do more than to take his hard length into my mouth.

Closing the gap between us, but not enough for our bodies to collide, I drop to my knees. My hand doesn't leave my clit, doesn't stop moving even if I'm slowing myself down.

I want my message to be clear: This is about what I want.

I take my time reaching out to drag my fingertips across the muscles at the base of his stomach. Curl my fingers around his hip—not that they make it that far around. Let the tips of my claws extend and brush them ever so lightly across his skin as I return to his front. I only retract them at the last moment before my palm closes around his cock.

I watch him the whole time and there's nothing but a gleam of anticipation in his eyes. Not a shred of fear even when my claws made an appearance.

Leaning forward, I run my tongue across his tip, surprised by how good he tastes. Slightly salty. Slightly sweet.

I plant my left hand against his stomach and take him into my mouth as far as I can, reveling in the sensation of his stomach muscles clenching beneath my palm.

Taking my time, I explore every inch of him, familiarizing myself with the strokes that make his breathing quicken or even out. His hand curls into my hair, his fingers gripping me, but he doesn't try to control my movements.

I'm so busy testing his responses, bringing him close to the crash, that I don't realize how near to orgasm my own body is.

The clench of my thighs warns me.

I'm right on the edge and I'm certain he is too, but I stop, my lips pausing on the tip of his cock, my left hand tightening around his hip, holding off the crash.

Silently telling him that this is mine.

I will give him release when *I'm* ready and when I choose to give it. Not because I need it.

His fist tightens in my hair and his breathing is beyond ragged. I sense his muscles clenching and understand the way he must be fighting the need to plunge himself into my mouth.

When I hesitate another beat, he lets out a groan, and the sound is a trigger for my body.

My finger slips across my clit and my orgasm breaks across me, my cries leaving my mouth even as I plunge my lips down his length, a final slide that makes him jerk against me.

"*Fuck. Veda.*" His muscles clench, his cock pulses, and I capture all of his length in my mouth.

His orgasm and mine extend through the moments, far longer than I expected. A complete release that ripples through me, making me shiver so hard that my hand around his hip becomes my anchor.

As the sensation eases, it leaves me with an intensely warm feeling throughout my entire body.

Diavolo's dark eyes glitter down at me while I lean to the side to spit, letting the shower swill everything away before I rise to my feet.

I don't bother hiding the satisfaction in my expression, but I make sure he's watching me when I tip my head to the side, gather up my hair, and start braiding it again.

He gives a soft chuckle a second before he sweeps me off my feet and up into his arms, pulling my legs back around his hips.

It's so quick that I don't even have time to gasp.

With a wave of his hand, the faucet turns off and several towels float across the distance.

"Bed," he says.

I arch my eyebrows at him. I slept all day and I'm not even a little bit sleepy. But I'm prepared to let him have this moment.

He carries me from the bathroom, wrapping a towel around me along the way.

The panthers raise their heads as we pass by, and I throw them a shrug. The males go back to their lounging, but Anarchy narrows her eyes at me.

Oh, don't judge. I was in control the entire time. I'm letting him have this.

If only she could hear my thoughts.

She huffs at me before she lowers her head back to the couch she's draped across.

Diavolo kicks the bedroom door shut behind us and places me on the floor. He finishes wrapping the towel around me before he turns to the bed.

I glare at his back because this has gone far enough. "You know how I feel about this bed."

But he's ripping the bedclothes off, starting with the puffy blanket, then the one below it, stripping the bed right down to a single layer of silky material that covers the mattress. He even throws the pillows on the floor.

He turns back to me and only now do I see the growing darkness beneath his eyes. Not shadows, but rings of what appear to be exhaustion.

It surprises me so much that I take a moment to reassess him. "What's wrong?"

"It's been millennia since I did anything like that. If, indeed, I ever did," he says. "I need to sleep. It's up to you if you sleep with me."

My eyes widen at his admission of what could be a vulnerability. I'm certain it's not so much the sex that has drained him as the use of energy and power.

It only now occurs to me to wonder if he was drawing on dark magic or if it was an illusion when he held me against the wall. The light that had engulfed me was black. Much darker than any compulsion power he's used, and not sapphire or emerald like his other magic normally is.

I'm not sure I want to know the answer.

"I'm not sleepy," I say. "But I'll lie with you for a while."

He seems especially relieved when I say that I'm not sleepy, his exhale immediate and deep, but his reason surprises me.

"It would be best if you can stay awake," he says. "It's difficult for me to sleep when you do. Your heart hurts too much."

My eyes widen.

My heart hurts while I sleep because of my dreams. He told me that on the beach.

He pulls the flat sheet up off the floor and then he crawls onto the bed, pulling the sheet around himself before he closes his eyes.

"Well, I suppose this bed will have to do," I grumble, dropping the towel and slipping onto the bed beside him, my body still naked and my partially braided hair damp.

I'm happy to find that the mattress is firmer than I thought it would be, and I can't complain about the smoothness of the material covering it.

This sheet has certainly expanded my 'soft as' comparisons.

Soft as towels. Soft as sheets. Soft as...

Lips.

Diavolo's upper arm pulls me closer, his mouth brushing the edge of mine. Not so much a kiss as a brief, tingling meeting of skin on skin.

I wait for more, but his features smooth out and his breathing becomes even.

The deeper he falls into sleep, the darker grow the shadows across his features. I'm surprised by the way his face and body very slowly shift between personas, his skin color and even its texture changing, as if his body is settling into whatever form he needs to take so he can rest.

I'm surprised when he stops on a form he hasn't shown me before. Possibly his largest male silhouette with broad shoulders that cause the tucked sheet to tighten around him so much, it could rip. His skin is fair but it takes on a metallic-black sheen, almost like scales across the top of his chest where the sheet doesn't cover him.

When he stays like that, I finally close my eyes.

But there's something I need to say to him that I won't be able to say when he's awake, so I take my chance with him while he's asleep.

"Obviously, I've never had sex," I whisper. "There's going to come a point where I'll need to do something about that. And it can't be with you. Because if it's with you..."

I'll lose myself. I'll lose control.

My eyes fly open when his voice sounds.

"Why would you need to 'do something' about your virginity?"

Oh, fuck, I was sure he was asleep.

I stare back at him, taking in his fierce eyes. Their reptilian color is just like the hints of fire I saw in his irises when we were discussing the nature of our enemies.

His features are completely smooth, his expression more tightly controlled than I've ever seen. I'd like to think that this face he wears now is more peaceful, but far from it, it feels more volatile.

I blink at him and make myself focus on his question. "Virginity is a liability I don't need."

He considers me calmly. "Why would the experience of your vagina—or rather, the absence of experience—define anything about you?" The corners of his lips rise. "My hands have never held a rose. Does that make me any less than I am?"

The fact that he's so certain he's never held a rose makes me wary. He can't remember his past. Yet this voice he speaks with now carries conviction, as if he's telling the truth.

"Sex is different." I scowl. "Sex is about power and control."

He doesn't look convinced. "My hand has both."

Power and control.

He adds: "Despite all of the things I've never done with it."

I dare to brush my fingertips across his lips, curious when he barely reacts to my touch.

It dawns on me that he may not really be awake right now...

I relax a little.

"So... if I told you I wanted to fuck you," I say, "and I mean a full-on *cock and vagina* fuck, you wouldn't do it?"

His smile grows. "If you wanted me to, I would fuck you in every way a woman can be fucked, but my goal would be to give you pleasure. Your heart tells me that isn't *your* goal."

Dammit. My disappointment now is caused not so much by the fact that he can tell exactly how I'm feeling, or even that he will always have that power, but that a little pit has opened up within me.

It's small.

I tell myself I can ignore it.

I really can.

But it wasn't there before. Now that it exists, there's a very real possibility that it might never go away.

I remind myself that I'm a dark creature. I care only about spilling my enemies' blood. Even if it takes me a lifetime to cut to the bone.

It doesn't matter how many empty pits open up within me along the way.

I'm grateful there's a chance he's talking to me in his sleep, and in a form he's never taken when he's awake, because chances are he won't remember this conversation tomorrow.

Just as my jaw clenches and I prepare to turn away from him, he reaches across the distance.

His palm glides over my cheek and into my hair as he pulls me back to him.

His lips touch mine, warm and full against my mouth, a kiss so deep that it sends a burn to my toes and makes my thighs clench all over again.

When he pulls back, he doesn't say anything. Just closes his eyes, his arm still entwined with mine.

His breathing deepens again, but I'm left staring at him and trying to process the way he kissed me without reserve.

Soft...

Soft as kisses I don't control.

CHAPTER THIRTY-TWO

*T*he keeper stays asleep, and by the time midnight passes, I'm fighting the urge to go out and explore.

I take my time pulling on a pair of tight, black jeans, a bra that pushes my breasts up, and a black T-shirt with a plunging neckline. I could do without the cleavage, but the witch has few options that don't expose my breasts in some way or another.

I pull on a black denim jacket to ward against the cold of night and then I tie my hair up in a thick bun and pull a beanie over it to conceal the unusual color combination.

The final touch is a pair of sunglasses to obscure the color of my eyes.

Then I consider the panthers and ponder not only the wisdom of leaving them to watch over Diavolo, but of taking one of them with me when we aren't protected by our illusions.

First problem first.

"Riot, Rumble, Strife," I address the males. "If I go out, will you protect the keeper while he sleeps?"

The panthers are immediately on alert. In response to my question, Riot pads into the bedroom and positions himself on the end of the bed, facing the door. Rumble and Strife head to either side of the door on the lounge room side and rest there like guards.

They all bare their teeth and stretch out their claws, hissing at me as if to punctuate their point.

I acknowledge their ferocity with a nod. "Very good."

Anarchy nuzzles up against my thigh and hisses softly at me.

"You're coming with me," I say to her. "But we'll have to stick to the shadows, where you'll be camouflaged."

Especially when she closes her eyes. She can disappear completely into the darkness.

I pull one of my makeshift blindfolds from my jeans pocket to show her. It's the strip of material from Jonah's shirt. I chose it because it won't matter to me if I lose it.

"I need to test my eyesight," I say, pushing the material back into my pocket, where I can retrieve the blindfold if necessary. Then I tap my ears, which are without earplugs this time. "And my hearing. So I know I can manage in the outside world."

Coping with the quiet of night is a far cry from the busyness of the city during the day, but it's a start.

Anarchy gives me an acknowledging snarl and heads to the door.

I pick up the keys from a little bowl on a table near the entry.

Thank you, assassins, for leaving everything so neat and tidy after you dispatched this witch.

The keeper simply translocated us inside when we returned last time, so it's my first time using keys.

It takes me a minute to figure out which key is for which lock and how the fuck the door handles work, but I get there.

I check that the corridor is empty before I lock the door behind me and head straight for the fire stairs—because who the fuck knows how to work an elevator? Not to mention, Mom warned me about things called cameras that take pictures and record everything they see. Humans put them in elevators, shops, and even on the street. She told me to look up because who knows who might be watching?

After carefully navigating the foyer at the bottom of the building, I slip out into the city, the mental map Mom gave me firmly fixed in my head.

I know exactly where I want to go.

The sunglasses protect me from the worst of the streetlight that inevitably gleams or reflects across the surfaces around me, but I'm pleased with how my eyes are coping.

Anarchy and I stick to the shadows, darting from spot to spot as we head toward Central Park. She stays beside or behind me, concealing herself in every dark space, disappearing when humans are nearby.

Our path becomes more precarious when I sense supernaturals in the distance. Encountering humans is one thing. Supernaturals are another.

I veer off course to avoid them, and Anarchy leads me from shadow to shadow until we can angle back toward the park again.

Finally reaching the trees, I carefully navigate my way to the statue Mom once spoke about.

By the time we reach it, it's the darkest time of night, and the only human we come close to encountering is a woman dressed in old pants and a threadbare shirt. Her feet are bare. She's huddled beside one of the nearby trees, muttering quietly to herself, a brown paper bag held loosely in her hand.

Homeless.

Mom called us that, too. We were women with nothing more than the clothes on our backs.

I shudder as I remind myself of her words: *This cage is not our home. Better to be fucking homeless than to accept these walls.*

Anarchy stays behind me, keeping to the shadows, and even though I don't think the human woman will notice us, I skirt around her position as widely as I can.

I head for the monument in the paved clearing up ahead.

It's made up of multiple smaller statues, all connected: A girl, a rabbit, and a little man in a top hat. They're sitting on top of, and are surrounded by, several toadstools.

It's right out of a children's book Mom read to me.

I'm glad it's the warmer months on this side of the world, since Mom described this statue as being covered in snow in winter. Which would make my task harder.

What I'm looking for is a little spot, the size of my forefinger, that's out of place. The place where Mom hid a scroll when she ran from my father's murderer.

In her last moments before she died, she told me it was here. She didn't tell me what was on it, only whispering, *"We were loved."*

I search and search, running my fingertips over the statues for so long that I'm ready to give up.

Then my thumb brushes the underneath of the smallest toadstool, finding its surface bumpier than the others. Stooping to see beneath it, I finally spot a darker place where it looks like there's a plug of chewing gum pressed against the metal. I can only hope it's concealing the hole at the end of the hollow she dug with her claw. The plug is under the mushroom, where humans wouldn't see to clean it unless they were lying on their backs beneath it.

Anarchy has positioned herself in the shadows behind the statue, but I know she'll warn me if someone's coming. With that thought, I slip under the statue, dig away the gum with my claw, and use my claw's tip to carefully drag at the edge of the tightly rolled paper within the hollow.

The scroll finally falls into my hand.

The parchment is tightly wound and inky black—the paper so dark that it seems to pull at the shadows around us. It's maybe only four inches wide and one edge is rough, as if it might have been torn.

I hold the scroll to my chest for a moment. Another rare physical connection to my mother. Then I slide out from under the toadstool and prepare myself to see what's written on it.

My heart is in my throat as I unroll the parchment, needing to use both of my hands to keep it from snapping closed again.

I try to breathe.

A moving image appears on the page, full of color against the black backdrop.

It's a family.

A man with black wings stands behind a woman with golden hair, who holds a baby in her arms. The man is as tall as the keeper, with hair as black as mine and golden eyes, also just like mine.

"My father," I whisper, my throat closing up as I try to process how much I look like him.

The woman is my mother as I remember her in my youngest years, before life in a cage depleted her. Her eyes are alive, her smile vibrant, nothing like the gaunt features of the woman who died in my young arms. "Mom."

As I watch, the man's left wing slowly extends and curves around the woman, enveloping her and the baby.

I can't stop the hot burn behind my eyes as she turns her face up to him, a soft smile on her lips.

The baby is in swaddling clothes. I can't see its face, but I know it's me.

I know in my head that this moment never happened. I was born in the cage. Mom never held me while she stood beside my father. This image is a dream, but all I can hear is her voice and the message she gave me, over and over.

We were loved.

My chest aches for a moment and then it's gone. Gone with the power in my heart.

Still, my tears defy the absence of feeling, slowly becoming tears of rage.

My family. Taken away from me.

It's past midnight. Later today, I'll begin my path into the inner circle. A first mission for Vanguard that must succeed if I'm going to achieve vengeance.

Gritting my teeth, I roll the scroll back up and tuck it beneath my bra strap, making sure my shirt is also tucked in. I can't risk losing the scroll on the way back to the apartment.

Stepping away from the statue, I call softly for Anarchy, who leads me back into the shadows at the side of the path.

But there I pause, causing Anarchy to stop and turn back to me.

Across the way, the homeless woman has remained huddled beside the tree, but now she's shivering.

It isn't freezing, but it's the coldest time of night and without my jacket, I'd be shivering too.

I hover on the balls of my feet before I make a decision.

"Anarchy, stay hidden."

The panther gives a soft snarl and stays in the shadows, where her body disappears from sight.

I pull off my boots and my jacket, bundling them in my arms, and then I approach the human very carefully, watching in case she makes any sudden moves.

I get within a few feet of her before she becomes aware of me.

She startles and her faded eyes widen, but all she does is wrench the paper bag closer to her chest. "Don't take my family."

She smells like piss and alcohol—the same sort of liquor that was on the tables when I met Vanguard and Jonah—but that doesn't mean she doesn't deserve to be warm.

"Your family isn't in that bag." I give a snarl as I stoop to her. "Hold still if you don't want to get hurt."

As quickly as I can, I shove each of the boots onto her feet. They're a good fit. Then I push the jacket over her like a blanket.

As a last thought, I pull off my beanie and yank it over her head, pulling it down over her wrinkled forehead.

She stares up at me with frightened eyes.

"Be warm," I order her with a dark scowl. Then, as an afterthought, I bend closer to her and look directly into her eyes over the tops of my sunglasses. I know full well she'll see my golden eyes.

She's frozen as she stares back at me.

"Tell anyone where you got this clothing, and I'll come back and kill you," I growl. "Do you understand?"

She blinks at me.

It's the best I'm going to get.

I hurry to my feet, pull the sunglasses back into place, and sprint back to Anarchy in the shadows. I'm not worried about my bare feet. The callouses on them will protect them.

We creep home as fast as we can.

When I step back into the apartment, I've barely had the chance to lock the door when Diavolo appears behind me in a literal cloud of rage, looking very much like the keeper of dark magic that he is.

Dark mist swirls across his blue-eyed form and the ring on his finger gleams so darkly that it's more painful to my eyes than the streetlight was.

I place the sunglasses on the little table by the door as he advances on me. Somehow, he manages to cut across the space diagonally so that he ends up between Anarchy and me. "Where were you?"

Anarchy growls at his back, but I incline my head toward the other side of the room, indicating she should go there. There's no need for her to get involved in this.

"You were supposed to be sleeping," I say to Diavolo.

"Impossible," he replies, ramming his fist against his chest. "Impossible to sleep."

"Oh."

My heart. The moment I saw the picture on the scroll, I felt pain. "I woke you up."

"What happened? Are you hurt?" he demands to know, but his focus flies to my breast, as if he's suddenly drawn to the parchment hidden there. He takes another step toward me, his focus intensifying. "What have you got there?"

"Breasts," I say without budging. "You've seen them."

He narrows his eyes at me, clearly not even remotely amused, and the heat of his glare makes my instincts prickle.

The closer he steps toward me, the more his ring glows.

The darker his fury grows, the more my own anger rises.

My hand closes over the front of my shirt where the parchment sits, and my lips draw back from my teeth in a warning.

"It's mine," I say. "My mother left it for me."

"*Yours?*" he asks. "If it is what I think it is, then it belongs to nobody. Should be held by nobody. Should not even be looked at." He stops to draw breath, his chest rising and falling harshly. "Not by any creature who values their life."

My eyes widen and I take a step back, a shiver passing through me. I'm close to pressing up against the door and I don't like the feeling of being cornered. Still, I clamp down on my ire and try to reason with him. "I'm not carrying anything dangerous."

"Prove it to me. Show me."

My hand tightens around the material of my shirt and the scroll beneath it.

It's a damn picture, for fuck's sake.

I snarl back at him. "Don't try to take it from me."

When he makes no further move toward me, I slowly reach into my shirt and pull the parchment free.

The black paper gleams in the light of the keeper's magic, its surface glittering in a way it didn't in the park.

EVERLY FROST

I begin to unroll it, but his voice is sharp. "Stop. Don't show me what's on it."

Looking up, I find his face turned away. His entire body is stiff with tension and the corners of his lips are turned down.

He speaks more softly now, but not once does he look at me. "I don't understand why your mother would give you something that could destroy you, but she has. Don't let anyone else touch it. Not me. Not even the panthers. Find a place to put it and leave it there. Don't keep it next to your skin for longer than you need to."

I'm having trouble reconciling his response with what I saw on the page, and when I hesitate, he snaps.

"Do it!" he snarls. "*Now!*"

I jolt at the fear in his voice, finding it difficult to accept that the keeper of dark magic can feel dread at all, let alone that it's being caused by something as simple as a piece of paper.

Especially one that, as far as I'm concerned, contains an image that can only motivate me to achieve my goal.

But I can also see that there's no way we can have a conversation until I put the parchment away.

Stepping as wide of him as I can in the entrance, I hurry into the bedroom since that's the only place with nooks and crannies to put the scroll. I reach for a jewelry box I noticed earlier and place the parchment in the bottom of it, pulling other pieces of jewelry over the top of it.

I hesitate before I close the lid.

I nearly reach back in and pull the paper out, fighting the sudden impulse to return it to its spot against my skin.

It's a compulsion that makes my senses tingle and my eyes narrow.

Hmm.

I'm not too proud to wonder if there's something in what Diavolo was saying after all. Even if the power in the parchment is based purely in emotional attachment. Putting this picture away is like putting away my mother. A hard thing to do. In fact, it might be impossible if I were still a slave to the power of love in my heart.

But I'm not.

I close the lid and the compulsion lifts.

Placing the box firmly on the shelf, I position it next to my makeshift blindfolds. All the things that remind me of my mother.

When I return to the lounge room, I find the keeper sitting with his elbows on his knees and his hands clasped in front of himself.

I pause opposite him. "Explain."

He lifts his gaze and scrutinizes me, searching my eyes before his focus lowers to my lips, and then down to my hands, where the tips of my claws have made an appearance.

The tension disappears from his shoulders, the friction lifting from around his eyes and mouth. He looks so incredibly relieved that for a moment, I think he's going to stand up and cross the distance between us.

He stays where he is, but when he speaks, his voice is soft. "There aren't many creatures who can hold a page from *The Book of Dark Magic* and resist its power, but it seems you're one of them."

CHAPTER THIRTY-THREE

"*The Book of Dark Magic*," I whisper, startled by this information. My focus flies back toward the bedroom and the parchment I left there. "I know of it. Mom told me about it when she spoke about the keepers of magic."

Just as there are four keepers, there are four books.

Each book works differently, true to the nature of the magic it embodies. As of twenty years ago, three of the books were either lost or hidden. Only one was out in the open and it wasn't *The Book of Dark Magic*.

The keeper exhales heavily. "Then you should also know that tearing a page out of any of the four books is a very difficult feat. In fact, I would have said completely impossible."

Again, his focus falls to my claws.

Claws that can cut through anything. My mother may not have had the same black canines that I do, but she had the same claws.

"Your mother must have really wanted you to have that page."

"It has a picture of—"

"Don't tell me," he says. "What you see in the book is for you alone."

Again, he turns away, his chest rising and falling with a deeply indrawn breath. But he winces and rubs his heart with the heel of his palm.

My voice is small. "For what it's worth, I didn't mean to wake you."

He shrugs. "You should get some rest. We have to be at the train station this evening."

The glimmer of light through the nearest window tells me that dawn is on the horizon. My focus now has to be on the mission ahead.

No distractions. Including my treacherous body's responses to Diavolo's nearness.

I give a nod and head to the bedroom.

His voice sounds behind me just as I reach the door. "You should know, Veda, in case your mother didn't warn you…"

I turn back to him.

The dark light in his eyes intensifies. *"The Book of Dark Magic* only serves itself."

I give him a short nod to indicate that I heard him. And I did. The parchment will remain in the box. The message my mother wanted to give me is clear enough: I had a family. Now, there is only vengeance.

Heading into the bedroom, I pull off the witch's tight clothing and choose one of the few larger, softer shirts to sleep in. I consider returning to the floor in the living room and piling in with the panthers, but I tell myself it will be easier to keep my distance from Diavolo if I stay in here.

I toss and turn before I finally fall asleep, but it isn't the parchment that clouds my senses and keeps me awake. It's Diavolo's scent on the sheets.

~

The train station is loud and bright, both of which set my teeth on edge.

We're all wearing our illusions again. Me with my completely black hair, slate-gray eyes, and sweet-as-a-pixie facial features, along with tight, black clothing and a pair of black flats that I can slip off if I need to. Even though my ears are plugged, I've opted for sunglasses instead of a mask, and I'm already regretting it.

Anarchy has resumed her canine appearance, although she now has a harness, which I'm holding on to. Every now and then, she tries to gnaw on the straps, and I don't blame her one bit.

The main hall inside the station is massive, wide-open, and exposed, but it lets us see in all directions.

We're early, so we find a spot next to a pillar to wait, quietly cataloguing all the other supernaturals we spot loitering among the early evening commuters. So far, I'm one up on the keeper.

True to his word, Jonah finds us soon after we arrive.

He's dressed in a business suit, navy this time. It looks a little tight in the shoulders, but it brings out the white-blond of his hair and the hints of fire in his eyes. His features are relaxed, but his gaze is sharp as he surveils both us and our surroundings as he approaches.

He doesn't bother with niceties. "This way," he says. "The train departs in fifteen minutes. Vanguard and the package are already on the platform, along with several other members of our team."

I step to Jonah's right and the keeper steps to his left, which is possibly a little disconcerting for him, but it allows us to keep our voices down.

"There's a fire mage in ripped jeans to our left," the keeper says, avoiding glancing in that direction. "Another one carrying a duffel bag to our right."

"Always with the fucking fire mages," Jonah snarls beneath his breath.

"They aren't part of your team?" I ask.

"No."

I give him a wry smile. I imagine it would be quite an accomplishment for a fire mage to survive a fight with Jonah, although I'm not sure if they know what he truly is.

Diavolo continues to quietly list off the other supernaturals we've identified, who are now all following after us. Some more furtively than others.

When he's finished, I add, "There was also a witch in a red coat off that way and a bear shifter sporting a significant beard lurking on that far corner, but they moved away a few minutes ago."

Jonah's response is grudging. "You've identified twice as many potential opponents as our team did."

I arch an eyebrow at him. "*None* of the supernaturals we spotted are on your team?"

"Not a single one," Jonah replies. "There are seven on our team—not including me and both of you, which makes ten in total. Our team is already split between the platform and in the sky along the tracks. I'll introduce you to the three on the platform. They'll move onto the train with us and the package."

Which means every supernatural now skulking after us is an enemy.

Anarchy stops gnawing at her harness and gleams up at me.

Funny how I can almost read her mind.

"First chance you get," I murmur to her. "Just don't eat them in front of any humans."

Jonah catches my speech and follows my line of sight to Anarchy, who gives her best doggie growl and frightens some human passerby.

I can see the cogs in Jonah's mind working and I imagine

he's picturing the speed with which Anarchy took down one of his men the other day.

I nudge his arm, ignoring the fact that any contact with his body is potentially lethal. "We have eleven on our team, not ten."

He grins at Anarchy. "So we do."

Moments later, we step onto the platform, and I pretend that this isn't the first time I've seen a train. It stretches out along the platform as far as I can see, like a metal beast made of multiple cars, which passengers are already boarding.

Way up ahead near the far end of the platform, I spot the witch in the red coat stepping into the first car. A moment later, the bear shifter with the beard enters the car beside it. Several other supernaturals we spotted earlier are loitering in the distance, while more have remained at a distance behind us.

We pass two supernaturals, who peel off from nearby pillars, but Jonah tips his chin at them, so it appears that they're part of the team.

They settle in behind us.

One of them is a woman about my height who has multiple piercings and wears boots, jeans, and a tank top. Her short sleeves show off her defined biceps while her cheekbones are high, her features chiseled. Her right wrist sports a solid black bracelet attached to which is a thin, metal thread that has the appearance of supple wire. It winds around and around her forearm to her elbow, where it's clipped to another solid, metal band. It looks like jewelry, but I'm not so sure.

She's chewing gum, her focus twitching from one side of the platform to the other, as if it would take a very small spark to set her off.

The other is a man wearing a gray suit with a crisp, white shirt. When he turns his head, I catch sight of a rattail at the back of his otherwise well-cut hair. He grins at me when he spots me scrutinizing him, his teeth the most brilliant white I've ever seen.

There's a spot of blood on his otherwise immaculately white collar.

I think he's a vampire, but I'm not sure what the woman is.

Jonah introduces the two supernaturals in the next moment.

"Valki is a berserker. She's our muscle. Don't get in her way," Jonah says, calmly inclining his head at the woman.

She bares her teeth at me, biting her chewing gum between them. I suspect it's her version of a smile.

"Gad is a vampire. He'll take care of anything that needs to be dealt with at speed."

Before I can blink, a fob watch appears in Gad's hand and then disappears again. I'm pretty certain he pulled it from his pocket and then put it back, but he moved so fast, I couldn't follow it.

"Our warlock is Orlan. He'll block other witch and warlock powers and control the humans if necessary," Jonah continues. "Orlan is already waiting with Vanguard and the package up ahead."

Farther along the busy platform, I catch sight of Vanguard standing near the open doors of one of the central train cars. Like the other day, he's dressed in a pinstripe suit, but he isn't carrying his sword across his back.

A slightly shorter man, although he's nudging six feet, stands beside Vanguard. He's dressed more casually, also in a suit, but with his shirt unbuttoned at the top and his jacket undone. He's younger in appearance, probably only a few years older than me. Neatly cut hair, bright eyes, a strong jaw.

My sharp eyesight catches the ink on his palms. Some sort of tattoo or image on the inside of each hand.

He's the one who will make sure any humans riding the train can't be mind-controlled. Of course, if Diavolo needs to use some sort of power that an enenra isn't supposed to have, he may need to control the *warlock*'s mind, but that will be a last resort.

Both Vanguard and the warlock—Orlan—are standing close together, half-turning as they keep watch over their surroundings, but what raises my curiosity is that neither of them is holding any kind of suitcase or box or any other object that could be the package they're so determined to protect and deliver to Boston. Both their arms are by their sides and their hands are empty.

Of course, the package could be a simple piece of paper tucked into someone's pocket. After all, I myself recently discovered how powerful a single piece of parchment could be.

For that matter, despite Jonah's claim that the package is with Vanguard, Jonah himself might be carrying it. His jacket is unusually tight. Maybe it isn't a wardrobe malfunction so much as an object pulling the lining taut.

We're only twenty paces away from Vanguard and I decide to come right out with my question.

"Are you going to tell us what the package is?" I ask Jonah.

"You'll see for yourself soon enough." The fire jotunn surges ahead, leaving Diavolo, Anarchy, and me to follow behind him.

I'm conscious of both Gad and Valki also picking up the pace, veering out on either side of us.

They slow down when they draw level with us and give us a onceover, both scoffing and smirking at each other.

"What's a blind chick doing here, Gad?" Valki asks, throwing the question across to the vampire.

My forehead creases. I'm not sure what gave Valki the impression that I can't see, although I remember Jonah talking about harnesses being associated with mobility assistance animals.

Gad presses his tongue to the edge of one of his eye teeth as if he's dying to let his fangs extend.

"She's my walking blood bag," he replies. "I've been trying to convince Jonah to give me one."

Beside me, Diavolo wears a chilling expression that says he

isn't amused. If we didn't have to make nice with these supernaturals, I'd encourage him to express his feelings.

I lay a hand on his forearm, grateful when he lets me speak first.

"Sipping on my blood can only hurt your bones," I reply, calmly allowing my teeth to sharpen, knowing that my canines have turned black and as sharp as blades. I retract them quickly because I can't risk humans seeing them. "I like to gnaw right down to the marrow."

Gad's smirk slips and Valki withdraws a little.

They appear to have the same thought at the same time, steering clear of me and surging ahead.

"Remind me to kill them once I'm in charge," I mutter to Diavolo, who simply inclines his head at Anarchy.

"If you get to them first," he says.

I can only smile down at my beautiful panther, whose teeth are bared at the backs of the berserker and the vampire. I imagine her ripping out their spines. They'd be dead before their bodies touched the ground.

"Soon, Anarchy," I promise her. "Soon."

We're now only ten paces away from Vanguard and Orlan. Jonah has joined them already and he's standing between them while Valki and Gad are boarding the train.

As we approach, Jonah steps to the side and so does the Orlan.

Another figure comes into view. A much smaller figure.

Vanguard is already speaking, but his voice washes over me. "Veda, Diavolo." He gestures to the little boy standing beside him. "Meet Elijah."

The kid can't be more than four years old. Five, at most. Unless he's little for his age.

He's wearing sunglasses on his face and some sort of leather-looking contraption over his head and ears, but he's turned in our direction and, even though I can't see his eyes, I'm struck by the sense that he's looking right through me.

All the way into my hollow heart.

"This is the package?" I whisper, struggling to find my voice. "A child?"

Vanguard's jaw clenches. "My son."

CHAPTER THIRTY-FOUR

*O*h, fuck me.

When Vanguard first spoke of 'the package,' he described it as extremely valuable. He said that many supernaturals would want to use it while others would be determined to destroy it.

I now see why.

This sort of leverage against Vanguard would be priceless.

He also said that 'the package' was being sent to a powerful supernatural who would secure it where it couldn't be found again, but that supernatural would try to kill Vanguard should he attend in person. The emotion in Vanguard's voice when he spoke about never associating with the package again makes a whole lot of sense to me now.

He's sending his son away to be raised by an enemy.

Must be some fucking honorable enemy for Vanguard to believe his child will be safe with them.

But, fuck... To trust strangers like me and the keeper with the safe passage of his child...

It speaks of a level of desperation that unsettles me.

Particularly when Vanguard made it clear that his sister will take the chance while the boy is out in the open to destroy him.

If our theory about Vanguard and his sister is correct, then I'm now looking at the son of an old god.

A very vulnerable four-year-old son of an old god.

With another old god coming to kill him.

I cast a glance at Diavolo, who's staring down at the kid, his expression blank. No doubt, he sees the potential to use the kid as leverage.

I probably should, too.

But I narrow my eyes at Diavolo until he seems to sense the heat of my stare.

He arches his eyebrows at me.

I shake my head. *No fucking way are we treating a kid as leverage.*

He tips his head, as if to ask: *Are you sure?*

I suppose, after collecting the magic of countless dark creatures, no doubt including children, he's hardened to the possibility.

I scowl at him. *I'm completely sure.*

I was the leverage used against my mother. I'm not repeating history with this kid.

Diavolo shrugs, as if he's prepared to drop it.

At that, we both turn back to Vanguard and Jonah.

It seems our silent communication hasn't gone unnoticed.

There's a new tension around Jonah's eyes and a glimmer of fire around his hands as he asks, "Everything okay?"

He isn't a fool. He'll know exactly what we were thinking. Particularly now that we know what 'the package' really is.

I meet his narrowed eyes without missing a beat. "I was wondering: What is that contraption on the boy's head?"

Jonah's forehead creases, as if I should know perfectly well what it is. "Headphones."

"Of course," I say quickly, noting the description, "but is he wearing them for a particular reason? I'd like to know if verbal communication will be difficult. It's important if we're to keep him safe."

The crease in Jonah's forehead clears. "Elijah needs to be shielded from the noise around him. He can remove the headphones if necessary, but only for short periods of time."

"And the sunglasses?"

Jonah arches his eyebrows at my own sunglasses. "The light hurts his eyes."

I bend down to Elijah, reaching as close to his eye level as I can. I'm under no illusions that the boy is unaware of our conversation, despite the headphones and the sunglasses.

"You and me both, kid," I say, pressing a finger to the edge of my sunglasses before turning my head slightly and tapping the earplug in my right ear. "The world bothers me."

The boy tips his head back to look at me, the corners of his mouth pulling down, his little shoulders hunched. I was hoping that by moving closer, I could see his eyes, but the sunglasses are curved to the shape of his face and sit close to his skin.

I can only assume that the boy's sensitivity to light and noise has something to do with his power. Judging by the slight tan across his fair skin, and the way Jonah and Vanguard lean so protectively around him, I highly doubt it's because he's been kept in a dark cage.

Jonah seems to have relaxed again, although it's impossible to miss the way he continues to scrutinize the platform around us.

I've already ascertained that the two fire mages we noticed earlier have approached the cars behind us. They're bound to step onto the train once we do.

I raise myself up and keep the fire mages in my sights while Jonah gives us an explanation of what to expect.

"Orlan will stand guard at the back of the car," Jonah says. "Gad and Valki will be at the front. We have seats in the center, and we'll remain with Elijah at all times. There are five stops between here and Boston. We can expect the occupants of the car to change at every stop. No matter what happens, we don't leave Elijah's side unless we have no other choice. We're his final line of defense."

"Got it," I say, but my speech is drowned out by the very loud voice that blares through the air and announces that the train will depart in two minutes.

I flinch at the booming voice and so does Elijah.

It's not the first time the loudspeaker—as Diavolo called it— has set my teeth on edge tonight, but it's so much worse on the platform, where the noise echoes and seems to strike through my head.

I shake out the tension in my shoulders, hating that both Vanguard and Jonah would have seen me jump. Thankfully, they're both focused on Elijah now.

Vanguard bends to his son, scooping up the boy's hands.

The corners of Elijah's mouth turn down even further. His voice sounds for the first time and it's very small. Very lost. "I don't want to go."

Vanguard's shoulders are tense, and his response is quiet. "You know why you must."

The boy's shoulders hunch even further. Tears trickle from beneath his sunglasses and his voice is bleak. "Please, Daddy, don't send me away."

Vanguard presses his forehead to his son's forehead. Tears fill his eyes before he squeezes them closed. "Sending you away is the hardest thing I'll ever do, Elijah. But I won't risk you being killed. The people you're going to stay with will protect you and teach you how to use your power." His voice breaks, strained as he continues. "Don't follow in my footsteps. Find your own way."

With that, he lurches upright, spinning to Jonah. "Don't trust anyone. Not even our own team."

Jonah taps his heart with his fist. "I'll protect Elijah with my life."

At that, Vanguard plows away along the platform, not once looking back.

I'm struck by how bleak this moment is. Vanguard loves his son so much that he'll send him away to keep him safe. To enemies, no less. It makes me wonder, if my mother had had the same option, would she have chosen to keep me at her side, or would she have set me on a new path even if it meant giving me up?

I'm startled out of my darkening thoughts when a cool hand slips into mine.

I look down to find Elijah beside me, his little fingers gripping my hand, his face upraised.

I can only blink down at him. I would not have expected him to gravitate toward me, since surely, he knows Jonah well.

Jonah doesn't look happy about it, casting glances at Elijah's hand around mine, but even when I tug a little, the boy doesn't let me go.

He's got a mighty grip, I'll give him that.

I cast Jonah a helpless shrug. His lips press together in a stern line, but he steps toward the open doors, never quite turning his back on us.

Ahead of him, Orlan enters the car, and I sense the keeper close at my back.

Elijah doesn't say anything to me, doesn't even swipe at the tears trickling to his chin, as he tugs me after Jonah.

Once inside the car, I spot Gad and Valki in the distance. They're sitting in the aisle seats in the front row, facing inward. There's a transparent door into a small corridor situated behind and between their seats, through which the next car is visible.

We pass silently by Orlan, who takes an aisle seat in the first row near the doors at the back of the car. I catch the way his forefinger runs across every surface he can reach, noting the little swirls he makes. Drawing spells, perhaps.

We maneuver past multiple humans, who are all finding their seats. As soon as they catch sight of Anarchy in her harness, they step aside, squeezing themselves between seats if they have to. I'm not sure if it's because they think my vision is impaired and they're trying to be considerate, or because she's fierce and they don't want to be anywhere near her.

Finally, we reach the center of the car, where there are two larger seating areas on each side of the aisle. Each area is made up of two seats facing each other with leg space between them. Perfect for families or groups of friends, I imagine.

Jonah indicates that we're to enter the seating area on the right.

Elijah tugs me forward and takes the window seat facing the front of the car. He hasn't let go of my hand and it compels me to sit beside him, also facing in that direction.

Great. The seats may be high, but both Gad and Valki can smirk at me this way.

On the upside, there's plenty of room for Anarchy, who stretches out on the floor perpendicular to our legs, facing the aisle.

Jonah looks even more unhappy about where I'm sitting. He probably intended to sit beside Elijah—if I were him, I would have preferred that, too. As it is, he makes way so that Diavolo can take the other window seat facing Elijah, while Jonah takes the aisle seat facing me.

Diavolo and I are now facing opposite ends of the car. Not bad since we can watch each other's backs this way.

A group of human teens plonks down in the seating area to our left, their loud chatter washing over us. A far cry from the silence among our group as the train begins to move.

Elijah stares out the window, still gripping my right hand,

and I take a few moments to assess each of the passengers—the ones I can see down the aisle and over the tops of chairs.

Most of them are human.

Three are supernaturals I recognize from the station earlier, although none of them is the witch in the red coat, the bear shifter with the beard, or one of the fire mages. The supernaturals in the car with us now have an aura I think belongs to shifters. Not wolves or bears. Lions, maybe. I can't quite tell, although the aura is the same for each of them.

They're all bushy-haired, blond males. All sitting in different positions, but each has a row to himself.

It irks me that I have to let Orlan, Gad, or Valki deal with them if they become a threat.

Jonah gave clear instructions: We stay with Elijah at all times. Unless danger reaches our location, I'm stuck in this seat.

A few minutes after the train sets off, Jonah rises out of his chair, apparently to take off his jacket.

His big body blocks my view for nearly a whole minute and when he sits down again, I stare at the three empty seats that the lions occupied only moments before.

Gad now sits in one of them.

Narrowing my eyes, I shift slightly, making out the shape of what could be a body slumped in the window seat next to him. I'm sure Gad will make it look like the dead man is sleeping.

Then I take note of the way all of the humans are staring out of the window nearest to them. They have glazed expressions. When I cast a quick glance back at Orlan, I catch a glimmer of fading light where it appears he drew a spell on the side of his seat.

I can only assume he compelled the humans to look the other way and clouded their senses while Gad dispatched the lions.

A second later, the humans resume their conversations as if nothing happened.

Gad grins at me from across the distance, licking the tips of his retreating fangs as if I'll be his next meal.

I shiver a little at the speed with which he took the lions out, but I tell myself to sit tight. We're all on the same team here.

Probably.

Vanguard warned Jonah not to trust anyone.

I give Gad a slow, cold smile.

Getting Elijah to Boston is my path to the usurper Ultima Nostra, and nobody is going to fuck that up for me.

CHAPTER THIRTY-FIVE

At the first stop, a few humans disembark and other humans get on while the teens in the seats near us remain where they are.

Then, a minute after the train leaves the station, the bear shifter appears at the front of the car near Valki, his hulking form filling the doorway.

At the same time, I hear the doors swish open at Orlan's end and a quick glance tells me that the two fire mages have appeared there.

It's impossible to tell if the mages are working with the bear shifter or if they've timed their approach to coincide with his, hoping they'll have a better chance if our defenses are split.

Craning my neck while trying not to make myself too conspicuous, I catch the quick movement of Orlan's hand and this time, I sense the very gentle shift in the air right before the chatter ceases and the humans become intensely focused on the landscape outside the train.

Vanguard said he was hoping the presence of humans would limit the attacks, but I guess that only works to a point. At least this way, Orlan is the only one controlling the humans' minds.

The two fire mages move fast, but they're forced to proceed single-file along the aisle.

Orlan rises up behind the second one—the one with the ripped jeans—who spins to the threat behind him.

Fire blazes from the mage's palm, shooting at Orlan's face.

At the same moment, Orlan crouches and claps his hands together. Before his palms collide, I see for the first time the full extent of the inked markings on his palms: elaborate and glowing.

The clap of his hands sounds like thunder as magic explodes between his palms.

He evades the mage's fireball, which hits the seat behind him and catches alight, and at the same time, he pulls his palms apart. It's like he's stretching magic between his hands, sharp blades of it, that separate into the shape of daggers.

Spinning deftly and evading another blast of flames, Orlan rams the first dagger into the mage's throat and the second into his eye.

Thud-thud.

The mage hits the ground.

That's all I see before the second mage reaches us, moving at a run now, pulling a rifle from his duffel bag. The rifle's barrel glows with heat, and I can only guess at the fiery bullets it's loaded with.

Opposite me, Jonah is up in his seat, appearing ready to tackle the enemy, but the mage passes me first and my claws are already out.

My left hand swipes the air, cutting right through the rifle's barrel and sending the cut portion spiraling into the area at the feet of the oblivious teens.

The mage gives a shout, skidding to a halt, and I prepare to launch myself up and out of my seat when a glowing spear thumps through the mage's chest from behind.

Orlan is poised there, arms forward, a thin line of magic

connecting his hands to the spear, which he yanks out of the mage in the next moment, calling his magic back to himself.

The mage drops to his knees where he stands, blood bubbling up between his lips, half-turned to me. "Fucking pixie."

I'm not sure why he's cursing me.

Sure, I broke his gun, but I didn't stab him in the back.

The mage falls forward onto his face. He's tall enough that his head lands near Jonah's feet. The fire jotunn promptly reaches down and presses a single finger to the dead mage's forehead.

Heat bursts from Jonah's hand. The mage's body glows hot like a coal, and then, startlingly, it completely disintegrates into ash.

Orlan spins to focus on putting out the fire that the mage started, dousing it in blue light and extinguishing the flames.

But ahead of us, the fight between Gad and the bear shifter has turned nasty. The bear shifter punches Gad, knocking him into the side of one of the seats, wasting no more time on the vampire before he pounds up the aisle toward us. The bear is partially shifted, his claws extended and his chest so broad, he nearly doesn't fit within the aisle.

A second later, Valki gives a scream and storms up behind him. Her muscles are visibly pumped and corded, her neck is thicker than before, and her eyes are so bloodshot, I can see the crimson color from here.

My own eyes widen. I'm not sure how she triggered her berserker nature, but I sure as fuck would not want her running up behind me.

She leaps onto the bear shifter's back, right up between his shoulder blades, the black wire from her bracelets held taut between her hands.

He roars as the impact against his back knocks him to his knees, but he doesn't have the chance to get up before Valki wraps the wire around his neck.

It tears through his beard and cuts across the front of his throat. She's pushing with her knees against his back and pulling with her enormously muscled arms, and the shifter doesn't have a chance.

A heartbeat later, she lets his body drop to the floor.

She stands over him, her shoulders hunched and her chest heaving. Her bloodshot eyes rake over us and she twitches when Gad steals close to her.

He stretches out his hand as if he doesn't want to get too close.

He's holding out a stick of gum. "Easy, Valki."

She snatches the gum from him, shoves it into her mouth, and begins to chew, her jaw muscles working over it.

Opposite me, both Jonah and the keeper have turned in their seats to watch Valki carefully while Orlan has paused in the aisle, and even Anarchy has edged forward, as if she believes Valki could be a threat to us.

Slowly, very slowly, Valki's chest deflates, her eyes clear, and her muscles visibly relax. She rolls her shoulders, stretches her neck, and shrugs. "All good."

She turns back to her seat and everyone around me seems to exhale with relief.

Too soon.

There's a flash of red only three seats away from us.

A red coat!

The witch materializes from nowhere, leaps up toward the ceiling, turns herself upside down, and scuttles along the top of the car like a damn spider.

I've barely shouted a warning when she veers toward the window seats, headed straight for Elijah.

The keeper was already facing that direction and so was Anarchy.

The panther leaps upward.

The keeper sees her coming and drops, turning his shoulder. "Up!"

It happens so fast I've barely blinked when Anarchy launches herself onto the keeper's back, using him as a spring board to leap at the witch.

Her jaws close around the back of the witch's neck, wrenching her down.

They're right above Elijah's seat.

My muscles are firing and I'm pulling him out of his chair and into my arms, getting him out of the way just in time before Anarchy and the witch crash downward.

Anarchy lands on her feet like the cat she is.

The witch's broken body drops partially onto Elijah's seat as well as onto the keeper's head and shoulders since he'd moved into the open area between the chairs.

I try to cover Elijah's eyes, nearly knocking off his sunglasses in the process.

No kid needs to see this much mess.

Jonah seems to have the same thought. With a horrified glance in Elijah's direction, he lurches forward, his outstretched hand full of fire. With a quick tap on the witch's back, she bursts into dust, blood and all.

The thick cloud of remains settles over Anarchy and the keeper, coating both of their bodies.

Jonah jumps back before he gets any on him.

The keeper coughs.

Anarchy growls.

Jonah gives them a sheepish grin. "Apologies."

The keeper squints at him, coughs again, and then both he and Anarchy shake themselves off.

I'm on alert for further threats, but all is quiet.

Orlan approaches us with a quick, "Sit tight. I'll take care of the bodies." He glances at all the dust in the aisle and around our seats. "And other remains."

Within minutes, he has lifted the bodies of the bear shifter, the first fire mage, and the three lion shifters into the air, along with the piles of ash from the other fire mage and the witch, pulling everything along with him to the doors at the back of the car.

I help Elijah into his seat and, a moment later, I catch sight through the window of the bodies and dust flying out into the dark landscape. We're passing close to the coast and everything drops into the dark water, even the clouds of dust descending as though every particle is weighted down.

A second later, the train has moved on.

Orlan returns to his chair, the air shifts, and the humans resume their conversations around us.

At the next stop, many of the humans disembark, including the teens, who vacate the seating area directly to our left. Only a few humans get on and none of them approach the now-empty space to our left.

When the train leaves the station, Jonah says, "These next two legs of the journey are the longest. Eventually, we'll pass through a State Park and then the final stations are close together within Boston."

As he speaks, he glances at the empty space on our left and I sense the growing tension in his shoulders.

"What's wrong?" I ask.

"Those seats are supposed to be booked by humans for the entire journey. In fact, we made sure of it."

At my raised eyebrows, he explains, "We have supernaturals placed inside many human organizations."

Of course they do.

Jonah continues. "The fact that those seats are empty—"

He stiffens, his eyes widening as he focuses on a spot behind me.

The keeper has also tensed. He's dust-free since Orlan

gathered it all up, but the shadows that have suddenly grown around his features send a chill down my spine.

At my feet, Anarchy lifts her head, alert once more.

Beside me, Elijah barely moves, but his little hand clamps so tightly around mine that his grip is painful.

His knuckles are turning white.

The sound of soft footfalls reaches me over the gentle hum of human conversation.

The back of my neck prickles a heartbeat before a shadow falls across me.

CHAPTER THIRTY-SIX

*I*t's an impossible shadow. The lights in the car should send it in the other direction.

An unfamiliar male voice sounds at my shoulder, but the speaker directs his greeting at the fire jotunn. "Jonah."

The owner of the voice is standing right beside my chair, but I'll have to actively turn to see him.

Around us, all of the humans—of which there are now only a handful scattered throughout the car—are suddenly staring out of their windows once more.

Poor things must be getting cricks in their necks by now. I wonder what sort of daydreams Orlan might be giving them that they won't be aware of the interaction happening so close by.

At the front of the car, within my line of sight, Gad and Valki are watching us with suddenly bright eyes. Unlike Jonah, they look delighted to see the newcomer.

Slowly and carefully, I look up and around.

The man standing near me is as big as the keeper's current form, but he appears younger, possibly the same age as me.

His hair is inky black like the darkest pit, his skin is fair, to the point of a brightness akin to the stars in the beautiful night sky, and his eyes, well, I can't see them because, like both Elijah and me, he's wearing sunglasses. Multiple golden rings glint on his fingers, where he rests them on the top of my chair at the corner of my vision. The edge of a tattoo on his bicep is visible beneath the sleeve of his black shirt. He's dressed casually, but nothing about his demeanor is relaxed.

This man wasn't among the guys in the room behind the green door when I first met Jonah and Vanguard, and he isn't one of the supernaturals we spotted at the station, but he clearly knows Jonah.

Jonah definitely knows him.

The way the fire jotunn's eyes spark with molten flames as if he's ready to summon his power is another indication that he isn't happy to see the newcomer.

Jonah takes a glance at the oblivious humans before he rises from his seat and speaks more plainly than I was expecting. "Why are you here, Lucian?"

"Isn't it obvious?" Lucian replies.

"Not to me."

Lucian scoffs. "I'm here to ensure Elijah reaches his new home safe and sound." And in the next breath, he adds: "That would be the home the Ultima Nostra arranged for him. In case you're confused."

"Obviously, we're on our way there," Jonah replies without blinking. "The Ultima Nostra's allies in Boston are ready and waiting to receive Elijah."

I fight the crease in my forehead. Vanguard made it clear that the people we're taking Elijah to are enemies, not friends. Of course, the false Ultima Nostra's allies may be Vanguard's enemies, but I don't think that's what's going on here. Not if I'm judging Jonah's tension correctly.

My teeth grit and my gaze flicks to Diavolo as I put two and two together.

Vanguard must be defying the Ultima Nostra. He's attempting to get his son to safety while appearing to follow orders. Because, of course, the Ultima Nostra would also love to use Elijah as leverage, ensuring Vanguard's complete cooperation for years to come.

What unsettles me is the question of how helping Vanguard in this situation will get me into the inner circle?

Oh... fuck.

I smother a sigh as I realize I may have been played. Vanguard was never going to get us in. I can see it now, and it explains why Vanguard would trust this mission to two strangers: We're the fucking scapegoats.

When the boy doesn't get where the Ultima Nostra wants him to go, Vanguard and Jonah can blame it on us. Maybe they'll say we stole Elijah or killed him. We're powerful enough that it's a real possibility.

Of course, it's all just a theory on my part for now, but hell, if I were trying to get my kid to safety and didn't want to blow my cover, it's what I'd do.

I glance across to Diavolo, wishing I could tell him my thoughts, but I can see his thoughts churning, the way he's quietly scrutinizing Jonah and the newcomer. Even the way he's sitting back in his chair and smoothing out his features, somehow making himself look less threatening.

Just like a predator would.

Don't let your prey know they're in danger.

Well, we're here now, and for now, I'll play along, too.

I squeeze Elijah's hand.

This child is the only one not playing a game. If there's any truth in all this, it's that Vanguard loves his son, and Elijah loves his father.

I'll find a way into the empire. *After* I get Elijah where he needs to go. Wherever the hell that safe place actually is.

At Jonah's reply, Lucian has given a dismissive wave, his

fingertips grazing the air near my face. If he cares about my presence, he makes no sign. "Well, obviously, that's where you're headed because only a fool would defy the Ultima Nostra."

He inclines his head sharply at the empty seats on the other side of the aisle and it takes me a moment to realize he wants Jonah to move there.

The fire jotunn hesitates. He hasn't left Elijah the whole time and he promised Vanguard he wouldn't. Stiffly, he obeys, stepping into the aisle, but he doesn't go so far as to sit in one of the other seats.

My attention returns to the newcomer.

Who the fuck is this guy anyway?

The shadow he casts is like an aura, but I can't make heads or tails of it. *What* is he?

Lucian slips into Jonah's seat opposite me, moving with the confident manner of someone who never encounters resistance and doesn't have to work hard to get his own way.

He ignores Anarchy, who hasn't stopped staring at him.

She's awfully restrained in her reaction. Her nostrils flare as if she's dragging his scent into her lungs, but she doesn't bare her teeth. If anything, the flicker of her brown eyes to me indicates that she's confused.

"Well, this is cozy," Lucian says, finally focusing on me, then Diavolo, then Elijah. "But wait." He points from Diavolo to Jonah with a laugh, leaning slightly out of his chair to single them out. "Get yourselves some fucking sunglasses, would you?"

Jonah doesn't appear amused and neither does the keeper. He may be making an effort to appear non-threatening, but his brown-eyed persona is in danger of slipping, a hint of blue clouding his eyes. With a shock, I make out a thread of black light, as thin as the finest wire, winding around the fingers of his left hand, where he's concealing it at his side.

Dark magic.

I'm uncertain where he's drawing the power from, but it's

most likely the environment we're passing by. We've left the coastline and have entered a forested area.

But it's the fact that he feels the need to draw on his darkest power that unsettles me. He didn't even use dark magic when we first fought Jonah and Vanguard.

Exhaling my tension, I smile across at Lucian, giving him my softest, most welcoming smile.

His focus was passing across me, dismissive of my existence, but now he pauses. I imagine he isn't accustomed to garnering smiles from potential opponents.

"You know you're being very impolite," I say, tipping my head a little and causing my long, black braid to swish across the tattoos down my right arm. "You haven't introduced yourself."

His lips purse, as if he's now studying me with interest.

"You first," he says.

Risking the worst of the light, I slowly reach up and pull off my sunglasses. I'm not afraid to show him my full fake face, especially since I look too sweet to squash a fly. Even the fire mage thought I was a pixie.

"I'm Veda," I say, and then I gesture at the keeper. "This is Diavolo."

Lucian doesn't deign to glance in the keeper's direction, fixated on me, his gaze passing down my seated body.

I'd like to think he's sizing me up out of respect for my possible strength, but his growing smile tells me otherwise.

I lean forward a little, resting my elbows on my knees and giving him a full view of my cleavage.

Come on now. Come closer...

"And you are?" I ask, gesturing to his sunglasses. "Unless you wish to continue being impolite."

Lucian chews the inside of his lip for a moment before a smile breaks across his face.

His teeth are perfect.

A perfect smile for an overly perfect mouth in a starlit face.

He slowly reaches up and removes his glasses, his focus cast down for a moment so it takes another beat before he looks up.

Golden eyes gleam at me.

The unnatural eyes of a predator. The same color as mine.

So much the same that it's like looking in a mirror.

My smile doesn't falter. My expression doesn't change.

I am neither confused nor disturbed because the fact that this man has eyes like mine can only mean he's related to my uncle, my father's brother. The man Mom never trusted.

It would certainly explain his strange aura—the eerie shadow of a dark angel. It could also be why Anarchy seems confused. If I'm related to Lucian, then she will likely smell the blood connection.

What I need to confirm is whether Lucian is my uncle's *son* or—dark saints forbid—another brother Mom didn't know about, and where both he and my uncle sit in the current empire. If not at the top, then high up, given the way Lucian ordered Jonah about.

Lucian continues to survey me with the kind of calm that belongs to someone who always has the upper hand. Without taking his eyes off me, he crooks his fingers at Jonah.

The fire jotunn doesn't seem to be in any doubt about what's required of him. He clears his throat.

"Veda. Diavolo," he says. "Allow me to introduce Lucian Nostra, the Ultima Nostra's son."

"Well, well," I whisper. "The son himself."

My smile grows, because now I know whom I need to kill.

CHAPTER THIRTY-SEVEN

"*W*ell met, son of the Ultima Nostra." My voice is soft as I acknowledge Lucian with a nod. "It's a pleasure."

Inside me, the deepest, darkest, most delighted pit has opened up. It's a pit inside which there is a well of fury and malice, and until this moment, I've kept it closed. Because I didn't yet have a target.

Now I know where my vengeance will begin, the steps I'll take to make sure my uncle feels all the pain I can possibly inflict on him.

It will start with the death of his son.

Oh, I'm going to end you slowly, and I'm going to enjoy it.

Beside me, Elijah's hand has loosened and opposite me, the keeper has kept his dark magic from burgeoning.

Maybe it's the smile I'm wearing that's calming them. Who knows?

I lean forward again, and my fucking cousin gives my breasts another onceover. Of course, he doesn't know we're related.

"You can rest assured, son of the Ultima Nostra," I say. "We're taking Elijah where he needs to go."

I'm not yet certain how we'll evade Lucian in this endeavor, but if I can manipulate this situation so that it looks like a failure on his part—to make it so that *he* lost the boy—then that's what I'll do.

I have no idea if his father is the forgiving type, but it will be a first step in bringing both Lucian and my uncle down.

Soon enough, the train begins slowing again, pulling into the next station, and my mind is working at a million miles an hour, since the crucial point will come when we need to disembark in Boston. Luckily, Jonah said that this leg of the journey takes a while, so I've got a little time to figure it out.

My biggest problem is that I don't know exactly where Elijah's supposed to go. If I did, I could wrangle it so that the keeper could translocate us right there.

It would have helped if Jonah had shared that information.

The train pulls to a stop, and my attention is drawn to the humans.

Every single one of them stands up, bags in hand, and moves down the aisle to disembark. Their eyes are still dazed and it suddenly dawns on me that Orlan hasn't released them from their mindless haze since Lucian appeared.

Jonah and the keeper are watching them too, and even Lucian's forehead is creased.

A quick glance through the far doors tells me that the humans in the next car are also disembarking.

Within seconds, every one of them is gone. I suspect—but can't know for sure—that the entire train has emptied of human passengers.

Jonah casts an alarmed glance at Elijah, clearly torn about leaving the boy before he hurries toward Orlan. "Orlan! What the fuck?"

Orlan has risen out of his seat and is following the last human out. He half-turns and raises his hand to his forehead in some sort of salute before he slips toward the door. "Sorry, Jonah."

Then he picks up his pace, racing from the car, dragging his hand across every surface he passes: the doors, even the air, sparks flying from both of his palms.

The doors slam shut behind him, the train takes off with a sharp lurch, much faster than it should be going, and the pressure within the car increases dramatically.

Fuck!

My earplugs only seem to worsen the pressure in my ears. I rip the plugs out with my free hand, just as Elijah wrenches his hand from mine and grabs at his headphones, tearing them from his head and rocking forward with a cry. He knocks off his sunglasses in the process, but his eyes are squeezed shut, so I still can't see them.

I reach for him, wrapping my hands across his ears.

"Try swallowing!" I cry. Not that my own attempts to clear my ears have helped.

Across from me, Lucian is up and out of his chair, the confident smile he wore only seconds ago vanishing from his face. "Jonah!" he shouts. "What the hell is going on?"

Jonah's voice sounds before he reappears in the aisle beside me. "We've been betrayed."

Heat radiates out from his form and all the visible veins running across his skin are turning to lava. "It can only be Halle."

Lucian's golden eyes widen. "Vanguard's sister?" He shakes his head. "My father dealt with her years ago."

Jonah stares back at Lucian with clear derision. "If you thought she was dead, that's what she *wanted* you to believe. Now get out of the fucking way."

Lucian isn't *in* Jonah's way, so it's a confusing order.

Jonah inclines his head sharply in Diavolo's direction.

Oh.

Diavolo smiles and the temperature around us lowers to freezing cold as he rises out of his chair. The acidic scent of smoke fills my chest, hot and cold at the same time, a mind-spinning combination.

His eyes turn white, his skin becomes gray like burned ash, and his size increases so fast that his shirt tears. The ripped material floats off his body while his pants stretch dangerously tight around his thighs.

Lucian jolts in his seat, finally paying attention, but not in time to save himself from what must be the very unpleasant experience of Diavolo's enenra arm sailing through Lucian's chest.

Diavolo plows past Lucian into the aisle.

"Fuck!" Lucian shouts, recoiling against his seat.

Diavolo pauses beside him. His voice is cold. "You should hide now, boy." And to me, he says, "Protect Elijah until we can make a move."

"Hide?" Lucian snaps, jumping up from his seat. "Fuck you." He lowers his voice, facing up to the keeper. "When this is over, you're dead."

Diavolo stares back at him, a mountain of ash and smoke beside Lucian's starry sky appearance.

"You first," Diavolo says, gesturing for Lucian to step ahead of him in the aisle.

Lucian's eyes narrow before he pushes in front of Diavolo. "We'll see who lives, old man."

When Lucian turns his back on the keeper, Diavolo throws me a smile. It's a wicked grin. Maybe he's tuning in to my thoughts about making Lucian fail. Certainly, he goaded Lucian into joining him in the first line of defense.

Assuming Halle attacks from that direction.

If my ears weren't so full, I might be able to hear her approach, whether or not it's from the sky or some other direction. Of course, she might already be on board—could have been on board the whole time, and will merely stroll on in to our car.

Jonah has remained in the empty space of the seating area beside ours. He draws closer to me, true to his promise to guard Elijah with his life.

He gives me a brief nod before he returns his attention to our surroundings.

I want nothing more than to demand to know where Elijah needs to go, but I have to wait until the fight starts so there's no chance Lucian will overhear.

Outside in the darkness, the forest has thickened. The train is traveling much faster than it should be—so fast, it doesn't take the next curve of track so well. Elijah is jostled against my side. I snatch up his sunglasses before they can slide across the floor, push them into his hands, and then haul him up into my arms. Anarchy draws closer to my legs, placing herself between me and danger.

No sooner have I lifted Elijah onto my lap than the roof of the car only five rows in front of us explodes upward, metal shrieking.

The pressure in my ears releases just as dark ropes snake through the opening above.

Not ropes.

Vines.

They're black, charred, and dead-looking, but they twine across the ceiling, tearing it up as if they were made of something stronger than metal.

Within heartbeats, the vines rip through every seat around their point of entry, wrenching the chairs up from the floor, wrapping around them and crushing them against the sides of the car. It happens so fast that the seats may as well be made of nothing more than paper.

I've barely blinked when eight rows have been ripped up,

four in each direction, creating an open space only a row ahead of me.

Gad and Valki are on the far side of it, both poised for a fight.

Lucian positions himself on this side of the open area with Diavolo at his side while Jonah continues to stand guard beside me and Elijah. Anarchy has risen to her feet and bares her teeth at the hole in the ceiling.

A woman drops through the gap above us, landing lightly on her feet.

She has auburn hair and bright, green eyes. A dusting of freckles across her nose. A slight cleft in her chin. I'm surprised to see that she's petite, thin, practically a whisp of a thing. She's wearing a mere slip of material masquerading as a skirt and a leafy-green sleeveless crop top that shows off a hell of a lot of her pale skin.

Damn, I thought *I* looked sweet. This woman could rot my teeth.

If the vines around us weren't slowly crushing chairs, I'd believe this lady was harmless.

She's unbelievably calm as she ignores Gad and Valki and seeks Jonah first.

"The harpies you had monitoring the sky are dead, Jonah. Your warlock, Orlan, belongs to me. You know you don't have a hope of beating me, so I'll give you one chance."

She smiles. "Give me the child now, and I'll let you live."

CHAPTER THIRTY-EIGHT

I growl a response before Jonah can speak. It's a very un-pixie-like sound for me to make. "You can fucking *try* to take him."

I rise to my feet, holding Elijah close as I make my presence known. It wasn't the wisest move since the train is hurtling along so fast and Elijah is heavy in my arms, making my footing unsteady. I have to lean against the side of the chair to keep my balance. But she would have spotted us within seconds anyway, and this way, I can let her know she'll have a fight when she gets to me.

Halle's lips twitch as she shifts her focus off the men and onto me. "What a slip of a girl to say such a thing to me."

I smile. "You're not so intimidating yourself."

I guess my comment makes her mad because her perfect features disappear. For a second, one half of her face and body appears blackened and charred, her eye on that side gleaming red. Even her clothing is split right down the middle, gleaming, black leather on the charred side.

Not so sweet after all.

Fucking Goddess of Death.

Half alive. Half living death. Certainly, she's a mistress of her own illusion.

Within a blink, she resumes her full auburn-haired façade.

She plows toward me, but Gad and Valki rush at her from behind. At their approach, she turns, crouches, and throws her hands out. Vines shoot from her fingers, growing in length the longer she extends her arms and moving with her.

Gad is ahead of Valki and the vines thump into him first, wrapping around his torso, lifting him off the floor, and driving him against the side of the car.

Valki leaps, making it within inches of Halle's side, but more vines fly from Halle's shoulder, punching into Valki's chest. One of them impales her shoulder and spears right through it.

Blood bursts from Valki's shoulder and she screams as the vine curls up and around the back of her neck and whips around her throat. She gets her hands up just in time before the rope closes around her neck and she, too is hurled against the side of the car.

Gasping, she claws at the tightening vine. "This is my trick... bitch."

Halle pauses. "Oh, that's right. You like to strangle your victims. Well, if you don't want the vines to cut your head from your shoulders, I suggest you shut the fuck up."

Halle jumps back to her feet, and with a shake of her wrists, the vines break off from her fingers, freeing her to charge in my direction once more.

I'm surprised she didn't kill Gad and Valki on the spot, but quite possibly, she's keeping them alive for other purposes.

Halle screams as she rages in my direction. "Which fool wishes to get in my way next?"

She doesn't wait for an answer, spearing the space in front of her with vines that shoot toward both Diavolo and Lucian at the same time.

I imagine she intended to dispense with them as quickly as she dealt with Gad and Valki.

The vines sail on through Diavolo's smoky body and tear up the chairs behind him without doing him any damage to his chest.

As for Lucian, his wings thump out at his sides and shadows burst from his body, darkening the space all around us. His feathers are so black that they nearly disappear within the shadows while his skin only glows more brightly.

As the vines shoot toward him, he sweeps his wings. Not down so as to propel himself into the air, but across the space in front of his body. There's a flash, then multiple sparks, as he cuts across the vines with the tips of his wings.

My eyes widen as, for a second, I think he's managed to cut through them, which would be impossible since feathers are soft... *Aren't they?*

Then I see that he's deflected the vines, not severed them, somehow using his wings as shields, beating back Halle's attacks as he pushes toward her.

Diavolo leaps forward, too.

Halle gives a scream of frustration, backtracking a few steps, and that's all I see before I whirl to Jonah.

"Tell me where to take Elijah," I whisper. "Give me the location and I'll get him to safety."

Jonah shakes his head, one eye on the fight ahead of us. "No."

"Look, you don't trust me. Well, I don't fucking trust you. After all, you were going to use us as scapegoats."

His focus snaps to me.

"Yeah, I'm not stupid," I murmur, although I'm disappointed that his expression confirms my theory. "The fact is, neither of us should trust the other. But I *can* make you a promise."

I grab his arm with my free hand despite the molten lava covering his skin.

Searing pain bursts across my palm.

Jonah jolts, his eyes widening, but I don't let go because I've got his full attention now.

The light around the edge of my palm fades—a sign he's reducing his power there—but the residual heat is intense.

"I'm going to tell a lot of lies," I whisper. "That's my nature as a dark creature. But I'll give you a truth: When I look at this kid, I see myself. A pawn in a game played by adults. And I won't fucking allow it. Do you hear me?" I grip him harder, the pain searing me, burning to a point where I believe the agony will stop soon because the nerves will die.

"I won't. Fucking. Allow it."

Jonah stares back at me, searching my eyes. Then his focus drops to Elijah, who's buried his head in my shoulder. Then farther down to Anarchy, who's snarling up at both of us.

"Tell me where to take him!" I snap.

Jonah's jaw clenches. The furrow in his brow is deep. But he doesn't look away. Beneath his breath, he says, "St. Michael Cemetery."

I let him go.

I can't feel my hand.

The sensations in it are as dead as my hopes of getting into the inner circle tonight.

I tell myself I'll find another way. For now, I need to focus on the problems in front of me.

"Keep the witch busy," I say to Jonah.

I step back from him, my only purpose to get the keeper's attention so he can translocate us out of here.

But I was focused on Jonah for a moment too long.

I step directly into the path of an oncoming vine.

It strikes toward my right side, sailing on through the keeper's body, and it's not my own life I'm worried about.

It will hit Elijah first.

It will drive right through his little ribs and tear his chest apart.

In that heartbeat, my mind works through all the terrible options. No time to turn and take the blow on my left. No time to extend the claws of my right hand, and even if I do, I'll impale Elijah since my fingers are pressing into his back. No time to duck all the way since the vine will strike, not through Elijah, but through my own head.

No time for Jonah to throw himself in front of me, although his muscles are bunching, and I know that's what he's doing.

No time, no time, no time—

I'm dropping, turning, trying to get down and expose my left side to protect Elijah when a dark body flies up in front of me, taking the blow.

Anarchy.

No!

She yelps. Blood sprays across me.

A scream wrenches out of me and then we all go down.

I hit the floor, partially on my back, partly on my side, Elijah cradled in my arms, Anarchy on top of us.

I'm aware of Elijah screaming and crying against my chest.

I'm aware of the blur of amber light as Jonah rushes away from me, throwing himself into the fight with Halle, shouting for Diavolo to help me. "Fucking help her!"

I'm aware of the movement of black wings and shadows as Lucian continues to deflect Halle's attacks, briefly glancing back at me, without a hint of pity.

But it's the keeper's presence I need.

Like a dark cloud, he storms toward me, vaulting the chairs, tearing them apart to get to me.

"Veda!"

"Anarchy," I cry. "Help her."

She's so still where she lies on top of me, a protective shield, her doggie illusion peeling away until her silver claws are revealed, resting at my side while her whiskers tickle my arm.

The keeper's features are as wild as the ocean we once slept beside as his hands hover over her.

"Where?" he asks, a harsh, unfeeling question that must surely defy the pain I'm streaming into his heart.

I know what he's asking.

Not where is she hurt, or where am I hurt, but where do we take the child.

"St. Michael Cemetery."

His forehead creases. "But that's…" He glances at Jonah, as if he's perplexed.

I don't know why and there isn't time to ask.

Using all of my strength, I lurch into a sitting position, clutching at Anarchy's heavy body with my left arm, pushing Elijah toward the keeper.

I turn my eyes up to his. "We need to go. Help me with them."

He seems to shake off his misgivings, giving me a single nod before his big arms close around both Elijah and Anarchy, pulling them safely to his chest.

I lean in behind them, stroking Anarchy's head and pressing my cheek to hers for a moment. I'm splattered with her blood, but I ignore it.

I want to believe that her chest is moving and that her claws are twitching. I want to believe that, somehow, Diavolo will use his magic to save her. Heal the deadly wound that struck through her upper body and bring her back to me.

The haze of transportation energy builds around us, a swirling mist that squeezes my chest and will take me far away from here within seconds. To a cemetery, no less.

I keep my focus on the keeper, noting the way his white eyes are suddenly turning sharp blue and in that moment, I wonder: *Does he sense what I'm about to do?*

As the mist builds around us, I fight the pressure around my torso, pushing myself closer to him, managing to reach his lips. I press a kiss to them. A brief touch. Nothing more.

"Thank you," I whisper.

The magic takes hold, but I'm already pushing off him, propelling myself backward with all my strength, out of the mist and away from his power.

He shouts my name, but his arms are full. His magic streaks toward me, trying to pull me back in, but I'm beyond his reach.

The swirling mist draws in on itself and then the keeper, Elijah, and Anarchy are gone, leaving me with my rage.

CHAPTER THIRTY-NINE

I don't have a heart anymore.

If I did, I would feel now what I experienced when my dying mother gasped her final breaths. What I felt when she closed her eyes for the last time.

My mother was my pack.

Anarchy was my pack.

They're both gone.

I may not be able to feel the grief in my heart, but I know it within my mind. It takes the form of a festering fury that will never leave me.

I don't wait for Halle to realize that her target is gone, or for Lucian to see that he's lost Elijah. I don't make a sound, don't let loose the scream rising to my throat.

Quietly, I crouch and extend my claws, studying the fight in front of me, the way that Halle tries to strike Jonah even though his fiery skin burns her vines to dust, the way that Lucian tries to get close to her, only to be driven back again. She uses her vines like whips, striking and withdrawing them in a dance that would be deadly if she could get past Lucian's wings or Jonah's fiery flames.

It seems that she'll only separate the vines from her body once she's caught her prey, as she did with Gad and Valki, both of whom are now so encased in black ropes that their mouths and eyes are covered. I doubt they're able to hear or see a thing.

They may not even be alive.

Then, Halle manages to land a blow on both Lucian and Jonah at the same time, her vines twining around Jonah's neck for long enough to fling him backward and striking at Lucian's ankles hard enough to pull him off-balance.

Both men hit the floor and are now out of her immediate path.

Halle charges forward, her eyes wildly searching the cabin.

Searching for Elijah.

It's the opening I wanted.

My muscles coil beneath me. I ready my claws. As quietly as a shadow panther, I leap through the gap the two men created, the muscles in my legs giving me air.

Halle's eyes widen as I bear down on her. Her hands shoot out, new vines streaking from them, but I expected her defense.

My claws cut across the vines, slicing right through them. Just as I cut Vanguard's snakes apart.

Halle gives a scream of pain.

Blood bursts across her fingertips as though I'd cut her hands instead of the vines.

She recoils, her eyes wide, fear striking through her expression. She attempts to backpedal even as I land right in front of her.

Her scream of agony continues to peel from her lips while she fixates on my claws and stumbles in her attempt to get away. "No... It can't be..."

I don't stop.

My mother taught me to fight dirty, so that's what I do.

I slash at Halle's face, the tips of my claws slicing her

cheekbone, cutting through the illusion she wears on the dead side of her face.

Black bones are exposed through the wounds, and I want only to strike deeper, to slice right through them. I slash again, but she manages to throw her arms up in time, taking the cuts across her forearms.

With her arms up over her face, her chest is exposed, and I ram my other fist at her heart, my claws making it within an inch of her skin before her hand snaps down and closes around my wrist, stopping me.

But not my other hand.

My other claws slip between her ribs, puncturing one of her lungs. Desperately, she tries to defend herself, audibly struggling to breathe as I strike again. And again. Cutting open her shoulder, gashing her ribs, driving my claws straight through her bones until her blood flows freely across her face, chest, and arms.

Any other supernatural would be dead now, but a goddess, well, it seems she's hard to kill.

I wrench backward, giving myself space to kick her chest, right where I punctured her lung, and knock her to the ground.

She falls heavily, her arms held up over her face once more. "It wasn't me!"

Her words barely register. The strangeness of them. As if she didn't kill Anarchy.

I drop onto her, ramming my knee against her chest, gratified by the *pop-pop* when two of her ribs break.

"You killed her," I snarl.

"No," she screams—a breathy cry as she tries to drag air into her body. "I would never betray her! It wasn't me!"

I pause, my forehead creasing. "Betray?"

Who does she think we're talking about?

Now that I've stopped striking Halle, I'm aware that, in the background, Lucian is shouting and Jonah is restraining him— or attempting to. Lucian's fighting hard against his hold.

I can only assume Lucian has discovered that Elijah's gone.

"I'll fucking kill you, Veda!" he screams at me. "You're fucking dead!"

"Veda." Halle's whisper draws me back to her. "Is that what she called you?"

"Who?" I ask, but my hollow heart is sinking because I think I know the answer.

"Galeia," she whispers. "You have her claws."

I'm frozen as it hits me that this woman, who stood at my father's side, had to have known my mother.

It seems she has recognized my claws—the same claws my mother had.

Now, my mother finally has a name: *Galeia.*

But that knowledge comes at a cost and an awful realization.

Because if Halle so instantly recognized my claws, then why didn't Vanguard?

Well, damn.

Of course he did.

I squeeze my eyes shut for a dangerous moment because I'm not sure exactly what this means. I don't know what Vanguard's true motives are. Or Jonah's, for that matter.

At the very least, they thought to use me to get Elijah to safety. After all, Vanguard insisted I was strong enough to fight his sister, and so I am.

But what other motivations could he have had? Will he have warned my uncle already or kept my secret until he can use it to his best advantage?

How much does Jonah know?

My focus is drawn to the fire jotunn, but I can't read anything in his expression.

All I'm certain of is that I can't trust any of them.

I can't trust anything they say or do.

"I don't know what you did or didn't do to my mother," I snarl at Halle. "But she died in that prison. She fucking died gasping for breath, and still she fought to keep me alive. Nobody came for her, and for that, you'll pay."

With a cry of rage, I drive my claws toward Halle's face, surprised when she doesn't try to defend herself this time. She lowers her arms with a single, quick movement.

"Don't kill me!" she cries.

Her features have changed. Now she stares up at me with a wrinkled visage, her body covered in tattered clothing.

I recognize the beanie she's wearing since it previously rested on my own head.

She's the homeless woman I saw in the park!

"You." A deep growl drags out of me. I ram my claws at her shoulder. "You made me believe you were homeless!"

"I watched over that statue every night. It was my only connection with your mo—"

Her speech ends in a scream as I dig my claws deep into her shoulder. "I want my boots back."

She's gasping for breath but not so badly as before, and my instincts tell me she's stalling for time. Hell, I can slash her all I like and she'll heal right up.

She's the fucking goddess of death.

She tries again. "Your kindness the other night—"

"Don't insult me! *Kindness*? You've got to be fucking kidding me. I will never walk past a shivering woman. That's not *kindness*. It's simple decency. But *you*." My lips twist. "Pretending to be in need."

Her expression turns stone cold. "Pretending? I've spent years soaked in my own piss and that weak-as-fuck liquid humans call 'alcohol.' Anything to bury the past."

"Don't give me your sob story," I warn. "I don't have the heart for it."

As I speak, my instincts shout at me that I've paused for too long. I should have slashed her face off by now. Torn out her heart. Anything to get what I need.

Her hands were formed into fists when she held her arms across her face, but now she extends her fingers.

They're fully healed.

A vine streaks up at my side, shooting between our chests, thumping against my stomach like the side of her arm, strong enough to shove me off her. She pushes me so hard that I gain air, but I easily land at a crouch a few paces away.

She's already rising upward, the energy around her beating at the air, lifting her without wings.

"You're on the wrong side of this, Veda," she calls, and with that, she soars up through the hole in the ceiling and disappears into the night.

I'm exactly where I need to be.

I hold on to that thought even when Lucian rages toward me, his wings tucked into his sides. His cheeks are flushed, his lips twisted, and the starry quality of his skin has been replaced with dark shadows.

A cut on his cheek is oozing blood.

Red blood.

One of Halle's vines must have nicked him, but damn, that wound seems to be taking a long time to heal.

The color of his blood and the fact that the cut isn't healing quickly confirms what Mom told me: the second child—that is, my uncle—is always weaker, and so are their offspring. The power dilutes with every subsequent child.

In the background, Jonah crosses his arms over his chest.

Even if he knows who I really am, there's one thing I'm sure of: Lucian doesn't.

He's too young to have met my mother. At most, he would have been a baby when my father was murdered, if he had yet been born at all.

If he *had* realized my real identity when he saw my claws, he wouldn't be screaming about me stealing Elijah. He'd be focused on the fact that I'm his cousin with a claim to the empire.

I've remained standing in the middle of the cleared area, and I could easily duck the fist he aims at my face, but I choose not to, recoiling just enough that I won't bleed.

The last thing I want is for Lucian to see my black blood.

Anarchy's blood could camouflage it, but I can't be sure, and for now, Lucian may well believe her red blood is my own. There's so much of it that he may even believe me to be badly injured.

I drop to my knees, registering the pain in my face, holding my hand over my cheek as a safeguard.

I don't have any feeling in that palm, since it's the one I burned when I was trying to make Jonah listen to me.

Lucian roars at me. "Where's Elijah?"

Without waiting for my response, he reaches down, wraps his hand around my throat, and wrenches me into the air. His hand nearly slips in Anarchy's blood, but he holds on tightly.

"Tell me where you sent him!"

I glare down at Lucian, my throat too constricted to speak even if I wanted to.

"Tell me!" he roars before he throws me to the ground.

I let myself land hard on my side, and I take the kick he aims at my stomach.

As the air *whooshes* past my lips, I gasp, "I'll only speak to your father."

He crouches to me, his question sharp. "What?"

It's a good thing I heal quickly or the lacerations he left around my throat would prevent me from speaking at all. "You want to know where Elijah is?" I rasp. "Take me to your father."

With a shout of frustration, Lucian rams his fist down onto my head again. There's nowhere for me to go this time to lessen the blow and I sense the skin split across my cheek.

I throw my hands up over my face, just like Halle did, hoping to cover the blood, watching Lucian through the gaps between my arms, but he doesn't seem to be paying attention to my features.

He leans back on his heels, running his hands into his hair and gripping hard. "Dad's going to kill me."

Jonah's voice sounds from behind him and it's surprisingly worried. Probably because he thinks I'll reveal Elijah's location despite my vow to protect the boy. "Your father wouldn't go that far—"

"No?" Lucian jumps to his feet and whirls on Jonah. "You think he hasn't been waiting for an excuse?"

"Losing the boy is *my* failure."

Lucian's lips twist. "But my father needs you, Jonah. You're useful to him."

Jonah's brow furrows. "You're his heir. Without you—"

"He can fuck another woman. Have another heir."

Jonah seems to have no comeback for that.

When he remains silent, Lucian retracts his wings, and I notice again the way the edges of his outer feathers glint before they disappear.

I struggle up to my knees, groaning and not entirely faking my pain. It seems that my palm has some feeling left in it after all.

At least my vocal chords are healing and my voice is stronger. "Either kill me or take me to your father. It's your choice."

Lucian crouches down in front of me again. His focus finally lowers to my hands, which are now resting on my knees, but I retracted my claws as soon as Halle left. My left palm is badly burned.

His voice is quieter. "You must think I'm fucking stupid."

I remain silent and he raises his eyes to mine.

"I don't know how you cut through Halle's magic, but I know you could have killed me with those claws already." His hand whips out, wrapping around my throat again, squeezing slowly this time.

"Do it," he says.

I attempt to lean back from him, eyeing him warily. "Do what?"

"End me!"

Does he think I would be more merciful than his father?

My closed fist rams down on his arm, knocking his hand away from my throat. "Take me to your father."

His lips twist as he jumps to his feet again. "Jonah, restrain her! Or better yet, knock her out and keep her that way." His chest heaves as he continues. "I have my own people placed along this train line and we should reach their position in another five minutes. They can get us off this train. We'll be back in New York soon enough."

Jonah approaches me, his footsteps appearing cautious.

I imagine he wishes he could read my mind.

Will I betray Elijah's location? Have I figured out that Jonah knows who I am? What else might I know?

Have I come to kill him, too?

I have as many questions for Jonah as he must have for me, yet I can't ask any of them.

Even if I could, I wouldn't trust the answers he'd give me.

Oh, these dark paths we walk.

I don't speak, other than to turn my burned palm up as a reminder of my promise that Elijah would be safe.

Maybe Jonah will read it that way. Maybe he'll read it as a threat.

But his feelings don't matter to me.

My thoughts are now fixed on my purpose and turned firmly away from the knowledge that I lost Anarchy tonight.

The keeper will get Elijah to the people who can keep him safe.

The keeper will bury Anarchy.

And then, his vow to me will bring him back to me.

But by then, I'll be face to face with my father's murderer.

Jonah reaches down to me, his forefinger glowing.

I consider his hand warily, since I assumed he'd try to punch the lights out of me.

"What are you—?"

I scream as he presses his burning finger to my temple and a fire bursts to life within my mind.

Recoiling from him, I try to leap backward, but his other arm has scooped around me, trapping me, hauling me up against his chest even as I thrash against him, my screams splitting my hearing.

Then the fire goes out and takes me with it.

Into blessed darkness.

CHAPTER FORTY

J dream of a beautiful home.

It has inky-blue walls decorated with swirling, silver filigree. The sunlight is muted through gauzy, black curtains, a forest visible between the folds of material that lift in the cool breeze. The trees surrounding my home have broad branches and cold shadows beneath them, but no matter what I do, I can't seem to leave this house.

My mother's silhouette passes across the edge of my vision, and I can't reach her. I hear her humming in the kitchen as she cleaves meat. Her footfalls through the halls and the soft scraping of the tips of her claws against the walls. The plucking of black roses as she appears bent over a garden bed outside my window.

She's always out of reach.

The dream fades as I regain consciousness.

I return to a dull pain, a throbbing in my head and in my left hand.

I'm also upside down.

Hanging in the dark.

There's a soft, slow, dripping sound nearby.

My arms fall beside my face, my hands aren't tied, but the pressure around my ankles tells me my feet are bound together. As soon as I can bring myself to tense my stomach muscles, I'll try to see my bindings and whatever contraption is keeping me in this spot.

My shirt isn't covering my face. It's gone altogether, although I can feel that I'm still wearing a bra, and my long, black pants seem to be in place. My hair is tied back. I'm not sure how, but it isn't falling into my face.

It means I have a clear view all around me.

What strikes me first is the little metal device attached to the forefinger of my left hand.

My finger is cut, the smallest wound, and the metal contraption is keeping the wound open.

My blood is dripping to the ground below me, forming a black puddle.

My tattoo is all but gone. Maybe the lightest smudge of it remains, but I have no doubt my true features are fully visible.

So is most of the dark room around me.

It's not unlike the room I dreamed of.

The walls are inky blue with glistening spots like stars across them. Possibly a very high ceiling. Shadows lurk there, so it's hard to tell how far up it goes.

The whole space is maybe fifty paces from side to side and, other than what I suspect is some kind of pulley that I'm hanging from, the only furniture in the room is a pedestal. Its top is slanting away from me, so I can't tell if there's anything resting on it.

The shadows above me move at the corner of my vision.

A deep voice sounds, a low, rumbling whisper. "I'm surprised you haven't freed yourself already."

I fight against the pure chill that passes down my spine. I can't quite place its point of origin since the shadows I crane my neck to see are swirling at multiple points above me.

I wonder if the speaker is hanging from the rafters like a fucking vampire.

"I'm enjoying the view," I say. "It's really quite lovely from this angle." I shrug my shoulders, a weird-feeling gesture in this position. "In fact, you've given me a new perspective on life. I might do this more often."

The shadow closest to my right dives to the ground, landing with a soft *thump* before wings become visible. They separate with a *whoosh* to reveal the man they belong to.

He's the same height as the keeper's blue-eyed form. His hair is black and his skin is even fairer than Lucian's. Looking at him is like gazing at a distant star.

His golden eyes graze over me, as if I'm a curiosity, a thing to be studied.

He can only be my uncle. The false Ultima Nostra.

Mom once said there's no creature so ethereal, or so deadly, as a dark angel.

Of course, she never met the keeper, but even so, I can't disagree with her claim.

This angel is beautiful in every way. Every perfect angle of his face, every curve of muscle in his chiseled, yet lithe, form. Even in the softening of his eyes, as if he can convince me that he won't hurt me.

He has the same basic features as my father in the image I saw, torn from *The Book of Dark Magic*, but this usurper is leaner, gaunter, and his smile is cruel.

"Well, hello there," I whisper. "I've been waiting a long time to meet you."

Finally bunching my stomach muscles, I curl upward, my claws extending in a flash. I cut through the bindings around my ankles, twisting before I fall and landing at a crouch. I make sure I miss the puddle of blood in which I would surely slip.

Slowly, I rise upward, ripping the little metal contraption from my finger while I keep my uncle in my sights.

I take a moment to reach back to my hair, loosening it from the looped braid it was caught up in and checking the strands. They're black with golden ends once more.

My real hair.

No more illusion.

My uncle doesn't appear alarmed that I've freed myself so easily. He himself said he was surprised I hadn't done it already. Although I do wonder that he didn't try harder to chain me in the first place.

No doubt he wants to play a game now. Like the dark creature he is.

"My son tells me you call yourself 'Veda,'" he says. "Did your mother give you that name?"

"No." It might be one of the few truths he gets from me. "She gave me the power to name myself."

"So very like Galeia." He chews the inside of his lip, a similar mannerism to his son's. "I would ask you why you're here, but your name tells me everything." He steps closer. "You've come to kill me."

My claws remain extended. "I have."

He gives me a nod.

Then he calls out, "Lucian, come down here."

A second shadow shifts on the ceiling before it dives to the floor.

My cousin opens his wings, folding them to his sides, and I hide my surprise at what I see.

His face is cut up. Far more than the wounds Halle inflicted on him. There's a red ring around his neck that looks like it was made with knotted rope. He's wearing a long-sleeved T-shirt, but bruises are visible at the sleeves and his knuckles are busted up.

His skin was already pale in color, but his cheeks seem to have drained of blood.

"You can't be real," he says, shaking his head at me.

I read the disbelief in his eyes, the struggle to comprehend what he's seeing—what he must have been seeing for the last little while. My real features slowly revealing themselves.

My uncle, the usurper, gives me a slow smile. "I'll give you one chance to fight me, Veda." He folds his arms across his chest. "But first you have to go through my son."

Lucian tenses. "Father—"

"*You lost the boy!*" my uncle screams at him, the starlight in his skin turning to shadows.

Lucian recoils, his wings suddenly shivering, as if he's fighting the instinct to fly to safety.

"You know I can't beat her," he says without a hint of cunning in his voice. "She'll kill me."

"Really?" The usurper advances on his son. "Why don't I make sure of it."

Lucian's eyes widen. "No... You don't have to—"

He attempts to backpedal, but his father grabs his left wing by the upper bone, yanking it toward himself. In the same instant, he smacks his other fist across Lucian's face. The force of the punch knocks Lucian backward, but his father is still holding on to his wing.

Crack!

Lucian screams and stumbles backward before he collapses to the floor, hunching his shoulders. His broken wing flops at his side.

The usurper bends to his son, dragging his fingers across one of the cuts on his face. "The color of your blood sickens me."

I marvel at his hypocrisy. Even if he siphoned all of my father's power—which is a possibility I can't ignore—it could not have changed the color of his blood to black since he wasn't born with it.

But then, Mom warned me that those who crave power

often ridicule the weaknesses in others that they most loathe about themselves.

The usurper pushes his son away. "Veda will kill you soon enough."

He returns his attention to me, his lips parted as if he's about to speak, but I'm already beside him.

"Hiding behind your son?" I say. "Fucking pathetic."

I ram my claws toward my uncle's neck.

He lurches backward, his reflexes fast. He deflects the blow, knocking my arm clear of his neck, but in moving backward, he has to steer clear of his son's location, and it makes his evasion clumsy.

I didn't expect to take him down easily, so I'm not disappointed that I don't draw blood.

Yet.

"You killed my mother," I say as I follow him around to the right, the hollow in my heart allowing my voice to remain detached. "You took the first twenty-three years of my life."

I don't see any weapons on him. It's possible he prefers to work with his hands.

"You left us in darkness."

"But look how strong you've grown," he says, his white teeth flashing at me. "Despite the odds."

"Strong," I snarl. "And vengeful."

His smile broadens. "Clever, like your mother."

He leaps toward me, using his wings like arms, sweeping them so that he would have taken my feet out from under me if I didn't have the reflexes to jump so fast. Not back, but forward, my claws aimed at his face. I nick his jaw and sense his indrawn breath before he retaliates.

My heartbeat hammers as we trade blows, but I evade nearly every strike. He, too, manages to avoid the worst cuts I aim at his chest and neck.

I wanted to make him suffer. I wanted to kill his son and tear apart his empire and then, only when he felt the pain of losing everything, did I plan to kill him.

But I'm here now, and I won't lose this chance.

As I beat him around the room, I'm aware that he could fly up into the air away from me, but he doesn't seem inclined to do that.

Not until I scratch my claws down his chest, tearing up his shirt.

Then he beats his wings, lifting off the floor and veering backward. Only to use his wings to increase his speed and ram forward into me instead.

The wall is close at my back and I knock into it.

His wings close in on either side of me, the steel-like upper bones pinning my arms against the wall. His hand closes around my throat, choking me and lifting me off the ground at the same time.

My feet can't find purchase and my arms are immobilized, but my fingers are free, and I remind myself that my claws can cut through anything.

There's a cold sort of justice in slicing up his wings.

With a grunt of effort, I flick my claws downward on both sides. Without the movement of my arms, they don't have the same impact, but it's enough to scrape across the tops of his wings, slicing into the bone.

With a shout of alarm, he leaps away from me, but this time, I'm not letting him go.

My right fist closes around his wing, my claws sending a flurry of feathers into the air. I wrench his wing toward the ground, gravity helping me drag him down as I drop into a crouch.

He lands heavily on his knees, struggling to free his wing from my grasp. Before he can succeed, I punch my other claws toward his neck.

He tries to evade the deadly blow by lurching backward,

which, because of my hold on his wing, only takes him closer to the ground.

The worst place he could be.

My claws are at his throat as he lands on his back, and all it will take is a single downward thrust to end his life.

But that's when I notice he's bleeding.

A trickle of blood slides down his neck from the cut across his jaw, working its way around the tips of my claws.

But... that can't be right.

His blood is the color of the night sky.

My voice is strained. "Your blood is black."

Black blood only belongs to the firstborn.

"Of course it is," he says, his eyes softening as he looks up at me. The gentle gaze of a predator. "It always has been."

"No... That's not possible..." I can't breathe. My hollow heart has stopped within my chest. "You died."

What dark fuckery is this?

This can't be real.

He can't be...

Alive, after all.

"Come now." The dark angel bares his teeth at me, his golden eyes consuming my vision. "You wouldn't kill your own father, would you... Daughter?"

Keep reading! Bonus chapter over the page!

BONUS CHAPTER: THE KEEPER
OF DARK MAGIC

I land on my knees in the grass beside a gravestone, clutching Anarchy and Elijah tightly in my arms.

The heart Veda gave me is hammering in my chest, every beat tearing at me.

Her pain. Her fury. Every emotion I took from her when I seized the power in her heart and made it mine. All of it drives me to the ground, where I grit my teeth and fight to focus.

Above us, the beautiful darkness is sprinkled with stars. There are no artificial lights close by. The cemetery stretches out on every side of me. It's dotted with trees, and a paved pathway curves along the ground on my right.

I know this place well. Many dark creatures have died here. Well, not exactly *here*, but in the hidden compound that exists on this very spot unseen by both human and supernatural eyes.

Elijah trembles against my chest, a contrast with Anarchy's stillness. They need help that I can give.

But, dark saints, if it weren't for Veda's heart, I would leave them both to die.

A cold truth.

For hundreds of years, I lived shrouded in death, numb to

the magic I tethered. Unfeeling. As I had to be. It was how I survived.

Now, I feel *everything*.

Every damn blade of grass beneath my knees where my pants are torn. Every sobbing breath Elijah takes. The tickle of his soft hair beneath my chin. The damp of his tears against my neck.

I wish I didn't feel any of it, least of all the hot blood of Anarchy's deadly wound, slowly spreading between her body and mine.

When Veda gave me the power in her heart, I thought only of escaping my cage and of being alive again.

I never dreamed that the heart of the darkest creature—*her* heart—could be capable of feeling so much. No dark creature should have a heart like this.

I was so fucking unprepared.

Even now that we've been separated, I'm driven by her wants and needs as surely as if she were standing next to me, daring me to defy her.

Managing to focus beyond the pain, I scan our surroundings, but whomever Elijah was supposed to meet, they haven't arrived yet. It doesn't surprise me. Translocation has brought us here more quickly than if we'd traveled by train as originally planned.

"Shh," I murmur to him, lying through my teeth. "You're safe with me now."

"Puppy-cat..." he whimpers.

Puppy-cat?

His little hand is resting on Anarchy's face, right across her whiskers. Her canine illusion disappeared when she was wounded, and she is very much a big cat once more.

"The puppy-cat will be fine," I say. "But I need your help. Can you help me?"

Elijah nods against my neck and I carefully place him down

onto the grass, back on his own two feet, before I tuck him into my right side. His eyes are downcast. He appears to be focused on Anarchy, and that's just as well.

Far better for me to stay out of this child's unfettered gaze. I have a strong suspicion that the sunglasses he was wearing were muting his power and I have no desire to look him in the eyes any time soon.

I'm not completely sure what Elijah's power is. He's the son of an old god, which is concern enough, but his mother's power will have also influenced his nature and I can't pinpoint what she might have been.

Unlike Veda. I know exactly what she is. *Who* she is. The moment she revealed her claws in the fight with the angel back at the Cathedral, she confirmed her mother's lineage.

What surprises me is that Veda doesn't seem to know. It appears that her mother was selective in the information she passed on. I can only guess at her motives. Probably, she wanted to protect Veda.

Far from it.

She has doomed her.

Leaning forward, I place Anarchy carefully on the grass, quickly studying the wound from the vine that drove through her shoulders and upper torso. It tore through her ribs near her spine, but not low enough that it would have pierced her heart.

There's still a spark of life within her.

Or rather, a glimmer of living darkness.

"Okay, Elijah," I say. "I need you to stay very still. Can you do that?"

At his nod, I take a deep breath.

Placing my palms flat across Anarchy's wound, I exhale, opening the cage I've placed around my most lethal power, fighting the impulse to set it free.

I opened this cage when Veda needed healing.

I opened it again when she demanded that I kiss her.

Now, I'll open it because her heart will break if I don't.

Carefully... very carefully... I focus on the grass around us, drawing on the life within it. Not only the grass, but the bugs and worms that live within the soil. Then beyond them to the roots of the nearest tree. I tug on the energy that exists in every blade and leaf and in the soundless hum of sap flowing through the tree's trunk. All of it flows into my fingertips, into the crown on my hand, and then outward again through my palm.

I fight the flood of it, allowing only a trickle to flow into Anarchy's body, seeking out the spark of darkness within her. I need the dark magic I'm harnessing to connect with the malice in her soul like two frayed ends of a thread that must come together.

There.

I latch on to the pulse of energy within her heart, dripping the dark magic along it, slowly, very slowly sealing up the ragged edges like mending a rope, twining the two together.

A soft hiss tells me that she's regaining consciousness and I press my palms harder against her. "Easy, Anarchy."

I can't risk her jumping up before I've finished healing her. I don't want to spill the dark magic I'm using or it may shift to the boy, draining his life instead.

As quickly as I can now, I work to seal the broken flesh and bones, muscles and sinew, and finally her skin, building layers of darkness within her until the wound beneath my hand is no more.

She peers up at me with her silver eyes, her claws digging into the dead grass now surrounding us before I lift my hands, allowing her to find her feet.

Released from my grip, she whirls on me, baring her teeth.

If only Veda were here for this, her heart would feel happiness again and this pain in my chest might ease.

In the next moment, Elijah pushes away from me and throws his arms around Anarchy's neck. "Puppy-cat!"

He buries his face in her fur.

Anarchy narrows her eyes at me with a final quick, sharp glance before she turns her attention on Elijah, nudging his face, deep purrs dragging out of her.

I huff softly. "As if it were the boy who saved you."

In the distance, the tree whose energy I drained creaks and groans before it splits up the middle, shattering into smaller pieces and crumbling directly downward into a pile of rotted wood.

I have no remorse. It was the tree or Anarchy.

But then, to my astonishment, the tree's broken pieces pull together, each one rising rapidly upward, sealing and reforming like a puzzle of wood into the perfect, lush tree again.

Lusher, in fact, than it was before.

It happens within seconds and leaves me on edge. Especially as I sense the immense energy being poured into the trunk, branches, and leaves to bring them back to life.

Tensing and preparing myself for anything, I shift my position slightly to see around the angle of moonlight.

I'm certain I make out the transparent silhouette of a woman, her hands held out toward the tree, before she disappears.

Movement directly in front of me forces me to refocus.

In the moment that I was distracted, two figures have appeared out of nowhere only ten paces in front of us. Given how early we were, I experience a moment of surprise until I remind myself about the hidden compound that exists on this site. If they were within it, then my use of dark magic would have drawn them out.

A man and a woman stand between two monolithic gravestones.

The man is dressed in sweatpants and a T-shirt, a casual look that belies the power radiating from his tall frame.

Like Elijah, I can't pinpoint exactly what he is, but I have no doubt he's a dark creature like me, and I'm instantly wary.

The woman has crimson hair and gleaming, brown eyes. She's wearing a black dress and carries on her hip a multi-lash whip with deadly-looking metal spikes at the end of each lash.

I sense the blood draining from my face and fight to stay lucid as she turns her gaze on me, her irises briefly tinted with a blood-red hue.

The power and pain radiating off her as she captures my gaze strikes right into my chest, as sharp as knives that could shred me to pieces.

Fuck.

This woman is judge, jury, and executioner.

No wonder Vanguard couldn't bring the boy himself. I have no doubt, with the sins he's bound to have committed, she really would try to kill him on the spot. As for me... well, something must be stopping her.

My lips draw back from my teeth, and I suck in a breath, fighting the pain of her gaze until she lowers her eyes to Elijah.

By contrast, he's leaning toward the woman, his attention riveted on her, and I sense the sudden spark of joy within him.

Opposite me, the man has held up his hand with a warning directly at me. "Stay where you are, dark one. If you come near her, I'll fucking end you. Only the boy may approach."

I take note of the fact that he warns me about approaching *her* and not both of them collectively. He's clearly protective of this woman.

At his threat, she reaches out to him, her hand pressing to his forearm, her gaze turned up to his for a brief second.

The way she looks at him, the trust in her eyes, makes me feel like someone wrapped claws around my chest and is dragging cuts through it.

Fucking dark saints.

I pity the fool who ever tries to step between those two.

It certainly won't be me.

In the next moment, the woman's focus returns to Elijah.

She crouches to the ground, her dress swooshing around her legs as she holds out her arms to him. "Elijah."

Her chest has visibly stilled, as if she's holding her breath and waiting for the little boy to make his decision.

Elijah's head turns to me and for the briefest moment before I evade his gaze, I catch the thankfulness in his expression.

Gratitude.

Veda would be screwing her nose up right now.

Keeping my eyes turned away, I merely respond with, "Go on."

With a final hug for Anarchy, Elijah turns and runs straight to the woman, his little legs pumping so hard that he reaches her in three seconds flat.

She scoops him up into her arms and immediately turns away.

The man doesn't let me or Anarchy out of his sight as he backs away with them.

The air shimmers around all three of them, and then they're gone.

I don't waste time.

Now that I've done what Veda's heart demanded, I need to find her.

"Let's go," I say to Anarchy.

I take five steps before I realize Anarchy isn't following me.

Turning back to her, I find her snarling at me again.

I keep my voice soft. "We both want to find Veda. It will be easier together."

Anarchy continues to hiss at me.

"You know I want her to be safe."

I want *her*. More than anything. It's a mess of desire and need that threatens to consume me.

Anarchy's snarls don't abate.

I capitulate. "Fine. You love her more."

The panther's features smooth out, but she tips her head at me, as if she sees right through me.

This time, her hiss is as quiet as a sigh. Finally, she follows me from the graveyard.

I take a few moments to silently plot my next steps, although my thoughts now are frenzied.

Returning to Veda is my greatest need, even if Anarchy is right not to trust me.

When I took Veda's heart, I was determined that her power would be mine, but the bond between us has consequences. The kiss she gave me lingers on my lips, a reminder of the vengeance she seeks.

It's a revenge that intersects with my own.

I've tried to tell myself there's a world beyond vengeance, but the need for retribution burns within me.

I will do whatever it takes.

I am a dark king, after all.

∿

Find out what happens next in
Bond of Flames.

∿

ALSO BY EVERLY FROST

DARK MAGIC SHIFTERS

(Dark Urban Fantasy Romance)

1. Wolf of Ashes

2. Bond of Flames

3. Crown of Fate

KINGDOM OF BETRAYAL

(Fantasy Romance)

1. A Sky Like Blood

2. A Sin Like Fire

3. A Storm Like Iron

4. A Soul Like Glass

BRIGHT WICKED - COMPLETE

(Epic Fantasy Romance)

1. Bright Wicked

2. Radiant Fierce

3. Infernal Dark

STORM PRINCESS - COMPLETE

(Fantasy Romance)

1. Book 1

2. Book 2

3. Book 3

ASSASSIN'S MAGIC - COMPLETE

(Urban Fantasy Romance)

1. Assassin's Magic

2. Assassin's Mask

3. Assassin's Menace

4. Assassin's Maze

5. Rebels

6. Revenge

7. Rogue

8. Assassin's Match

SOUL BITTEN SHIFTER - COMPLETE
(Dark Urban Fantasy Romance)

1. This Dark Wolf

2. This Broken Wolf

3. This Caged Wolf

4. This Cruel Blood

SUPERNATURAL LEGACY - COMPLETE
(Angels and Dragon Shifters)

1. Hunt the Night

2. Chase the Shadows

3. Slay the Dawn

4. Claim the Light

DEMON PACK - COMPLETE
(Dark Paranormal Romance)

1. Demon Pack

2. Demon Pack: Elimination

3. Demon Pack: Eternal

ABOUT THE AUTHOR

Everly Frost is the USA Today Bestselling author of fantasy romance, urban fantasy and paranormal romance novels. She spent her childhood dreaming of other worlds and scribbling stories on the leftover blank pages at the back of school notebooks. She lives in Brisbane, Australia with her husband and two children.